CHUPA

CABRA

ROLAND SMITH

SCHOLASTIC PRESS
NEW YORK

FOR LITTLE NIK

Library of Congress Cataloging-in-Publication Data Available

ISBN 978-0-545-17817-4

10 9 8 7 6 5 4 3 2 1 13 14 15 16 17

Printed in the U.S.A. 40
First edition, October 2013

The text type was set in Garamond.
The display type was set in Bank Gothic.
Book design by Phil Falco

cryp·to·zo·ol·o·gy (krip-tə-zō-ä-lə-jē) *noun* The study of animals, such as the Sasquatch, the Yeti, the Loch Ness Monster, the Chupacabra, kraken, and others, whose existence has not yet been proven scientifically. There are thought to be more than two hundred ***cryptids*** in existence today.
—**cryp·to·zo·o·log·i·cal** (-zō-ə-ˈlä-ji-kəl) *adj.*
—**cryp·to·zo·ol·o·gist** (-ˈä-lə-jist) *noun*

Marty O'Hara: Wolfe's nephew. Grace's cousin (formerly thought to be her twin). Thirteen years old. Brown hair, gray eyes, a foot taller than Grace. Talented artist. Master chef. Scuba diver. Mountain climber. Skydiver. He has spent most of his life at the Omega Opportunity Preparatory School (OOPS) in Switzerland. His parents, Timothy and Sylvia (the most famous photographer/journalist team in the world), are missing after a terrible helicopter crash in the Amazon rain forest.

Grace Wolfe: Wolfe's only daughter (although for most of her life she thought she was Timothy and Sylvia O'Hara's daughter and Marty's twin sister). Black hair, blue eyes the color of robin's eggs like her mother Rose's. Born at Lake Télé in the Congo. Thirteen years old. Small for her age, but a foot *smarter* than Marty. The best student to ever "grace" the halls of OOPS. Fluent in several languages. Habitual journal-writer (uses a Montblanc fountain pen and Moleskine notebooks). Lock-picker. Genius.

Luther Percival Smyth, IV: Marty's best friend and former roommate at OOPS in Switzerland, where they managed to get into a tremendous amount of trouble. Coauthor/illustrator of Marty's graphic novels. Sleeps like a vampire. Eats like a wolf. Gangly, with wild orange hair. His father (Luther Percival Smyth, III) and mother are billionaires and often forget they even have a son. Expert computer hacker and video gamer.

Dr. Travis Wolfe: Cryptozoologist. Veterinarian. Oceanographer. Cofounder and owner of eWolfe with Ted Bronson. Called Wolfe by his friends — and foes. Grace's father. Marty's uncle. Sylvia O'Hara's older brother. Widower. Former son-in-law of Noah Blackwood. A giant of a man — just under seven feet tall. Unruly black hair, bushy black beard, brown eyes. Wears size-fifteen shoes. His right leg was bitten off by a Mokélé-mbembé as he tried to save his wife, Rose Blackwood, in the Congo. He now wears a high-tech prosthesis invented by Ted Bronson.

Dr. Ted Bronson (a.k.a. Theo Sonborn): Wolfe's closest friend and partner at eWolfe. Eccentric genius. Inventor. Recluse. Rumored to have not left the Quonset hut on Cryptos Island (where he develops his marvelous gadgets) in more than three years.

Theo Sonborn (a.k.a. Dr. Ted Bronson): Has been with Wolfe since the beginning. Surly. Pugnacious. Obnoxious. Jack-of-all-trades, master of none.

Dr. Noah Blackwood: Wealthy. Powerful. Owner of several animal theme parks around the world, all called Noah's Ark. Environmental television superstar — but he is not what he appears to be. He hunts and breeds endangered animals and cryptids, and displays them at his parks. In their prime he kills the animals, has them stuffed, and displays them in his private diorama. Father of Wolfe's deceased wife, Rose. Grace's grandfather.

Butch McCall: Noah Blackwood's henchman. Dangerous. Tattooed. Tough. Expert field biologist. More comfortable in the woods than he is under a roof. Sworn enemy of Travis Wolfe, whom he despises for "stealing" Rose Blackwood away from him.

Yvonne Zloblinavech: Freelance marine mammal trainer aboard the *Coelacanth*. Spy for Noah Blackwood. Ambitious, desperate to work her way to the top in Noah Blackwood's organization.

Dr. Laurel Lee: Wolfe's cultural anthropologist. Birdlike. Athletic. Former circus aerialist. Taught Grace to walk on a high wire to help her focus and overcome her many fears. Laurel and Wolfe are sweet on each other.

Mr. and Mrs. Hickock: Caretakers on Cryptos. Wild "Bill" Hickock remains on the island; Melanie Hickock (Ph.D. in Egyptology) is currently staying in a condo on Lake Washington with their son, Dylan, while she curates an Egyptian exhibit at the University of Washington.

Dylan Hickock: Sixteen years old. Caretakers' son. Just got his driver's license. He's new to the Cryptos Island crew, but not new to cryptids.

Dr. Strand: Noah Blackwood's chief genetic scientist. As pale as an eggshell, with a prominent nose and thick black-framed glasses.

Henrico: Noah Blackwood's personal taxidermist. Lives beneath the central Seattle Ark, has not seen the light of day in many years, and has no complaints about it.

Mitch Merton (a.k.a Mitch the Snitch): Former head maintenance chief on Cryptos; was Noah Blackwood's spy on the island. Current assistant to Henrico the taxidermist — a job for which he is ill-suited.

Bo: Female bonobo chimpanzee; orphaned and adopted by Wolfe years ago in the Congo when Wolfe and Rose were searching for Mokélé-mbembé. Especially fond of Luther's orange hair.

PD: Short for Pocket Dog; black-haired teacup poodle. Best friends with Bo. Jumps into a pocket upon hearing the word *snake*.

Congo: African gray parrot who belonged to Rose, Grace's mother, when she was in central Africa. Grace brought him back to Cryptos Island after their adventure with Mokélé-mbembé; he also accompanied her aboard the *Coelacanth* on the quest to capture a giant squid in the South Pacific.

Chupacabra is a Spanish name meaning "goat sucker." A beast of legend, its actual existence has yet to be verified, although sightings have been reported in the West Indies, South and Central America, and the southern parts of North America. The chupacabra's size is estimated at four to five feet in length. Its fur has been described as brown to black in color, and its head large, with huge fiery-orange eyes that appear to "glow" in the dark. Sharp fangs are said to protrude from its powerful jaws. Spikes, or hard knobby ridges, run from its head to the end of its spine. Accounts of a tail are inconsistent.

The chupacabra's hind legs are powerfully muscled. The front legs are thinner in comparison, and tipped with three-clawed toes, sometimes reported to be red in color.

An opportunistic predator by all accounts, the chupacabra hunts primarily at night, feeding on anything it can catch and kill. As its name indicates, it has a particular taste for goats. Its victims generally exhibit two or three puncture wounds in the neck, made by either the fangs or the claws, and from which the chupacabra can drain the blood on which it feeds.

CONTENTS

PART ONE | SQUIDARIUM

PART TWO | THE ARK

PART THREE | CHUPACABRA

THE CRYPTID HUNTERS SAGA SO FAR . . .

Fraternal twins Marty and Grace O'Hara are attending the Omega Opportunity Preparatory School (OOPS) in Switzerland when they receive shocking and tragic news: Their parents' helicopter has crashed somewhere in the Amazon rain forest of Brazil and they are missing. Two days later, their headmaster tells them they are leaving OOPS to live with a man named Travis Wolfe, who claims to be their mother's older brother.

Travis Wolfe, a giant of a man, with unruly black hair and a shaggy beard, lives on a volcanic island called Cryptos off the coast of Washington State. He and his genius business partner, Ted Bronson, own a very profitable tech company called eWolfe, headquartered on the mysterious island. But Wolfe's real interest is cryptozoology. He spends almost every dime he makes searching the world for mythical animals called cryptids. Now, though, much of that money is going toward finding Marty and Grace's parents in the Amazon.

A few days into Marty and Grace's stay on the island, a woman shows up, unannounced and uninvited, paddling a kayak. Her name is Laurel Lee. She's a cultural anthropologist recently returned from the Congo, where she was living with a tribe of pygmies near Lake Télé. While in the Congo, she met an old friend of Wolfe's from his time there, Masalito. Just before she left, Masalito gave her a large, dried-out egg, claiming that it belonged to a dinosaur called Mokélé-mbembé. The egg is one of three. The other two eggs had hatched. Masalito told her that the male had died recently and the female was ill. When Laurel got back to the U.S., she took the egg to a genetics lab owned by the famous wildlife conservationist Dr. Noah Blackwood to have it tested. Noah Blackwood's people stole the egg from her. Laurel managed to steal it back, but not without consequences. In a matter of hours, she lost her job at the university, all of her money was taken from her bank account, and her credit cards were canceled. The powerful Noah Blackwood is after her. She's on the run.

Travis Wolfe and Noah Blackwood have been archenemies for years. Noah is rich, famous, and respected, but he is not who he appears to be. His television show, *Wildlife First*, and his animal parks around the world are fronts to make money and hide his real purpose, which is to collect rare species for his Arks and "harvest" — that is, stuff — them in their prime.

Wolfe springs into action. They have to get to the Congo to save the last dinosaur on earth before Noah Blackwood and his henchman, Butch McCall, get their hands on it. Wolfe decides to send Marty and Grace back to OOPS. The Congo is too dangerous for kids. His plan is to have his pilot take Marty and Grace to Switzerland after he and Laurel are dropped off in the Congo.

Things do not go according to plan. As they are carrying out a supply drop over Lake Télé from Wolfe's converted bomber, Marty and Grace have an accident caused by a chimp, a bunch of bananas, and a teacup poodle. The twins reach

Lake Télé clinging to a parachute, days before Wolfe and Laurel can get there.

Alone in the treacherous jungle, with Butch McCall stalking them, Marty and Grace take up residence in a gigantic tree house built by Wolfe fourteen years earlier. While there, Marty and Grace discover that they are not twins after all, but cousins. Travis Wolfe, their guardian, was married to Rose Blackwood — Noah's daughter. To get away from her controlling father, Rose eloped with Wolfe and they hid out in the Congo. Grace was born there; she is their daughter. And Noah Blackwood is Grace's grandfather. But Rose, her mother, is dead, killed by Mokélé-mbembé, which bit off Wolfe's leg in the struggle.

Marty and Grace find the Mokélé-mbembé nest. The last living dinosaur, the sickly female, has died, but she has left behind two eggs. The cousins take the eggs and escape by hijacking Noah Blackwood's helicopter, leaving Butch and Noah behind to make their way out of the jungle on foot.

Back on Cryptos Island, Wolfe decides it's best to leave the country for a while. He knows that Noah is going to come after not only the eggs but also his granddaughter. Marty's best friend from OOPS, Luther Percival Smyth IV, joins them. Aboard Wolfe's research ship, the *Coelacanth*, they head to New Zealand to catch a giant squid for Northwest Zoo and Aquarium, the rival to Blackwood's Seattle Ark.

Butch McCall manages to get aboard the *Coelacanth* disguised as a researcher, with two co-conspirators to help him: Yvonne Zloblinavech and Mitch Merton.

The Mokélé-mbembé eggs hatch on the ship, producing two voracious and gassy baby dinosaurs.

Noah Blackwood catches up to them off the coast of New Zealand aboard his own research ship, manned with mercenaries and pirates. While Marty and Ted are in the deep on Ted's submersible, trying to catch a giant squid, Noah Blackwood attacks the *Coelacanth* with his hired pirates. The *Coelacanth* crew fends off the assault with sonic cannons, but the pirate attack is a feint. While they are fighting on the surface, Noah sends in scuba divers to place explosive charges inside the *Coelacanth*.

Marty and Ted manage to lure a giant squid into the *Coelacanth*'s Moon Pool, but before they can congratulate themselves on their historic catch, they discover the explosives. As they frantically try to disarm them, there is a standoff up on deck.

Butch, Yvonne, and Noah's mercenaries have bagged the Mokélé-mbembé hatchlings, and are holding Grace and Laurel at gunpoint. Noah lands his chopper on the *Coelacanth*'s helipad. Butch threatens to shoot Laurel if Wolfe and his men don't lay down their arms. To break the impasse and protect her father and friends, Grace agrees to go willingly with her grandfather.

Marty and Ted manage to find and disarm all of the bombs. The Cryptos crew heads back to Seattle with the first giant squid ever to be captured alive. But they are dejected. They've lost Grace. They've lost the dinosaur hatchlings. And Marty's parents are still missing. . . .

PROLOGUE: NINE'S MIND

From the darkness of his wooden den the chupacabra sensed everything. . . . The *whir* of fans. The *click* of the flickering lights. The *drip . . . drip . . . drip* of water. The *hiss* of doors opening. The grating sound of human voices before the doors hissed closed again. The sharp scent of his own urine in the corners of his cage. The scratching of rabbits and rodents against cold steel. The bleating of a kid goat. His belly churning with hunger. . . .

The kid goat bleated again. It had been several sleeps since the last one.

The night before, the woman with the box had made him go to sleep. At least he thought it was her. It only happened when she was nearby with the box she held.

"Sleep!" she had shouted.

A sharp, piercing pain in his head, then the darkness.

When he woke there was something wrapped around his chest and back. He tried to scratch it off with his razorlike claws, but his claws could not reach it. He tried to bite it off, but his long, sharp fangs were not long enough to pierce it. He had tried to rub it off on the bars of his cage, but that had made the chafing and constriction worse. Finally, he had given up and simply accepted the discomfort, crawling into his dark den, his head toward the opening, watching, listening, scenting the air.

The man with the white coat and shining mirror eyes opened the door down the hallway. The chupacabra moved farther back into his den, his powerful hind legs pressed into the corner. He was not afraid of the man, but he was fearful of the things that happened to him when the man was near.

"Hungry?" the man said.

The chupacabra did not move. He stared at the man's hand from the darkness. The hand was wrapped in cloth as bright as the man's coat. He had tasted the man's blood and wanted more, but he stayed where he was . . . still, silent, waiting.

"I have something that will get you out of that box," the man said.

The man disappeared from the chupacabra's view. His feet clicked on the concrete floor. The kid goat started bleating louder. Steel doors rattled. The bleating got closer with every door rattle. Closer. Closer. Closer.

The chupacabra knew what was coming. He felt liquid dripping from his jaw. His belly rattled like the doors. But he stayed where he was. Watching. Waiting.

The final door opened. The kid goat jumped into his cage, prodded by the man with a long stick through the steel mesh.

The kid goat pranced back and forth in front of his den, bleating, bleating, bleating. The chupacabra could smell its fear.

"Dinnertime," the man said.

The chupacabra wanted the frightened creature, but he didn't move. He wanted the man more. He had been studying this man for days. Watching him. Listening. Trying to lure him closer.

"Suit yourself," the man said. "Eat or don't eat. I don't care."

The door hissed open. The man stepped through. The door hissed closed. But the man did not go away. He watched through the small window in the door.

The chupacabra waited. He watched the man. He watched the kid goat pacing back and forth.

The door hissed open again. The man re-entered the room. The kid goat bleated.

"Are you okay?" the man asked. "Are you alive?"

The chupacabra didn't move.

The man stepped closer and squatted down to peer into the den, inches from the wire mesh.

This is what the chupacabra had been waiting for. He launched himself from the den and hit the steel mesh.

Bang!

The man screamed and fell backward. His shining eyes flew off his face and clattered on the concrete floor.

The man breathed through his mouth. Big, deep breaths.

The chupacabra tried to reach him through the mesh with his claws, but the man pulled his feet away and curled into a ball.

The kid goat bleated. It stood in the corner, shivering.

The chupacabra jumped on the kid goat, sunk his long fangs into its neck, shook it once, and began to feed.

As he lapped up the warm, salty blood, he looked at the man curled up next to the wall. He could smell the man's fear. It somehow made the blood taste better.

PART ONE | SQUIDARIUM

A VIEW FROM A ROOF

"I can't say I'm sorry to be rid of those vicious prehistoric gasbags," Luther Smyth said. "But I sure miss Grace."

"I miss her, too," Marty O'Hara admitted. He also missed his parents, who were hopelessly lost in the Amazonian rain forest . . . or dead. The vicious prehistoric gasbags Luther was talking about were a couple of Mokélé-mbembé babies that had hatched aboard his uncle Wolfe's research ship, the *Coelacanth*, on the way to New Zealand to capture a giant squid. Marty and Grace had snagged the dinosaur eggs in the Congo. Luther still had Band-Aids on his fingers where the meat-snappers had bitten him. He also smelled like the meat-snappers, even though he had taken at least twenty showers since the last feed. It was like the stink had soaked into the pores of his skin and the follicles of his flaming reddish hair.

"Look at all those people!" Luther said.

The boys were standing on the roof of the brand-new Squidarium at Northwest Zoo and Aquarium in Seattle, Washington. The structure was huge, but not nearly big enough to handle the football-stadium crowd waiting for the gates to open. According to the news, more than a thousand people had camped outside the entrance the night before with sleeping bags and coolers filled with food.

"You think Noah Blackwood is in the crowd?" Luther asked.

"Fat chance," Marty said, frowning. Noah Blackwood, Grace's grandfather, had snatched the hatchlings and kidnapped Grace. Marty would trade a thousand giant squids just to talk to her.

The NZA director, Dr. Michael Loch, opened the door to the roof and joined them.

"Quite a crowd," he said, grinning from ear to ear.

At fifteen bucks a head, Marty didn't think Dr. Loch was seeing the crowd like he and Luther were seeing them.

He's seeing a stream of endless cash flowing into his zoo, Marty thought.

"What time do the gates open?" Luther asked.

"As soon as we finish the media previews," Loch said. "There must be two hundred reporters down there right now, maybe more. We should be ready for the peds by about one o'clock."

Marty had learned that "peds," short for *pedestrians*, stood for zoo visitors. He looked at his watch. It was noon.

"How much did the Squidarium cost?" he asked.

"Thirty million dollars," Loch answered.

"Let me get this straight," Luther said. "You put up a thirty-million-dollar building on the off chance that Wolfe would bring in a live giant squid?"

"That's right."

"Even though this is the first *Architeuthis* brought into captivity alive?" Marty added, showing off a little by using the scientific name for the giant squid.

"I have a lot of faith in your uncle and Ted Bronson."

Ted Bronson was Travis Wolfe's reclusive partner, but he'd come out of hiding aboard the *Coelacanth* long enough to take Marty down into the deep to catch the giant squid. It was lucky they all weren't killed.

"Have you ever met Ted Bronson?" Luther asked.

Marty elbowed Luther in the side. Dr. Loch didn't notice because he was staring dreamily at the people lined up outside the gate, dollar symbols practically flashing in his eyes.

"No, I haven't," Dr. Loch answered. "I understand he hasn't been off Cryptos Island in years."

Cryptos Island was the secret island where Wolfe and Ted Bronson lived and ran eWolfe, a company that built everything from satellites to robotic flying bugs.

Luther was baiting Dr. Loch. At that very minute, Ted Bronson was inside the Squidarium, monitoring the giant squid with Wolfe and the world's foremost authority on giant squid, Dr. Seth A. Lepod. Dr. Lepod had gone into the deep with Marty and Ted, but missed a lot of the action because he'd puked inside his pressurized aquasuit and couldn't see through the visor of his aquahelmet because of the spew.

Marty was certain that Dr. Loch had met Ted poolside, and he was just as certain that Dr. Loch had no idea he was Wolfe's genius partner. Ted was a master of disguise. His other persona was a pugnacious jerk by the name of Theo Sonborn. No doubt Loch had shaken his hand within the hour. No one would mistake Theo for Ted Bronson in a billion years.

Dr. Jekyll and Mr. Hyde, Marty thought.

"How many people do you think you can get through the Squidarium a day?" Marty asked, getting him off the subject of Ted Bronson.

"If we stay open until ten at night," Dr. Loch answered, "— and there's no reason why we can't — I'd guess we could get fifteen thousand people in and out every day."

Marty did a quick calculation. At $15 apiece, that would be $225,000 a day. Wolfe was getting half the gate receipts for catching the squid, which left Loch over $100,000 a day. At that rate, the Squidarium would be paid off in a little less than a year. During that same time Wolfe would also rake in about $40 million dollars, providing that the squid lived that long.

Wolfe needed the money. He was nearly broke even before they shipped off for New Zealand to catch the squid. It took a lot of money to keep eWolfe afloat, organize cryptid expeditions, and, most important — at least to Marty — keep the search going for his parents. And now they had the added, urgent challenge of rescuing Grace.

That is, if she wants to be rescued, Marty thought.

"What do you think Noah Blackwood's reaction is going to be to the squid?" Luther asked.

Marty gave Luther another dig with his elbow. Harder this time. Luther grunted, but ignored it.

Dr. Loch's grin broadened, which seemed impossible considering how wide it already was. "Oh, he's not going to be happy. Not happy at all."

Marty wasn't so sure. If this many people were lined up to see a giant squid, how many would line up to see a pair of baby dinosaurs?

Loch looked at his watch. "I've got to get ready for the press conference. Are you coming?"

"Yeah!" Luther said.

Marty grabbed Luther's arm and held him back. "We'll be along soon."

Loch nodded and hurried through the door.

"What?" Luther asked, jerking free. "The press might want to talk to me."

That's exactly what Marty was afraid of. "We'd better find Wolfe and see what he wants us to do."

"Party pooper," Luther complained.

"Whatever," Marty said.

NOAH'S ARK

Noah Blackwood was sitting in his private office on the top floor of his mansion, located on a hill overlooking his Seattle Ark. The shades were drawn, as always. He was watching the news coverage about the giant squid on a flat-screen monitor atop his large snakewood desk. Snakewood was the rarest wood in the world — and Noah was in a rare good mood.

He may not have gotten the giant squid in his pirate raid in the Pacific as he had plotted, but he'd come back with a treasure worth far more than that denizen of the deep — which, in part, accounted for his good mood.

A couple of hours earlier, a network television crew had shown up at the Ark to interview him about the giant squid. Noah loved speaking in front of a camera, and the camera loved him. The only thing he liked better than speaking in front of a camera was watching himself on television after the fact. And that's what he was doing right now. . . .

"We are at Noah Blackwood's Seattle Ark today with Dr. Noah Blackwood himself, who is no stranger to our viewers. He has five zoos — or Arks, as he calls them — in five different countries."

In the solitude of his office, Blackwood frowned at the blow-dried anchorman reflected on his desktop monitor. He didn't like it when his Arks were called zoos, although he knew that was exactly what they were. He preferred the term *wildlife conservation centers*. If he'd heard the introduction, he would have corrected the idiotic reporter right on the spot. But his irritation faded as he saw himself appear on the screen. Longish white hair swept back like a lion's mane against a perfectly tanned face, mesmerizing blue eyes, and capped teeth as white as fresh snow. In the exhibit behind him were three adorable panda cubs, which the keepers had turned out early into the grassy yard for the interview. The cubs were a new addition to the Seattle Ark. The trio had been orphaned in China and personally rescued by Noah — allegedly. The truth was that Noah sent his right-hand man, Butch McCall, to China with enough cash to hire a poacher. Together Butch and the poacher stole the three cubs from three different mothers in the wild and smuggled them out of the country.

"Thank you for taking the time out of your busy day to talk to us, Dr. Blackwood," the reporter said.

"It's my pleasure."

"As you no doubt know, Northwest Zoo and Aquarium is about to put an endangered giant squid on exhibit for the first time in history. Your thoughts about this?"

"First of all, *unseen* does not mean *endangered*. We have no idea if the giant squid is endangered or not, but this takes nothing away from Northwest Zoo and Aquarium's remarkable accomplishment. I'm thrilled for them, and for the zoological community as a whole. We'll all learn a great deal about this interesting creature because of their efforts. Northwest Zoo and Aquarium is to be congratulated."

"But aren't you worried about the squid siphoning off visitors from the Ark?"

"I'm not in competition with Northwest Zoo and Aquarium. We're on the same team. They've accomplished what was thought to be impossible. I just hope the specimen lives long enough for us to learn from it."

"Are you saying there's a possibility the squid might die?"

"Everything dies eventually. That's the law of life. I just hope that the specimen they captured was young and didn't suffer any debilitating injuries from the transport. The longer it survives, the more we'll learn."

"I understand that you were also off the coast of New Zealand when they caught the giant squid."

"We had research ships in the area, yes."

"Were you asked to help?"

"We were dealing with a little crisis of our own around the time they caught the giant squid. In spite of that, we certainly would have assisted them if they had needed it."

"What kind of crisis?"

"Stay tuned — I'll give you more specifics on a future episode of *Wildlife First*."

"Can you give us a hint now?"

"Pirates. But that's all I'm going to say at this point."

"Well, we look forward to that episode!"

"Piracy is just one of the hazards of trying to protect our planet's wildlife. It was touch and go. We lost some crew members to the scoundrels, but we all do this knowing the risks."

"That sounds fascinating — you heard it here first on SeaTac News, viewers! Dr. Noah Blackwood, battling pirates! But, Dr. Blackwood, back to the subject at hand: Rumor is that you and Northwest Zoo and Aquarium have had your differences in the past. Wasn't there a falling-out between you and Dr. Loch over an expedition to catch whale sharks? Something about a fire, and —"

"You cannot believe everything reported by 'the press.' Dr. Loch and I are not only colleagues, we are friends. He regularly calls on my staff for assistance, and we're happy to lend him a hand. As I said, I couldn't be happier for him. In fact, as soon as I get a chance I'm going to go over there, take a look at his giant squid, and congratulate him in person."

Noah Blackwood and Michael Loch despised each other. Loch had publicly accused Blackwood of sabotaging their expedition to catch a whale shark by setting their research ship on fire. There was no proof, and Dr. Loch had to issue a public apology, but the truth was that Noah Blackwood had sent Butch McCall to torch their ship. And he wouldn't hesitate to send Butch to the aquarium if their new acquisition threatened his income. A couple of drops of an undetectable poison in the water would do the trick and kill off NZA's new main attraction.

"A few weeks ago, SeaTac News interviewed you after you returned from rescuing one of your employees, Butch McCall, from the Congo. You indicated at the time you had made an important discovery during the rescue. I'm wondering —"

"I'll repeat what I told you then: *Wildlife First*. That's the title of my bestselling book, that's the name of my internationally syndicated television show, and that's my policy. *Wildlife First*: It's not just a slogan, it is the lifeblood of my very soul. Wildlife first, without exception. Today is a day to celebrate Dr. Loch's and Northwest Zoo and Aquarium's achievement. I will not mar it by talking about my own exciting discovery. Now, I have an important phone call to take, so if you'll excuse me. . . ."

Noah watched himself walk away from the camera, pleased with how well he had handled the interview and how good he looked on television. The report moved back to Northwest Zoo and Aquarium and the mass of people waiting to get through the gates to see the giant squid. Noah switched the newscast off, smiling.

This time next week, it will be as if the giant squid never existed.

He called Butch McCall.

"Where are you?" Noah asked, knowing perfectly well where Butch was because he was staring at Butch through one of the dozens of surveillance cameras set up throughout the Ark.

"Pandas," Butch answered flatly, unaware that he was being watched.

"Is Grace with you?"

Another throwaway question. His granddaughter was perfectly framed on Noah's screen. Everyone on staff knew there were surveillance cameras at the Ark, but no one knew how many, or where they were. Noah was the only person who had access to all of the cameras at any one time.

"What's Grace doing?"

"Playing with the cubs," Butch mumbled.

"What's the problem, Butch?"

"There's no problem."

Butch's eyes rolled. Butch was lying. It was almost impossible for Butch to hide his true feelings, which was why Noah was careful to keep him in the background most of the time. It was a miracle that Butch had been able to infiltrate Wolfe's crew aboard the *Coelacanth.*

"Spill it, Butch," Noah said into the phone, although he already knew exactly what Butch's gripe was. If life was a chess game, Noah was always five moves ahead of the people on the playing board. In the case of Butch, he was ten moves ahead.

"Grace," Butch said.

"What about her?"

"There are a lot of other people who could be babysitting her besides me."

"Grace is my only living relative, Butch. And you're right, there are a lot of other people who could babysit her, but there is only one person I trust to protect her."

"Protect her from what?"

"Travis Wolfe!" Noah raised his voice. "Do you think he's going to sit idly by and do nothing about us kidnapping his daughter?"

"We didn't kidnap her," Butch said. "She came with us on her own."

"She came with us because you were holding a gun to Laurel Lee's head," Noah corrected.

"It was a standoff," Butch argued. "I wasn't about to shoot Laurel Lee with Al Ikes pointing his assault rifle at me. It was a bluff, and Grace knew it."

"And how do you know that?"

"She told me," Butch said.

Noah's blue eyes narrowed in suspicion. Butch had worked for Noah since he was a teenager, starting out as a zookeeper. Now he was his top field operative. Noah knew Butch McCall better than Butch McCall knew himself.

"It sounds like you and she are getting along splendidly," Noah said.

"I wouldn't go that far," Butch said. On the security camera screen, Noah watched as he cocked one eyebrow in doubt. "But I don't think she's going anywhere. Even if she had a chance to escape, which she doesn't."

Noah smiled. It seemed that Grace had inherited his charm and his guile. "A chip off the old block," he said.

"What?" Butch asked.

"Forget it," Noah said. "The more you trust Grace, the closer you need to watch her. She is being far too cooperative. I don't believe that she is as happy as she appears. She's up to something."

"Like what?"

"I expect you to find that out, Butch. Don't let your guard down. And make sure she doesn't return to her room for a while."

"Why?"

"Just do it! I'll let you know when it's clear."

Noah ended the call, then watched them on the screen for a few minutes. Grace did seem to be genuinely enjoying herself as she played tug-of-war with the three adorable panda cubs. He still couldn't get over how much she looked like his daughter, Rose. She had the same robin's-egg-blue eyes. The same raven-black hair. Even her smile was the same. He wondered what she would think of him if she knew what he had planned for at least one of the cubs she was playing with.

"I don't think you'd be smiling, Grace," he said aloud. "But you will come around to my way of thinking when you see the grand scheme. When you see what I've accomplished. When you see the impossible become possible."

He hit an icon on his computer screen, got up from his desk, and walked over to his precious collection, which very few people had ever seen, or even knew existed. If you looked at the wall across from his desk, you'd think you were looking at large glass panels as black as obsidian. The halogen lights on the other side of the glass illuminated the cases slowly, like the rising sun. Behind each panel was an animal. Dead. Beautifully preserved by his exclusive taxidermist, Henrico. The animals had been harvested in their prime. Frozen in magnificent poses against a stark black background so that nothing detracted from their natural beauty. They looked more alive in death than they had in life. Among the dozens of rare animals was a thylacine, or Tasmanian wolf, pulling a wombat out of its burrow. A flock of passenger pigeons winging their way to extinction. And the newest addition, a young female Caspian tiger named Natasha, in mid-leap, about ready to take down and devour an unlucky ibex.

Not that long ago he had been petting Natasha right here in his office. Now he would be able to view her raw symmetry forever.

But the bodies were just the shells of the animals. The essences of these long-extinct creatures were stored deep below the Ark in cryogenic tanks, frozen in time, awaiting the day when Noah's technicians could bring them back to life. And his geneticists were close. They had already created a living, breathing, mythical beast in his secret laboratory. With the unique DNA from the Mokélé-mbembé hatchlings now at his disposal, who knew what his team could duplicate or invent next.

Noah smiled, thinking about old Henrico and the new apprentice he had found for him. He wondered how they were getting along in the workshop several levels beneath the mansion. He carefully examined the glass. Not a smudge or speck of dust on the surface. It was as if he could reach through and pet the extinct animals, just as he had petted Natasha the Caspian tiger when she was still alive. Just the way he liked it.

He returned to his computer and brought the lights down. No time for pleasure. Time to make his daily rounds.

DUH *DU JOUR*

Marty and Luther followed Wolfe and Theo Sonborn down the hallway to Dr. Loch's office. The door was open. Loch was sitting at his desk, still smiling. "The crowd is massive," he said.

"So I've heard," Wolfe said. "Can we borrow your office for a short meeting, Mike?"

Filling the doorway, Travis Wolfe towered over Dr. Michael Loch, as he did over most people. He looked down at the zoo director with tired brown eyes, a full black beard, and long black hair.

"Of course," Loch said, standing up from his desk. "But what about the press conference? There are two hundred journalists waiting for us in the Squidarium."

"I'll pass on that," Wolfe said. "And the less you say about our involvement, the better. We don't want the publicity or the attention."

"In that case, make yourself at home," Loch said with a sweep of his arms. "I'll see you at the opening."

"Actually, you won't," Wolfe said. "I'm flying out right after this meeting."

"You're kidding?" Loch said.

Marty was surprised, too. Wolfe was notoriously camera shy and rarely spoke to the press, but Marty didn't think he'd miss the giant squid opening.

Wolfe shook his head. "I have some things to take care of."

"What could be more important than the catch of the century?" Loch asked.

Marty could think of a couple of things, like finding his parents and getting Grace and the hatchlings out of the clutches of Noah Blackwood.

"You'll be fine without me underfoot. Dr. Lepod is more than capable of handling any medical problems with the giant squid, and Theo Sonborn here can handle any technical or environmental issues that might come up."

Dr. Loch looked at Theo with serious doubt. Theo glared back at him with serious hostility.

"Don't worry," Wolfe said. "Theo's smarter than he looks."

Marty and Luther turned away so Loch couldn't see their grins. The pudgy, bearded, perpetually angry Theo Sonborn was probably the smartest person on the planet.

"All right," Loch said, switching on the lights over the conference table. "I guess I'll leave you to it." He looked at Theo. "Are you coming with me?"

"He'll be down after we finish here," Wolfe said.

Loch left and closed the door behind him.

"I don't think Loch likes me," Theo said, pulling off his wig and fake beard.

"I wonder why," Wolfe said.

"Because no one likes Theo Sonborn," Theo said, giving him a yellow-toothed grin before popping the fake teeth out of his mouth. "Which is the point of the disguise." He dropped the greasy wig on the floor.

Marty had seen Theo morph many times before. He turned away to check out the office. It was filled with books, wildlife photos, and zoo memorabilia. Luther wandered around, frenetically picking up or touching everything within reach.

"Try not to break anything," Wolfe warned.

The conference table was across from Loch's cluttered desk. A dozen chairs surrounded it. Wolfe pulled one out, sat down heavily, and began massaging his right leg, where his prosthesis attached to the stump. His leg had been bitten off years ago in the Congo by Mokélé-mbembé.

The rough-looking, not-too-bright Theo Sonborn had almost completed his transformation into Ted Bronson. "Is that thing bothering you?" he asked.

"A little," Wolfe admitted, kneading the muscles above his knee.

"Want me to make some adjustments?" Theo was now completely gone, replaced by a man who looked like an action hero from a Hollywood movie.

"It's fine," Wolfe said. "I haven't been off my feet in twenty-four hours. I just need to give the stump a little rest. It'll be good as new by the time I land in DC."

"You're going to Washington, DC?" Marty asked, surprised. It was the first he'd heard that his uncle was leaving town with so much going on.

"Believe me, the capital is the last place I want to go," Wolfe said. "But yeah, I'm taking off from McChord Air Force Base as soon as we finish here."

"To do what?" Luther asked, still prodding Loch's personal belongings.

Ted joined Wolfe at the table. "The expedition for the giant squid was not a complete failure. We lost Grace, we lost the dinosaurs, but we won in the scientific technology department. The Orb, the aquasuits, the molecular particle disruptor, the dragonspies, as you call them, and the micro-surveillance cameras: They're all ready for prime time. Which means we get paid."

The Orb was a miniature nuclear sub that looked like a golden beach ball and was big enough to hold three people. It was able to reach unheard-of depths without imploding the occupants. They had used it to lure the giant squid out from the Kaikoura Canyon into the Moon Pool of the *Coelacanth*. The molecular particle disruptor was a zipper wand that allowed them to get into and out of the Orb and the aquasuits. The Orb and aquasuits were made out of a brand-new alloy that Ted likened to "organic body armor," able to adapt instantly to any environment and impervious to just about everything.

The dragonspy, or bot-fly, was Marty's and Luther's favorite invention of Ted's. It resembled a dragonfly in shape and size, but that's where the similarities stopped. It was a miniature flying robot equipped with cameras and microphones that sent video and audio to the Gizmo — another invention of Ted's that made all other smartphones look stupid.

"What about Grace?" Marty asked. "What about my parents?"

"Duh *du jour*," Wolfe said.

Marty and Luther looked at him in shock. This was the boys' favorite saying, but it didn't sound quite right coming from Wolfe's bearded lips.

"This is why I wanted to talk with you," Wolfe said. "There are several new developments. Grab a seat."

Marty sat down at the head of the table, wondering if his uncle had good news or bad. Good news had been as rare as cryptids since they'd returned from the coast of New Zealand aboard the *Coelacanth*. Not even the successful delivery of the giant squid was enough to rescue them from the funk they had been in since Grace's abrupt departure.

Luther plopped down on Loch's desk, which would allow him to pick through the director's clutter while he listened to what Wolfe had to say.

"Let's start with your parents." Wolfe took out his Gizmo and consulted the screen. "There's no concrete news, but Robert Lansa sent me an email late last night saying that he's heard some rumors about a man and a woman being injured and taken by an uncontacted indigenous tribe to their village deep in the jungle."

"What do you mean by *uncontacted*?" Luther asked.

"A tribe that has had no contact with the outside world," Wolfe answered. "Ever."

"Can't be too many of those left," Marty said.

Wolfe nodded. "But I don't want you to get your hopes up. One of the problems we're dealing with now is that our presence down there is causing a lot of chatter. It's the same thing when you're looking for cryptids. When you go into an area making inquiries about something that's not supposed to exist, the rumors and sightings hit the roof. Most of the sightings turn out to be hoaxes, and the rumors lies."

"But the rumors in Brazil might be true," Marty said excitedly.

"We'll see," Wolfe said. "Laurel Lee and Ana Mika are on their way down there right now to help the Lansas check out the rumors. Jake Lansa's meeting them in Manaus and taking them to the jaguar preserve."

Ana Mika was an investigative journalist and Ted Bronson's longtime girlfriend. Laurel Lee was a cultural anthropologist, and maybe Wolfe's new girlfriend.

"If there's any merit to the information, those two will dig it out," Ted said.

"I wish I'd been able to go with them," Wolfe said.

"Why didn't you?" Marty asked, wondering why he hadn't been told about this beforehand. He would have liked to have gone down with them, too.

"Business," Wolfe said gloomily. "It's time to cash in on the technology we've been developing the past several years."

"I thought catching the giant squid would make you solvent," Luther said.

"*Solvent?*" Marty repeated.

"Rich," Luther explained. "At least that's what my dad calls having piles of cash."

Marty looked at Wolfe. "What about Grace?"

"We aren't going to be able to do anything about Grace until we have enough resources to take on Noah Blackwood," Wolfe answered. "That's why I'm heading to DC. In a day or two, we should have everything we need to start the process."

"What process?" Luther asked.

Wolfe sighed. "It's complicated. Our first problem is that Grace went with Blackwood voluntarily. The second is that I have no legal proof that Grace is my daughter. She was born in the Congolese jungle. No birth certificate. It's my word against Blackwood's, and to be honest, Blackwood's word carries a lot more weight than mine."

"At the moment," Ted added. "But that could change. Ana has gathered a very damaging dossier against him, but the allegations still need to be vetted and proved."

"Proved how?" Luther asked.

"Good question," Ted said. "Photos, video, documentation of some of his nefarious activities would help. Al Ikes is trying to figure this out right now, but the Ark is like an armed fortress. Noah has been keeping secrets for years and is very good at it."

Al Ikes was an ex–CIA agent who was in charge of eWolfe security. Marty had wondered why they hadn't seen him since the *Coelacanth* docked at the NZA pier.

"Is Grace at Blackwood's Seattle Ark?" he asked.

"We don't know," Wolfe said. "But we do know that Noah's there. Or at least he was earlier this morning. He did a press interview in front of his new panda exhibit."

"Cubs that Butch McCall poached in China," Ted added.

"Or so we think," Wolfe said. "If we could get proof of just one of these things, we could take him down."

"Let's get back to Grace," Marty said.

"We think she's at the Seattle Ark, too," Wolfe said. "I doubt that Noah would let her out of his sight."

"What about using the dragonspy?" Luther suggested.

Just before Grace climbed onto Blackwood's helicopter, Luther had landed a dragonspy in her shirt pocket. She had used it to communicate with them briefly before the helicopter flew the bot out of range.

"It's off the grid," Ted answered. "Which could mean one of several things. The dragonspy is somewhere in the Ark that our telemetry can't penetrate. Blackwood discovered the dragonspy and disabled it. The dragonspy simply ran out of juice. Or Grace isn't at the Ark with her grandfather."

"Or Grace doesn't want us to know where she is," Wolfe said glumly.

"Not likely," Luther countered.

Marty wasn't so sure. Grace didn't always take the *likely* path. After their terrifying trip to the Congo, where she'd discovered who she really was, she had ventured off the well-trodden path several times. She might be waiting to use the dragonspy until she absolutely needed it. But he wondered about that, too. Grace wasn't into electronic gadgets like he was. On their way back from New Zealand, Ted had loaned him his dragonspy. It was in Marty's cargo pocket right now, resting inside his Gizmo. He hadn't flown it in days, but Luther had . . . several times. Marty hated to admit it, but Luther was a much better dragonspy pilot than he was.

"What's your plan?" Marty asked.

"I'm still formulating it," Wolfe answered. "I'll know more when I get back from DC." He looked at his watch. "Phil and Phyllis are flying Laurel and Ana to Brazil. They're well on their way by now. Ted is going to stay here and make sure everything goes okay with the giant squid. The *Coelacanth* is heading back to Cryptos in a little less than an hour. You two will need to be on board before she sails, so you'll need to gather your things and get —"

"No can do," Luther said.

"Why not?" Wolfe asked.

"The parental units." Luther reached down and pulled his cell phone out of his sock.

"You carry your cell phone in your sock?" Wolfe asked.

"Yeah," Luther said. "Don't you?"

Wolfe shook his head. "What did your parents say?"

"Dad just texted me to say that he and Mom are flying in tomorrow morning to check out Mr. Squid. They've been reading the press reports, and they're excited to get a firsthand look. I told him that we'd be able to give them a behind-the-scenes tour of the leviathan. I hope that's okay."

Marty knew about the phone in the sock, but the text was news to him, which meant there was a good chance that Luther was lying about his billionaire parents flying in. In all the years he'd known Luther, Marty had met his parents exactly twice. He wasn't sure if Luther himself would recognize them on the street if he bumped into them, but they would recognize him, if by nothing else than his shocking flame-colored hair.

"I wish you would have asked," Wolfe said.

"I would have if I had seen you. I'll write Dad back and tell him no." He started to tap on his cell phone.

Wolfe held his hand up. "You don't have to do that. I just need to figure out what to do with you for the night and how to get you to the island tomorrow. What time are your parents flying in?"

"I'm not sure."

"Where are they flying in from?" Ted asked.

"They didn't say. Could be anywhere. They virtually live on their jet. They use it like a recreational vehicle."

Wolfe looked at Ted. "Can you keep an eye on these two?"

Ted shook his head. "I'm afraid not, partner. Theo Sonborn is going to be busy keeping an eye on *Architeuthis* today. And tonight he's going to change back into Ted to take care of some very important business. Business that can't wait and can't be done with company."

"What are you up to?" Wolfe asked suspiciously.

Ted smiled. "You don't want to know."

Marty looked at Luther, who was looking at Wolfe with a goofy grin. He knew Luther had a plan, too, that he hadn't let him in on yet. He could hardly wait to get Luther by himself and find out what he was really up to. Knowing Luther like he did, it had to be something insanely stupid, but incredibly interesting.

"The problem is, I don't have a way to get the boys back to Cryptos, with Phil and Phyllis flying to South America. The *Coelacanth* has to leave today. Another ship is scheduled for the slip," Wolfe thought aloud.

"How are you getting to DC?" Marty asked.

"Military jet. The Pentagon arranged it. I guess they're eager to see me."

"Wait until they see the video of the Orb," Ted said. "They'll kick the president out of the White House and give the place to you."

"I wouldn't take it," Wolfe said. "But I am going to talk to them about our lease for Cryptos and getting a replacement chopper."

Butch McCall had sabotaged their helicopter when he was aboard the *Coelacanth*. Cryptos Island, where Wolfe and Ted lived, had been a secret military base during World War Two.

Wolfe had gotten it in exchange for some work he and Ted had done for the government. Grace had tried to find the island on a nautical map, but with no luck. It was as if the island didn't exist. They weren't even sure if it was a part of the United States. The name *Cryptos* came from the word *cryptic*, which meant "secret" — and Marty could think of no better word to describe the mysterious place.

"I'll be stranded, too, until I can figure out a way back to Cryptos," Ted said. "Maybe the Hickocks can keep an eye on them."

"Who?" Marty said.

"Our new caretakers," Wolfe said. "You haven't met them yet. They started on Cryptos after we left for New Zealand. Bill Hickock; his wife, Melanie; and their son, Dylan, a few years older than you two. Dylan's down at the squid tank. Nice kid with an incredible story about an encounter with a Sasquatch during the last eruption of Mount Saint Helens."

"He saw Bigfoot?" Luther said.

"Big-time," Wolfe said. "Right here in Washington State. And it just so happens that the guy who helped Dylan and his dad on the volcano is a retired field biologist named Buckley Johnson, and he's working with Robert Lansa at the jaguar preserve in Brazil."

"Big coincidence," Ted said.

"Small world," Wolfe said. "How can they help us with our transportation problem?"

"Before Bill got hooked on cryptozoology, he was a real-estate guy," Ted explained. "He owns property all over the Pacific Northwest. His wife is staying at one of his condos on Lake Washington. She's teaching at the University of

Washington this summer. She'd probably keep an eye on these two until we can work something out. I'll be around for a couple of days before I head back to Cryptos. I can check in on them, too. I'll take them with me when I figure out how I'm getting back to the island."

"We'll have to get them to that Lake Washington condo," Wolfe said.

"Dylan just turned sixteen," Ted answered. "He has a license. I loaned him one of my cars."

"That'll work."

"Excuse me," Marty said. "We're right here." He hated it when adults talked about him as if he wasn't there.

Ted looked at him and grinned. "Sorry, I didn't see you there."

"Funny," Marty said.

THE SIXTH MOLESKINE

Grace and Butch stepped outside of the panda exhibit into the public area.

"Beautiful day," Grace said cheerfully. "But there aren't many people here."

"Squid," Butch grunted.

"Oh, that's right," Grace said, as if she had forgotten. "We have the park almost all to ourselves."

Noah's animal park was like the biblical Ark, but thousands of cubits bigger. All of his parks were of the same design. What visitors didn't know was that they were only seeing about ten percent of what was actually there.

The tip of the iceberg, Grace thought. *Or the deck of the ship. The most interesting things are below, invisible to the public.* She looked up at her grandfather's mansion. It sat atop a small hill, overlooking the park like a ship's bridge overlooking a deck.

"What do you want to do now?" Butch asked without enthusiasm.

Grace hid her grin. She had taken a page out of Luther's book by driving her reluctant babysitter crazy with polite, but very annoying, chatter and requests. She knew Butch was now long past wishing she had stayed aboard the *Coelacanth.*

"Let's go see the hatchlings!" Grace said.

"Again? We were just there a couple of hours ago."

"I know, but they change so quickly. It's like seeing new babies every time we visit them."

This was an exaggeration, but the hatchlings had grown a lot since they'd arrived at the Ark.

"Maybe we should go to the lunchroom and chill for a couple of hours instead," Butch muttered.

"You go ahead," Grace said, reaching for her cell phone. "I'll just call my grandfather and see if he can take me down to the hatchlings. Or you can loan me your key card." Everyone at the Ark had a key card hanging from a lanyard around their neck, except for Butch. He kept his key card in his coat pocket.

Butch flushed with anger. Grace used this tactic on him several times a day. When they got to the Ark, Noah had said that she could "go anywhere and do anything she liked." He gave her a cell phone that could only call one number . . . his. "If you have any problem whatsoever, I'm just a call away. I promise you that your problem will vanish." This was about as true as his telling her that she could go and do anything she liked. But threatening to call Noah Blackwood never failed to enrage Butch McCall. It was impossible to go anywhere behind the scenes without a key card. Grace had one hanging around her neck, but it only opened the front door of the mansion and the keeper work area beneath the Ark. Noah said he was working on getting her a card that opened everything, but that it was a complicated procedure that took time. Grace knew this was a lie, but she hadn't pushed the issue. She hadn't pushed any issue with him . . . yet.

"Let's go," Butch said grumpily.

He started walking. Grace followed slowly so Butch would

have to stop and wait for her. What Noah had really meant by *You can go and do anything you like* was *You can go and do anything you like as long as Butch, or Yvonne, or I am with you.*

No matter what time of day or night Grace left her room on the second floor of the mansion, Butch, Yvonne, or Noah would *bump* into her within a minute or two and accompany her wherever she wanted to go.

Grace had spotted the surveillance cameras inside her bedroom as soon as she was through the door. They were sophisticated and cleverly concealed, but they were not nearly as clever as the ones Ted and Wolfe had invented. The only place she hadn't found a camera was in the bathroom, which was only decent, but she supposed this wasn't beyond Noah's capabilities if Wolfe was correct about him — and she was beginning to believe he was.

Noah had been friendly, polite, and accommodating, but there was something dangerous lurking beneath his cheerful exterior. "A wolf in sheep's clothing," Wolfe had called him.

Grace was determined to uncloak the real Noah Blackwood and find out why her mother's dying wish was to keep her away from her grandfather.

Noah Blackwood completed his morning rounds by firing only two people. After he returned from a trip, he usually fired a lot more people than that, so it was a good day for the staff at the Ark. The first person he fired was a keeper who had no idea who Noah was. He'd bumped into Noah in the keeper area beneath the Ark and had the audacity to ask Noah who he was and what he was doing in the restricted area. The second person Noah fired was the assistant curator who had tried to defend the keeper who Noah had just fired. Noah had never trusted the curator anyway — *trust* being defined as someone who wasn't afraid of him. This was especially true at the Seattle Ark. His other Arks scattered around the world were what they appeared to be . . . zoos. But the Seattle Ark was different . . . very different.

Noah stopped at the security complex where six employees were glued to flat-screen monitors. They knew better than to glance away from the monitors when he entered.

"Where's Butch?" he asked.

"Level Two with the girl," the shift supervisor said without taking his eyes off the screen. "Lab 251. No surveillance cameras inside."

There were cameras in 251, but Noah was the only person who had access to them, and only a few people at the Ark knew what was inside.

"That *girl* is my granddaughter," Noah said, an edge to his voice. "Her name is Grace."

The supervisor tensed, but still didn't look away from the screen. "Yes, sir," he said.

"Let me know the second she leaves the lab. Call my private line."

"I will."

Noah scanned the monitors and the watchers one more time before leaving. As he closed the door behind him, he could almost feel the relief sweeping through the surveillance team.

It brought a small smile to his face.

Grace and Butch were inside Lab 251.

Yvonne was tossing chunks of bloody meat to the two Mokélé-mbembé hatchlings. The baby dinosaurs snatched the dripping pieces out of the air with lightning speed. They stood four feet tall now, most of it neck, and food passed through them almost as fast as they were able to gobble it down, their feces creating an eye-watering odor that was strong enough to collapse lungs. Butch grimaced and choked back a gag. He hated going into 251, which was one of the reasons Grace insisted on a visit every few hours throughout the day.

Yvonne, on the other hand, did not appear to mind the smell at all. She always had a smile for Grace when she walked into the lab — now the dinosaur nursery. Grace trusted Yvonne less than she trusted Butch and her grandfather. Wolfe had hired Yvonne to train the dolphins aboard the *Coelacanth*. Little did her uncle know that the woman was a spy who worked for Noah Blackwood. Along with Butch, she had been instrumental in kidnapping the hatchlings, and would have kidnapped Grace if Grace hadn't chosen to come with them voluntarily. Grace was convinced that Butch would have shot Laurel Lee if she hadn't broken the standoff by climbing into her grandfather's helicopter. But that was not the only reason Grace had volunteered.

"How are they doing?" Grace asked as she observed the hatchlings.

"As you can see, they are doing just fine," Yvonne answered with a cheerful voice but cold eyes. She glanced at her watch. "Just like they were when you were here two hours ago."

"Oh," Grace said, just as cheerfully. "I hope I'm not getting in your way by coming here so often."

"Not at all," Yvonne said. "You are welcome to visit as often as you like. I love having you."

Nothing could be further from the truth, and they both knew it.

"Any word about when they'll be put on display?" Grace asked.

"Again, not since you asked me two hours ago," Yvonne answered with the same fake cheerfulness. "Or yesterday. I thought you were going to ask your grandfather? The decision lies with him. I just work here."

"He's so busy," Grace said. "I hate to bother him." Actually, Grace had been very careful not to ask her grandfather anything about the hatchlings, or anything else. But she hoped that was about to change.

"He is busy," Yvonne agreed. "But I'm sure he'd tell you if you asked."

"How's the training going?" Grace asked, changing the subject.

Yvonne tossed a couple more chunks of meat, which were snapped up and swallowed with single gulps, followed by belches and an explosion of loud noxious gas in stereo.

"I'm still establishing a behavioral baseline," Yvonne answered. "As you can see, the hatchlings have a healthy appetite, or what we trainers call a good food drive. By manipulating it, I'll be able to train them to do whatever they are physically capable of. Operant conditioning, it's called. It's how all animals are trained."

Or controlled, Grace thought. *The person who controls the food controls the animal.* The night before, she had spent several hours in Noah's library reading about operant conditioning. But food was not the only way to control behavior.

"My grandfather was talking about you this morning at breakfast," she said.

"Really?" Yvonne's cold eyes showed some genuine interest.

There it is, Grace thought. Like the operant conditioning books said. Desire. Just a tiny glint, but it was there. Yvonne wanted to know what Noah had said about her.

"He said that he was lucky you were here taking care of the hatchlings," Grace lied. "That you were doing a fabulous job."

The truth was that Noah hadn't even mentioned Yvonne's name. Like any other morning when he joined her for breakfast, he had spent the entire time tapping on his smartphone and iPad. She had asked him for an iPad of her own. When she returned to her bedroom later that morning, a brand-new iPad was sitting on her bed. Just like the case of Moleskine journals she had requested the first day they arrived at the Ark. It seemed that her grandfather would give her anything she wanted except the truth. And an all-access key card.

"He said that?" Yvonne asked.

Grace nodded. "He also said there were a lot of things you could teach me and suggested I spend as much time with you as I could."

This wasn't true, either, but judging by Yvonne's pleased expression, it was exactly what she wanted to hear.

"Grab some meat," she said with a smile. "I could use some help feeding these two."

"I'll wait outside," Butch groused.

Grace tugged on a pair of disposable gloves and dug in.

Noah Blackwood slipped into his granddaughter's bedroom and closed the door behind him. Checking her room had become part of his "unofficial" rounds since his return. Unlike the three panda cubs, for example, Grace was not on public display, of course. But in a sense, Noah thought with cold calculation, she had to be managed like any other animal in his Ark. One of the most important aspects of zoo management was containment. You had to make sure the animals were secure. From his experience, escape was more likely early in an animal's stay rather than later. After a few days, or weeks, of regular food, shelter, and comfort, the desire for freedom faltered, replaced by resignation or contentment. Ideally, a well-adjusted specimen, upon discovering an open door, should walk right past the opening without a thought of walking through it. Noah knew that Grace had not yet reached this level of contentment, but he was confident that she would, eventually. Once she realized what he was offering her, and how she'd really come into the world, she would never return to the chaos that was life with Travis Wolfe.

The bedroom had belonged to his daughter, Rose, Grace's mother. The only changes Noah had made were the addition of cameras and a few framed photos of him and Rose when Rose was young. Rose had never liked framed photos on her walls. Noah didn't care about the staged family photos, either, but he wished he had installed the cameras when she was there. If he'd been able to keep an eye on Rose like he was watching Grace, he might have been able to prevent Travis from stealing her away.

Don't look back! he admonished himself with a grim smile. *There's nothing you can do to change the past. You have the future now. You have Grace.*

He looked at the nightstand next to the bed. The iPad he'd given her was still in the box, seemingly untouched. Stacked on top of it were the Moleskine journals. He ran his perfectly manicured fingers along the black bindings.

One . . . two . . . three . . . four . . . five . . .

He had ordered six for her. One was missing. She wasn't carrying it in her backpack in the panda exhibit — Butch had gone through it when she wasn't looking, as he did every day per Noah's request. And the Moleskine was too big for her pockets. He looked around the room, knowing he could run up to his office and go over the surveillance video instead, but it would be more fun to find the notebook on his own.

He looked in all the obvious places. Her coat, which was hanging on a hook near the door. The desk drawers. The dresser drawers. The bathroom cabinets. Under the bed. Beneath the mattress. In the pillowcases. On the closet shelves. He didn't find it.

The only reason she would hide the journal was so that no one could read what's inside.

Grace had been the perfect granddaughter since she'd arrived at the Ark. At least on the surface.

She might be able to fool Butch, Noah thought, *but she can't fool me.*

He redoubled his efforts, checking again in the places he had already looked. He called Butch to make sure Grace was still in Lab 251. It wouldn't do to have her discover her grandfather ransacking her bedroom.

"She's in the nursery," Butch said. "I'm right outside the door. Yvonne and her are watching the dinos belch and fart — you're going to have to put them behind hermetically sealed glass so the visitors don't faint. Yvonne and Grace are acting like they're long-lost sisters. I guess Grace has forgotten that Yvonne helped us snatch her from the *Coelacanth*. Can I get outta here?"

"No. Stay where you are. Call me the second Grace leaves the lab."

Noah ended the call and walked back into the bedroom's closet. The mansion was riddled with secret passages. He'd designed it that way. There wasn't a room in the house, including the bathrooms, that didn't have another way out. It was one of his most carefully guarded secrets. Not even Rose, when she was alive, knew about the passages, despite the fact there was one right in her closet. It had been years since he had used any of them. Some he had never used.

Click . . .

A panel slid open with barely a sound. He reached through the opening, switched on the light, and stepped in. It didn't look like anyone had been there in years. The dust was undisturbed. The Moleskine was not there.

He took a few steps down a narrow aisle. He pushed another button and a second panel slid open, revealing the shower stall in Grace's bathroom. He stepped through and closed the panel.

Where did you hide it, Grace?

He went through the bathroom cabinets again, then pulled the vanity drawers all the way out to see if she had hidden the journal behind them.

The only place I haven't looked is . . .

He walked over to the toilet and pulled the lid off the water tank. Inside, double-wrapped in Ziploc bags, which she had no doubt taken from Lab 251, was the sixth Moleskine.

DYLAN

"Exactly when did your parents text you?" Marty asked. He and Luther were on their way down to the dock where the *Coelacanth* was moored, to retrieve their gear.

"Good news about your parents," Luther said.

Marty stopped. "You didn't answer my question."

"Huh?"

"Spill it," Marty said.

"They didn't exactly text me," Luther admitted.

"What did they do . . . *exactly*?"

Luther shrugged.

"Where are they?"

Another shrug.

"They didn't contact you at all."

"I'm sure they would have if they'd had the time."

"You lied to Wolfe."

"I prefer to think of it as distorting the truth."

"Why did you lie?"

"I wish you'd quit using that word."

"Okay, why did you . . . uh . . . distort the truth?"

"Because of Grace, you dunce. Someone has to get her out of the clutches of Noah Blackwood."

"We aren't sure she's *in* his clutches. You and everyone else said she went with him willingly." When Grace was boarding the chopper, Marty was belowdecks trying to defuse a bomb.

"She didn't have a choice. She was under duress. If you'd seen it go down, that would have been crystal clear to you like it was to me. We need to get her away from Blackwood."

"What if she doesn't want to leave now that she's there?" Marty did not believe his cousin (and former fraternal twin sister) would choose Noah Blackwood over him and Wolfe, but she was up to something.

"We at least need to talk to her and find out if she's okay," Luther stated.

We need to talk to her and find out if she's lost her mind! Marty thought.

"As much as I'd like get back to Cryptos Island and look around," Luther continued, "we can't. If we leave the mainland, we'll be off the grid. Stuck."

There were a lot worse places to be stuck than Cryptos, but Marty got the point.

"How do you plan to contact her? Walk up to the mansion, knock on the door, and ask if Grace can come out and play?"

"That'd work," Luther said with his goofy grin. "Or we could just head over to the Ark, see where she's hanging out, and talk to her."

"Yeah," Marty said. "And maybe while we're there we can find Butch McCall and Yvonne and have lunch with them. Maybe Noah will join us for a bite. I'm certain they'd be happy to see us."

"You're right," Luther said. "We'll have to make sure they don't spot us."

"With your hair?"

"What's wrong with my hair?"

"Nothing," Marty said. "Except that it looks like it's on fire and it can be seen from the moon."

"Disguises!" Luther said. "Like Ted Bronson. I've been watching how he does it. I think I can do it better."

"You're dreaming," Marty said. "But there are a couple of things we could do. And we're the last two people they'll be looking for."

"So you're in?"

"Duh *du jour*," Marty answered.

Marty and Luther had loaded two small backpacks with things they thought they might need. Sitting on the nightstand in their cabin aboard the *Coelacanth* were Rose's last two Moleskine journals. On the trip back from New Zealand, Marty had read all but these last two. He'd discovered virtually no useful information about Rose and Noah Blackwood. He thought about leaving these last two behind, then thought better of it. If he didn't get time to read them ashore, maybe he could pass them on to Grace. He slipped them into his pack.

He and Luther were just about to leave when a boy with dark hair stepped into their cabin.

"Are you Marty and Luther?"

"Yeah. I'm Marty."

"I'm Luther."

"I see that," the boy said, staring at Luther's hair. "My name's Dylan Hickock. I guess we're going to be bunking with each other for the next couple of days. I've been looking for you. Did you know the ship's about ready to cast off?"

"Now that you mention it, yeah," Marty said, noticing the vibrations and loud rumbling of the engines. "We better hurry. Cap doesn't care who's on board or who isn't. When it's time to go, it's time to go."

A small yapping black dog the size of a squirrel ran into the cabin between Dylan's legs, making him jump. "What's that?" he blurted out.

"Teacup poodle," Marty said. "PD. Short for Pocket Dog."

A second later a gray parrot flew in, screeching. Dylan covered his ears.

"That's Congo," Marty said.

"You're kind of jumpy for someone who's seen Bigfoot," Luther quipped.

"You heard about that," Dylan said.

"Not in any detail, but Marty had a Bigfoot encounter, too. Of course, it really wasn't Sasquatch, it was a chimp."

"Shut up, Luther," Marty said.

Luther grinned. "Are we going to take these two with us?"

Congo had landed on his perch and started to loudly crack sunflower seeds. PD had stopped yapping and was running circles around Marty's feet.

"They're too much trouble together. I'll take PD." He held his baggy cargo pocket open. "Snake!"

PD jumped into the pocket and disappeared.

"Hence the name," Dylan said.

"Yeah." Marty said. "She's terrified of snakes. Saying *snake* works every time."

The three boys hurried out of the cabin and ran across the deck, reaching the gangway just as it was being winched up.

"Jump!" Luther yelled.

They leaped the four-foot gap. Marty and Dylan made it with several feet to spare. Luther stumbled and plunged into the cold waters of Puget Sound.

"Can he swim?" Dylan shouted.

"Not very well."

Dylan ran back toward the gangway and dove off the dock and into the water like a cormorant. By the time Marty reached the edge and looked over, Dylan had the sputtering Luther in a headlock and was towing him toward a ladder attached to one of the pilings. Marty helped them onto the dock.

"I can't believe we fell!" Luther said. He looked at Marty. "And I can't believe you didn't, as clumsy as you are."

Marty was a natural athlete and didn't have a clumsy bone in his body, which Luther was well aware of. Luther also knew that Dylan had jumped in after him, but Dylan didn't correct him — it would have been bad form to do so. In fact, his cold bluish lips were grinning. You either loved Luther or hated him. There was no in-between. Luckily, Dylan seemed to like him.

"We need to go to the Ark," Luther said through chattering teeth, pouring salt water out of his backpack. "Where's the car?"

"In the lot," Dylan said. "Maybe we should stop by the condo and get dried out first."

"I'm fine," Luther said, wringing out the bottom edge of his T-shirt, "but if you need to, I guess that would be okay."

Marty gave Luther a humongous eyeball roll.

"What?" Luther said.

They followed Dylan to the parking lot, where he unlocked a battered crew cab truck with a cracked windshield and a missing hubcap.

"You've got to be kidding me," Luther said. "Ted . . ." He looked at Marty. "I mean Theo Sonborn drives a junker?"

It seemed Ted did not limit his disguise to his body. A trashed truck was exactly the kind of vehicle that Theo would drive.

"Not much to look at," Dylan said. "But it runs. I'm just happy to have wheels. It was nice of him to loan it to me."

"How long have you had your license?" Marty asked.

"A couple of months."

"Shotgun!" Luther jumped into the passenger seat.

Marty wedged himself unhappily into the crew cab but was soon redeemed when Luther started sneezing from his plunge into Puget Sound.

"We need windshield wipers on the *inside*!" Dylan said, his head pressed against the driver's side window, trying to duck the fallout.

Marty decided that he liked Dylan.

Twenty-seven sneezes later, they arrived at a condo that overlooked Lake Washington.

"Nice digs . . ." *Haa-choo!* ". . . dude."

As soon as they were inside the foyer of the condo, Dylan handed Luther a box of tissues. Farther down the hallway, he opened a door. "My bedroom's in here. Spare clothes in the closet. The bathroom has a washer and dryer."

"My clothes don't need washing," Luther said, "but the dryer will come in handy." He looked at Marty. "Lucky I fell in the drink and not you. You have the graphic novels in your pack. That would have been a disaster."

Marty had more important things than their novels in his backpack, like the Gizmo and the dragonspy and the Moleskines. It would have been an even worse disaster if they'd lost any of those. He fished the Gizmo out of his backpack and slipped it into another cargo pocket for safekeeping. PD was still dozing in his makeshift papoose.

"Graphic novels?" Dylan said.

"We're artists," Luther said grandly.

Marty gave him an eye roll, which Luther ignored.

"I love graphic novels," Dylan said. "Can I see them?"

"They're kind of rough," Marty said.

"Two volumes so far," Luther said. "They recount our adventures all over the world."

Our adventures was an exaggeration. Luther had not been in the Congo when Marty and Grace found the Mokélé-mbembé eggs, but he had been aboard the *Coelacanth* when they hatched.

"The third volume is a work in progress," Luther continued. "We live these stories. That's where our inspiration comes from. I can't promise, but we might be able to turn your Bigfoot encounter into a graphic novel — if it's interesting enough."

"It's pretty interesting," Dylan said. "I actually wrote the story down, but didn't want to put it out there for public consumption."

"You have a title?" Luther asked.

"Right now I'm just calling it *Sasquatch*."

"Bet I can come up with a catchier title," Luther said.

Marty gave Luther yet another eye roll, then looked at Dylan. "I'd like to read it."

"Sure. As long as you keep the story to yourself." He turned to Luther. "I'm surprised Dr. Wolfe let you write about his exploits. I thought he liked to keep what he does quiet."

"They're not just his exploits," Luther said. "He'll come around." He walked into the bedroom and closed the door behind himself.

Dylan looked at Marty. "Is he always like this?"

"Sometimes he's weirder," Marty answered. "And he's wrong about my uncle. Wolfe will never change his mind about going public. He likes to keep things secret."

"Cryptic," Dylan said.

"Yeah," Marty agreed.

Dylan reached into his pocket and pulled out a folded sheet of paper.

"What's that?"

"A note to you from Wolfe." He handed it to him. "Theo gave it to me."

DYLAN IS ON THE TEAM. YOU CAN TELL HIM ANYTHING. NO RESTRICTIONS. STAY OUT OF TROUBLE. I MEAN IT.

WOLFE

"What do you know so far?" Marty asked.

"I know about the dinosaurs and that Noah Blackwood nabbed them from the *Coelacanth.* I know your cousin Grace went with Blackwood. I assume that's why you want to go to Noah's Ark?"

Marty nodded.

"Does your uncle know?"

"Not exactly."

Dylan grinned. "Like in, not at all."

"He wouldn't be too happy if he knew."

"I'm not your babysitter."

"Lucky for you," Marty said. "When we were kids, Grace and I drove every nanny we had stark raving mad."

"Imagine what Luther did to his sitters," Dylan said.

"I think he had keepers rather than sitters. You want to look at the graphic novels?"

"Yeah. And if you're hungry, there's plenty of food in the kitchen."

Marty let PD out of his pocket and followed the poodle into the kitchen.

Forty-five minutes later, Marty came out carrying a huge platter of food with PD at his heels.

Dylan looked up from the dining room table, where he was reading the second graphic novel. "These illustrations are great."

"Thanks. Half of them are Luther's." Marty set the platter on the table.

"What's this?"

"Middle Eastern food. Stuffed grape leaves, hummus, baba ghanoush, flat bread, and tabouli."

"There wasn't any Middle Eastern in the kitchen the last time I checked."

"Yes, there was," Marty said. "It was just in a different form, except for the flat bread."

"So you cook, too?"

"I can get around a kitchen." This was an understatement. The only thing Marty liked doing better than drawing was cooking. "Where's Luther?"

"Haven't seen him."

That can't be good, Marty thought, looking at the bedroom door.

Dylan pointed at one of the drawings. "Is Theo Sonborn really Ted Bronson?"

Marty nodded. "The illustration doesn't do the real transformation justice."

"You've got that right," Luther said, coming through the door.

PD barked and jumped back into Marty's cargo pocket.

Marty and Dylan stared at Luther in shock. He was completely bald, except the bits of tissue stemming the flow of blood from dozens of nicks on his pale scalp.

Luther gave them a triumphant grin. "I bet Noah Blackwood wouldn't recognize me now if we tripped over each other."

"I bet Noah Blackwood would run if he saw you from a hundred yards away," Marty said. "You look like an extraterrestrial that got his head stuck in a wood chipper. You may need stitches."

"Head wounds look worse than they are." Luther spotted the platter on the table. "Food!" He started gobbling down stuffed grape leaves and shoveling baba ghanoush into his mouth with flat bread. "Aren't you guys eating?"

For some reason, Marty and Dylan had lost their appetites.

"Do you have a beanie?" Marty asked Dylan.

"I think so," Dylan replied.

"I hope so," Marty said back.

BAIT

Grace walked into the mansion smelling like dinosaur emissions. She was in for a brutally hot shower, where she would have to scrub herself raw to get rid of the odor. But it was worth it. She loved hanging out with the hatchlings in spite of the resulting stench — and having to be near Yvonne.

As soon as she stepped into her bedroom she knew someone had been going through her things. But she disguised her dismay, breezing in and kicking her tennis shoes off with a bright smile on her face. *Remember the cameras*, she thought. She crossed over to the dresser and opened a drawer as if she were getting fresh clothes. The drawers had clearly been gone through, but she kept her smile, acting as if her biggest concern was what to wear. She had arrived at the Ark with virtually nothing but the clothes on her back. Her grandfather had taken care of that by setting up a generous credit account on the Internet for her. All she had to do was find what she wanted, press the BUY button, and the item would arrive the next day. There was a laptop on the desk, which she had only used to order things. She was afraid to set up a private email account or surf the web for fear that her every keystroke would be monitored.

On the bed was a pile of freshly laundered towels. She picked them up and walked into the bathroom. As soon as she had closed the door behind her she let out a sigh of relief. Acting cheerful when you weren't cheerful was very taxing. She looked around the bathroom again for cameras, but didn't see any. Next she went over to the toilet, disappointed to note that the water tank did not look disturbed. She removed the lid and set it on the seat. A smile spread across her face, but this time it was a genuine smile. The Ziploc bag was floating zip side down. She had left it floating zip side up. There wasn't enough room in the tank for it to flip upside down on its own. A fish had nibbled on the bait. But which fish? Had Noah Blackwood searched her room, or was it someone else? There was only one fish she was trying to hook.

Her grandfather's mansion was nothing like Wolfe's house — or fort, as Wolfe called it — on Cryptos Island. In fact, the two homes could not be more different. Noah's mansion was ultra-modern, Spartan, antiseptic like a hospital operating room. The only other person she had seen within its stark white walls was her grandfather. Her bedroom, and the entire house, was cleaned within an inch of its life every single day, but she had yet to lay eyes on a maid. Breakfast, lunch, and dinner were lonely affairs. By the time she got to the massive dining room, the food was already laid out no matter what time she arrived. No servers or cooks. Noah Blackwood certainly wasn't preparing the food and setting the table. She had visited the kitchen several times at different times of day. Not once had she found anyone in there. It was like the meals were cooked by ghosts. When she had asked her grandfather about this, he answered, cryptically, that he preferred his help to be neither heard nor seen. "They are employees. This house is for family," he had said. As far as she knew, she and her grandfather were the only two people in the Blackwood family. Half the time, her grandfather didn't show up in the dining room for meals and she ate alone.

Grace missed Wolfe's cluttered fort, which looked more like a Gothic castle than a home. Jammed into every room was a mishmash of antique and new furniture in total disarray. Meals were communal affairs. The kitchen and dining room were free-for-alls, with everyone participating in the food prep and the eating.

She pulled the Moleskine from the tank and shook off the water in the sink. She had written several pages. It was the most difficult writing she had ever done, because it was filled with lies.

I suppose that's what bait is, Grace thought. *A lie dangling on the end of an invisible line.* She opened the Moleskine. *But to hook a fish, the bait has to be believable.*

She skimmed the first several pages and got to the section she had penned that morning, hoping it was convincing enough to negate her grandfather's suspicions.

Timothy and Sylvia lied by letting me believe they were my parents and Marty was my twin brother. Wolfe lied by letting me believe he was my uncle when in fact he was my father. As far as I know, the only adult who hasn't lied to me is Noah Blackwood, my grandfather. Wolfe and the others say he's the biggest liar of them all. But I'm not so sure now.

It's not bad here. I miss Marty of course, and I'm a little lonely, but when I think about it, I'm pretty happy, all things considered. Butch lets me do whatever I want. I know he's not thrilled to be hanging out with me, but I think he enjoys it in his own way. He's not nearly as tough as he'd like people to believe. When I finish my entry for the day, I'm going to ask him to take me down to play with the panda cubs. They are so adorable! Afterward I want to spend some more time with the hatchlings and Yvonne. She's not as bad as I thought, either. She's already taught me a lot about animal behavior and training.

Grandfather wasn't there for breakfast today . . . again. I really miss his company and I hope he shows up for lunch. I want to spend more time with him. He's my only relative. We have a lot of catching up to do, but we can't do that unless we're together.

Grace hoped this wasn't over the top. She knew that Noah Blackwood, being one of the most accomplished liars of all time, was no doubt equally skilled at spotting liars. When she'd arrived at the Ark, she'd held on to a small hope that Noah Blackwood was not as bad as she'd thought. But after a few days the hope had all but vanished. Beyond his smiling, pleasant exterior there was something fundamentally wrong. It was clear from watching his interactions with his staff that they were all terrified of him. Even Butch, although he tried to hide it, was afraid of Noah Blackwood.

She looked at her ridiculously expensive Swiss watch. It had cost her grandfather twenty-three thousand dollars. He hadn't batted an eye. Trinkets like this were *his* bait. The iPad was another one. Shiny, irresistible lures. If she didn't nibble at the bait, he would think the fish wasn't biting. Grace had never worn a watch in her life, she couldn't care less about jewelry, but she had made a huge fuss over the timepiece. The more things, or trinkets, she accepted from her grandfather, the more she had to lose if she ran away. The more she accepted, the more he would trust her. It was an hour before lunch. If her grandfather showed up for the meal, she'd know the bait was working.

She slipped the Moleskine into the Ziploc bags and put it back into the tank, noting the exact position. With the Moleskine back in place, she took off her dinosaur-soiled clothes and dropped them down the laundry chute.

Laundry elves, she thought. Noah had bought her thousands of dollars' worth of clothes, but she had only worn two outfits so far, simply switching the dirty clothes for the laundered ones. In a couple of hours the clothes she'd dumped would be back in her dresser, cleaned, pressed, and folded.

"Sorry for the stinky clothes!" she yelled down the chute, then listened. She didn't get a reply, and didn't expect one, but she felt it was important to try to make friends, even if they couldn't, or wouldn't, acknowledge her.

The marbled shower was almost as big as her cabin aboard the *Coelacanth*. She turned the water up to a notch below scalding, then stepped under the stream with her eyes closed. As she reached for the soap dish to her right the marble wall seemed to move. She opened her eyes and stared in disbelief. The wall *had* moved. There was a six-inch gap in the white marble.

Noah was standing in his state-of-the-art DNA laboratory on the third level beneath the Ark. His biochemistry company was called GeneArk. Above ground, the company did very standard biochemistry research. Below ground, under his direction, it had taken biochemistry to unheard-of places. In the Middle Ages, his scientists would have been called witches and warlocks. Their experiments would have been called dark magic.

Noah was talking to his chief genetic scientist, Dr. Strand. The scientist was as pale as an eggshell, as if he hadn't been out in the sun in a decade. But in truth it had only been six months. He was wearing red surgical scrubs. He had a bandage wrapped around his left hand. Perched on the bridge of his prominent nose were the thickest black-framed glasses Noah had ever seen, making the scientist's dark eyes pop from his bald skull. The effect, Noah thought, was irritatingly squidlike. He noticed that Strand's glasses had been damaged, the bridge crudely repaired with silver duct tape.

"What happened?" Noah asked, pointing, and not really caring.

"Nothing," Strand said. "Dropped them on the cement."

Noah gave him a nod and got on to more important things. "How are the samples?" he asked.

"Pristine," Dr. Strand answered excitedly. "There is nothing even remotely like them."

"Can they be cloned?"

"Absolutely. But of course we will have to transport them south for the real work to begin. When do you think—"

"When I say!" Noah cut him off. Strand had been complaining about being stuck at the Ark for months, and Noah was sick of it.

"Of course . . . of course . . . ," Strand whined, backing away as if Noah was about to take a swing at him.

Noah smiled. He had never hit the scientist, but knowing that Strand thought he might gave him a feeling of great satisfaction.

"Can the samples be mutated and recombined?" Noah asked.

"I'll need more time to work with the material, but I don't see why not."

"And did you take care of the implants?"

"Of course . . . of course. Subcutaneously, at the base of the tail, just as you requested."

Noah nodded. Although he already knew the implants had been taken care of. He had watched the minor procedure on one of his secret cameras.

"Where did you find these remarkable creatures?" Strand asked, his excitement overtaking his fear for a minute. "They are absolutely incredible."

Noah frowned. Questions like this were not allowed at the Ark. Information was strictly segregated. One level had no idea what another level was doing. Most of his staff didn't even know how many levels there were at the Ark.

"I-I'm sorry," the scientist stammered, realizing his mistake. "It's just that the material appears to be millions of years old, but it's still viable. If I could learn the country of origin, I could—"

Noah cut him off again with a cold blue-eyed stare. "You'll know soon enough."

"Of course . . . of course," Dr. Strand sputtered, backing farther away like a frightened crawfish.

"How is CH-9?"

"Yvonne was down here early this morning working with him. She said the training was going well. He has a very strong food drive."

"What about his implant?"

"Well, his is very different from the implants we placed in the dinosaurs, of course. Yvonne aptly calls it a steering wheel."

Noah thought about this for a moment. "Is it possible we could use that implant in a human subject?"

"I don't see why not. It would involve brain surgery, which is always a risk. And we would need a willing subject."

Noah nearly laughed. Willingness had nothing to do with a subject's willingness. It had to do with Noah's will. And he had the perfect subject in mind.

"We managed to come up with a harness for CH-9," Strand went on enthusiastically. "It doesn't impede his movements in any way, and with the new camera we can see everything CH-9 sees."

"We won't be using the camera in the next field tests," Noah stated matter-of-factly.

"Of course . . . of course," Strand sputtered again. "That's a given, but as a training tool it's perfect. CH-9 is fast. He gets ahead of us. Without the camera to see where he's going, we might lose him. We've left the camera harness on him so we don't have to tranquilize him every day. He's a little hard to handle." Dr. Strand rubbed the bandage wrapped around his hand.

Noah smiled. CH-9 had bitten Strand three times. The last two requiring stitches.

"I'm glad to hear the camera is working well," Noah said. Ted Bronson's high-tech camera had been an added bonus to the Mokélé-mbembé raid. Butch had stolen it from the *Coelacanth*. Noah's technicians had modified it to fit the harness.

"It's unbelievable! The video is almost as clear at night as it is during the day."

Noah glanced at his watch. He had just enough time to take a look at the final cut of his syndicated television show before sending it off. It was due to go out early the following morning and air the following evening all over the world. It was a dramatic episode. All he had to do was add an announcement at the end that would shake the scientific community and the general public to their very core. He was looking forward to it.

THE GIZMO

Luther scooped up the last smudge of baba ghanoush and popped it into his mouth. "So your mom teaches at the University of Washington?"

"Just for the summer," Dylan answered. "She's an Egyptologist."

"So she's not really your mommy she's your —"

"My mummy." Dylan finished the old joke and gave him an eye roll.

Luther grinned. "I guess you get that a lot."

"Only when I tell someone what she does for a living. There's a good chance you won't even meet her. She's putting together an exhibit at the university. That's why Theo, I mean Ted, loaned me the pickup. She's been spending her nights in the exhibit hall. I didn't have a way to get around."

"Can I drive?" Luther asked.

"No!" Marty said.

"Just asking."

Dylan laughed. "What's the plan?"

"We don't have a plan," Marty admitted. "We thought we'd just go to the Ark and see if we could spot Grace and maybe get a chance to talk to her."

"And maybe get those hatchlings back," Luther added.

"Fat chance," Marty said.

"And Noah Blackwood is going to be on the lookout for you?" Dylan asked.

"Yeah, and his thug Butch McCall."

"Don't forget that snake Yvonne."

"The animal trainer," Dylan said.

"She's worse than Butch," Luther said.

"Nobody's worse than Butch McCall," Marty said. "He tried to throw me overboard, and he murdered a guy aboard the *Coelacanth*."

Dylan pointed at the graphic novel. "I read about that. I thought you were kidding."

"It's no joke," Marty said. "These guys play for keeps. You may not want to get involved with this. We just need a ride to the Ark. Do you have a cell phone?"

"Of course."

"Good. We'll just give you a call when we're ready to be picked up."

Dylan shook his head. "No way. You need me. I'm the only one of us that Noah Blackwood and the others don't know on sight. I'm going with you."

Marty looked at Luther.

"It'd be nice to have one more person — to call the undertaker if things don't work out at the Ark," Luther joked grimly. "And he's right about Blackwood not knowing him."

Marty turned back to Dylan. "Are you sure?"

"Positive," Dylan said.

Marty nodded. "When we get there, we should enter the gate separately."

"Why?" Luther asked.

Marty looked at Luther's shaved head. "Because we'd be humiliated to be seen anywhere with you."

"Feeling's mutual," Luther said.

Marty smiled. He and Luther had been throwing smack talk at each other since they were in first grade at Omega Opportunity Preparatory School in Switzerland (OOPS for short).

"Seriously," Marty said. "If we go in together and they recognize one of us, we'll all get busted. We can stay in touch by cell phone. Providing your phones work after getting dunked in Puget Sound."

"Mine was in the truck," Dylan said.

"Mine's in the bathroom next to the blow-dryer blasting it," Luther said. "I've dropped it in the toilet half a dozen times. The blow-dryer always revives it." He looked at Marty. "You don't have a cell phone."

"But I have the Gizmo, which works like a smartphone."

"The Gizmo is real?" Dylan said.

"It's all real," Luther said. "And the Gizmo isn't a smartphone, it's a genius phone. Show him, Marty."

Marty didn't have to be asked twice. He pulled PD out of his pocket so he could get to the Gizmo. He handed PD to Luther. She growled.

"I don't think she likes me."

"She doesn't recognize you. You look like one of the walking dead."

"I told you the disguise was good."

Marty *and* Dylan each gave Luther a heavy-duty eye roll.

"What?"

They ignored him. Marty fished out the Gizmo and turned it on. It was a little bigger than a standard smartphone and had the same functions: phone, camera, video, email, texting, web browsing, etc. But there were a couple of other functions that made it very different. The first was its tracking capabilities. Everyone officially connected with eWolfe wore a color-coded tracking tag around their neck. They could be tracked anywhere in the world in real time.

Marty demonstrated by clicking Wolfe's icon. He was currently forty-thousand feet over Montana, traveling at seven-hundred miles an hour.

"Hope he's in a jet," Luther said.

Dylan laughed.

"Don't encourage him," Marty said, randomly clicking through a few other names. Ted Bronson was at the Squidarium. Not surprisingly, Theo Sonborn was in the exact same position as Ted. Laurel Lee and Ana Mika were passing over Columbia, South America, on their way to Brazil.

Marty wished Wolfe had thought to give his parents tags. If he had, Marty would know exactly where they were.

"What about Grace?" Dylan asked.

"Blackwood tore off Grace's tag before he took her," Luther said.

Marty nodded. "She's off the grid."

"Show him the dragonspy!" Luther said.

Marty knew Luther well enough to know that what he really meant was: *Let me show him!*

"Here."

Luther eagerly grabbed the Gizmo and pushed the WAKE icon. A drawer slid open, revealing a tiny gold insect the size of a dragonfly. Its wings unfolded. There were two working dragonspies in existence. Grace had one of them. The second one belonged to Ted. He had loaned it to Marty and forgotten to ask for it back.

"What's it made out of?" Dylan asked, watching the bot in shock and wonder as it stretched its spidery legs out one at time.

"Some kind of organic bug material that Wolfe discovered in the Congo," Marty answered. "Ted Bronson synthesized it into a new compound. He used it to build the Orb, the aquasuits, and —"

"His coolest invention," Luther interrupted. He pushed a button and the dragonspy rose into the air on two sets of wings. He flew it around the room, then brought it to a hover just above Dylan's head.

Dylan stared up at the tiny bot in amazement. "What powers it?"

"Light," Marty answered. "The wings double as solar panels."

"So," Dylan said. "The dragonspy Luther flew into your cousin Grace's pocket could still be active."

Marty still wasn't used to people calling Grace his cousin after all their years believing they were twins. "If she still has it, the dragonspy is out of juice. Or Blackwood might have taken it from her. But that's not the problem. She can't fly it without a Gizmo."

"She couldn't fly it even if she had a Gizmo," Luther said. "It's not easy, and video games were never Grace's thing. Whoa, dude! You didn't do the dishes."

Marty and Dylan looked at the Gizmo screen. Luther had flown the dragonspy into the kitchen and was hovering it over the sink.

"You know the deal," Marty said. "If I cook the food, you do the dishes."

"I didn't ask you to cook," Luther said. "I wasn't even hungry."

"That's odd. You ate most of the food."

"I was just being polite."

"I'll do the dishes," Dylan said. "I can't believe how clear the video is. The camera must be microscopic."

"Cameras, plural," Luther said. "And I'll help you with the dishes."

"Audio, too," Marty said. "With speech-to-text."

"Speech-to-text?" Dylan asked.

"Yeah. Ted figured it out on the way back from New Zealand. You can land the dragonspy and it will stream the conversation and video to Wolfe's satellite and play it back later."

"Wolfe has a satellite?" Dylan said.

Marty nodded. "Two, actually. One in the air, one being built."

Luther moved the dragonspy and found PD sniffing around for crumbs near the kitchen table. She heard the buzz of the wings and barked. Luther pushed the speech-to-text icon. The bark came out: *arrgh . . . ugrk . . . shlep . . .*

"Guess it doesn't understand teacup poodle," Marty said.

Luther grinned. "That Ted is such a dunce, creating an app that doesn't speak dog."

"Are we taking PD with us?" Dylan asked.

Marty shook his head. "Not this time. It's going to be hard enough for us to get past the gate without getting busted. She lets out a single whine and it'd be all over for me."

"Let's get going," Luther said. "The Ark will be closing in a few hours."

"Dishes first," Dylan said.

"We can do them when we get back," Luther said.

"Better do them now," Marty said. "In case we're murdered." He looked at Dylan. "Are you sure you want to go with us?"

Dylan shrugged. "Why not?"

LUNCH

Grace walked into the dining room, her head still spinning with the discovery of the secret passage. She hadn't had time to explore it like she wanted, but she'd seen enough to know that it was extensive and there were more passages, connecting somewhere behind the walls of her grandfather's mansion. And as far as she could tell, there were no surveillance cameras in the passages.

But enough of that, she thought. *It's time to find out if I'm getting a nibble.*

Twenty-two white chairs sat around the glass and chrome table. The chairs were empty, but Grace wasn't discouraged. Not yet anyway. The few times Noah had joined her for a meal he had been late.

She sat down near the end of the table. On the white linen placemat was a steaming bowl of crab chowder; a beautiful green salad with tomatoes, avocado, and olive oil dressing; and a plate of calamari ceviche. An identical meal was set out next to her, at the head of the table, for her grandfather, but she knew from experience that there was no guarantee he would show up to eat it.

Grace frowned at the plate of raw squid. The choice of entrée was not a coincidence. She suspected that Noah Blackwood carefully planned all of the menus.

Looking at the beautifully prepared and plated food, she couldn't help but think of Marty and his love of cooking. She wished she'd been able to talk with him before she had left with Noah Blackwood. She could only hope that he understood why she had gone.

"Calamari!"

Grace jumped. One thing she had not gotten used to was Noah Blackwood's ability to enter a room without a sound, as if he were a ghost.

He smiled at her. "One of my favorite dishes."

"Mine, too," Grace lied. She didn't like any kind of food that reminded her of crawling animals.

Noah pulled out the chair at the head of the table and sat down. "I apologize for being late. I was reviewing the final tape for my television show. I'll send it out first thing tomorrow morning. It will air tomorrow evening in nearly every country on earth. It's a wonderful segment. Pirates off the coast of New Zealand."

"Pirates?" Grace said.

"Surely you remember the attack?"

"Of course," Grace answered, not mentioning that she and the *Coelacanth* crew all believed the pirates were sent by none other than Noah Blackwood himself.

"They attacked our ship first," Noah said. "Fortunately, we were able to repel them. When they couldn't board us, they tried their luck with you. We were preparing to come to your assistance when your . . ." Noah hesitated. "When Dr. Wolfe broke out the sonic cannons. I wish he'd used them on the pirates when they were attacking us, but that's neither here nor there. I'm just happy the casualties were low."

"Casualties?"

Noah nodded sadly. "I lost two of my best soldiers in the war for wildlife. They will be greatly missed. I'm dedicating the episode to them."

"I'm sure their families will appreciate the gesture," Grace said.

"It was the least I could do." Noah picked up his fork, stabbed a tentacle, and popped it past his perfectly aligned, unnaturally white teeth. "Delicious! Aren't you hungry?"

"Yes." Grace started in on her salad, hoping to forego the raw squid entirely.

Noah Blackwood sucked down the squid like a famished sperm whale. When he finished the last tentacle, he started in on the crab chowder. In between spoonfuls he said, "I know it must be lonely for you." *Slurp.* "It's my fault." *Slurp.* "I've been so incredibly busy since we returned." *Slurp.* "But I've blocked out some time today." *Slurp.* "What would you like to do?"

The crab chowder was gone.

Her grandfather had read the Moleskine.

He had taken the bait.

Grace smiled. *Now I need to set the hook.*

"I'd like a complete tour of the Ark. There are places I haven't seen yet."

"It would be my pleasure," Noah said, eyeing her untouched ceviche. "Are you going to eat your calamari?"

Grace shook her head. "No, I'm full. Go ahead."

Noah took her plate and gulped the squid down.

PART TWO | THE ARK

A ZOO BY ANY OTHER NAME

"Not too many people here," Marty said.

"Duh *du jour*," Luther said. "Everyone's at Northwest Zoo and Aquarium trying to get a peek at the giant squid."

Dylan had just pulled the pickup into the half-empty Ark parking lot. Over the entrance was a billboard of a thirty foot tall smiling Noah Blackwood surrounded by wild animals, looking like Doctor Dolittle.

"I think what Marty is getting at," Dylan said, "is that you two are going to have a hard time losing yourself in a crowd if there isn't a crowd."

"In Marty's case, I think you're right," Luther said. "A pair of sunglasses and a Seattle Mariners baseball cap isn't going to cut it."

"I don't think a scabby bald head is going to cut it, either," Marty said. Luther had refused to wear the stocking cap, but begrudgingly consented to stuffing it into his damp backpack.

"I'll go first," Luther said. "Do you guys have any cash?"

"I thought your parents were billionaires," Dylan said.

"They are, but they don't give me cash." Luther pulled a credit card out of his pack. "This is how their certified public accountants keep track of how I spend their money. If I pay with plastic at the front gate, they'll know who I am."

Dylan handed him a twenty-dollar bill.

"What if I want to get something to eat?"

"You just ate lunch," Marty pointed out.

"That little snack?"

"You ate most of it."

"I didn't want to be rude."

Marty gave him a second twenty.

"I guess we should set up some ground rules," Marty said.

"What do you mean?" Luther asked.

"We're bound to run into each other inside. When we do, should we talk to each other?"

Luther shook his head. "We can call or text each other. What else?"

"I don't know." Marty looked at Dylan. "Can you think of anything?"

"How long do you want to stay?"

Marty hadn't even thought about this, and he was sure Luther hadn't, either. "I guess we stay until we find Grace and talk to her."

"What if we don't find her?"

"If she's here," Luther said, "we'll find her. I wonder what the Ark is like after dark?" He jumped out of the pickup and headed across the parking lot.

Dylan looked at Marty. "Does he mean that we're going to stay inside after the Ark closes?"

"Yep," Marty answered. "When you get inside, you might want to find a good hiding place so they don't boot you out."

• • •

Luther handed the woman at the ticket booth a twenty and gave her a smile.

The woman did not smile back. "Were you in an auto accident?" she asked bluntly.

"Shaving accident."

"How old are you?"

"Almost fourteen."

"So you're thirteen."

"That's what I said."

The woman gave him his change, which wasn't very much.

"Where's the concession stand?"

"We have concessions throughout the Ark. You can't miss them. I hope you enjoy your visit."

Luther sent a text to Marty as he headed toward the concession stand.

I'm in. The disguise worked perfectly. The woman at the ticket booth was clueless.

Marty showed the Gizmo screen to Dylan. "Do you want to go next or should I?"

"Go ahead," Dylan said.

As Marty walked across the parking lot, he put on the sunglasses and the baseball cap.

Not much of a disguise, he thought. *But at least it won't attract attention like Luther's scabby head.*

There were people in front of him, and he had to wait his turn to get a ticket.

"One juvenile," he said, handing the woman his money.

"I hope the sun comes out for those sunglasses," the woman said.

So much for not attracting attention.

Marty changed the subject. "Is Noah Blackwood here today?"

"A fan, huh?"

More like an archenemy, Marty thought, but he nodded.

"He's on the grounds, but it's unlikely you'll see him. The best time to catch Dr. Blackwood is when he's doing his morning rounds."

"I'll keep that in mind the next time I come."

She passed him a ticket. "I hope you enjoy your visit."

Marty hoped so, too. He walked through the gate, keeping an eye out for Butch, Blackwood, Yvonne, and anyone else who might want to kill him.

He had been to Noah's Ark in Paris — a school field trip when he and Grace were at Omega Prep in Switzerland. The Seattle Ark looked like it was set up pretty much the same way. It was *zoogeographical*, meaning the animals were grouped together by where they were found in nature: North America, South America, Antarctica, Australia, Africa, Asia, and Europe. He thought a good place to start would be to go to Grace's favorite animal, until he realized he didn't know what her favorite animal was. In all their years together, he had never asked her. Up until she had gone to the Congo, Grace had been afraid of animals. In fact, Grace had been afraid of almost everything.

He began to wonder if he knew his cousin at all. She had taken off with Noah Blackwood without even saying good-bye.

Of course, he had been belowdecks disarming bombs, but still. . . . He shook the negative thoughts away, knowing from experience that whenever he started thinking like this, disaster soon followed.

He headed for the Africa exhibits, because that's where Grace was born — a fact neither he nor she had known until recently. When they were in the Congo searching for Mokélé-mbembé, they had come across several rare species of animals. It seemed to him now that Grace might hang out with the same animals she had hung out with as a baby. That is, if Noah Blackwood let her hang out anywhere.

He walked up to the okapi exhibit. Okapi looked like a cross between a giraffe and a zebra. There were very few in the wild. Noah Blackwood had twenty of them, as far as Marty could see. Next stop was the bonobo chimpanzee exhibit. Bonobos were a rare subspecies of chimpanzee. Wolfe had rescued one during his first trip to the Congo. "Bo" had free reign on Cryptos Island, and everywhere else. She lusted after Luther's strangely colored hair. *Maybe Luther shaved his head to stop Bo from trying to scalp him,* he thought. *I should try to retrieve the cuttings back at Dylan's condo and make something out of them for her, like socks or gloves or a muffler.*

The bonobo exhibit was huge and lush with plants and had several places for the chimps to hide from the gawking eyes of visitors. This was how the exhibits in all the Arks were constructed. There was no guarantee you'd see any animals. Marty had watched Noah Blackwood's television show dozens of times. With his photographic memory he could repeat verbatim almost everything Blackwood had ever said on the show. . . .

"My Arks are not zoos. They are built for animals, not people. Like on safari, there is no guarantee you'll see the animals you've come to view. But I do guarantee you'll learn something valuable about them, and the cost of admission will go directly to the wildlife we love so mu —"

The Gizmo buzzed. Marty took it out of his pocket and looked at the screen.

Why are you talking to yourself?

Marty hadn't realized that he was talking to himself, but he wasn't surprised. His photographic memory often went verbal on him without his realizing it. He looked around the viewing platform. There were a handful of people trying to spot the chimps in the exhibit. None of them looked remotely like Luther Smyth IV.

Where is he?

"Look!" a woman said. "The chimps are starting to show themselves!"

She was right. Two chimps popped their heads up from their tree nests. Another came out from behind a rock. They were all looking in the same direction. And they didn't look happy.

"What are they looking at?" the woman asked.

Two more chimps appeared. Marty followed their gaze. They were staring up at the trees behind the viewing area. That's when he spotted Luther sitting on a branch about twenty feet off the ground. Grinning.

Marty sent him a text.

Apparently chimpanzees have a thing for you. Understandable.

Luther sent him a text back.

You're right. They're agitated. Don't want to attract attention to myself. I'm outta here.

When Marty looked back up at the branch, Luther was gone.

It took Dylan a long time to get to the entrance gate.

As he watched Marty cross the parking lot, he thought about the possibility of spending the night on the wrong side of the fence. He wasn't thrilled about that idea. In fact, he thought it was crazy. But if they were going to stow away in the Ark, they needed to do it smart.

Dylan was certain there were security people wandering the grounds at night. Surveillance cameras, too. They might be able to stay off camera if they knew where the cameras were, and they might be able to dodge the security staff if they could figure out where and when they made their rounds. But if security found the pickup in the parking lot, they'd know someone had stayed in the Ark after hours. If they ran the license plate, they'd know it was owned by none other than Ted Bronson a.k.a. Theo Sonborn.

When the Hickocks arrived on Cryptos Island, they underwent a briefing by Wolfe's head of security, Al Ikes. Al was a no-nonsense guy in a three-piece suit, silk tie, and black shoes shiny enough to reflect a pimple on your face. After having the

Hickocks sign a nondisclosure agreement as thick as a book, Al proceeded to lecture them for six straight hours about corporate espionage, international spies, terrorism, and Noah Blackwood.

"Of all the real threats against eWolfe and Cryptos Island, the most persistent and viable is Noah Blackwood and his agents," Al had said. "You've only been here one day, but I guarantee that Blackwood already has detailed dossiers on each of you. He knows where you've worked, where you went to school, every disease you've contracted. He knows your friends. He knows what you own, who you owe, and what you desire. He has people spying for him here on Cryptos that we have not been able to ferret out, which means they are very good at what they do. . . ."

Dylan pulled out of the parking lot wishing he could get his five-dollar parking fee back. He drove around the Ark's upscale neighborhood until he found a parking space in front of one of the large houses. They would have to walk, or run, two blocks to get to the pickup, but it was better than revealing who they were, or having the pickup towed.

Halfway back to the Ark, it started to rain. By the time he got to the gate, he was drenched. He gave the woman his money.

"They sell rain slickers at the gift shop," the woman said, giving him his change.

"I guess I'd better pick one of those up. Hey, I'm doing a report about the Ark for school. Would you have a few minutes to answer some questions for me?"

"Sure," the woman answered. "I've been working here since it opened."

When he finished with his questions, he jogged over to the closest concession stand to dry out and see about buying one of those rain slickers. As soon as he stepped inside, his phone vibrated. He looked at the screen and the text message from Luther.

Get me a couple of hot dogs. Mustard, no ketchup.

Dylan shook his head, stunned at Luther's bottomless appetite, got in line, and sent him a text.

I'll leave your dogs near the garbage can outside. Enjoy.

BENEATH

Noah and Grace were beneath the Ark on Level Three.

Room 305 . . . 306 . . . 307 . . .

Grace had asked her grandfather for a complete tour of the Ark, which was turning out to be anything but.

It's like someone offering to give you a complete tour of their house, then walking you around the outside.

They were walking counterclockwise along a circular cement corridor that seemed to have no end. The walls were painted antiseptic white. The floor was gray and covered with some kind of rubbery material that muted their footsteps. The corridor was lit by bright halogen lights concealed in the ceiling. Every thirty steps or so was a metal door with an electronic lock that could only be opened by a magnetic key card. Large red numbers were stenciled on the doors. Noah Blackwood had a key card hanging around his neck on a lanyard, but had not slid it through a single lock.

308 . . . 309 . . . 310 . . .

"How many rooms are there?" Grace asked.

"Dozens."

"What are they used for?"

"Storage, mostly."

The first level beneath the Ark had been very active with keepers cleaning holding areas and observing their animals on color monitors, people driving electric carts filled with food, and white-aproned staff chopping vegetables and fruits and meats in large kitchen areas. The second level, where the hatchlings were, was quieter, but still busy, with lab-coated researchers hurrying in and out of the numbered rooms as they consulted electronic pads. The third level, where they were now, had no one in it at all, at least in the corridor.

"Where is everybody?"

"All the levels below Level One are secured. Limited access."

"Why?"

Blackwood gave her a slight frown.

"I mean," Grace stammered, "the Ark is just a zoo."

Her grandfather's frown deepened. He took a deep breath and the frown disappeared as quickly as it had formed. "My Arks are not zoos, Grace. They are wildlife conservation centers . . . the last stop before extinction. The animals on the surface are mere representatives of the real work, which lies below. There are many people who would like to get their hands on my research and discoveries and exploit them for a different purpose than I intended. This is why I have security in place."

Grace wanted to know how many of his discoveries were stolen like the hatchlings, but she didn't ask. She wanted to keep Noah Blackwood thinking that she didn't care about what had happened aboard the *Coelacanth*.

"How many levels are there?"

"Oh, several," Noah answered. "But the deeper levels are unfinished and unsafe."

His pleasantly vague answers were maddening, but there was nothing Grace could do about it. He wasn't lying; he just wasn't telling her the truth. If she pushed him harder, she might push him away. It was important to make their time together as comfortable as possible.

Comfortable for him, Grace thought. *My comfort doesn't matter at the moment. Just like in the books on operant conditioning. His reward for the right behavior is a brighter smile. For the wrong behavior a disappointed frown. Positive and negative reinforcement. The only thing he wants is my genuine affection. It's the only way to reward . . .*

"Penny for your thoughts," her grandfather said.

315 . . . 316 . . .

Grace knew her thoughts were worth a lot more than a penny, but she wasn't going to haggle with her grandfather, nor was she going to tell him what they really were.

317 . . .

"My mind wanders sometimes," she said.

"Head in the clouds," Blackwood said. "Just like your mother."

This was the first time he had mentioned her mother, which was the main reason she had decided to leave the ship with him. She wanted to know more about her. She wanted to know why her mother, with her dying words, had made Wolfe promise to keep her away from Noah Blackwood.

"What was she like?" Grace asked.

Her grandfather paused outside room 318 and looked down at her.

"She was exactly like you," he said.

AROUND THE WORLD

Marty walked across Kenya and Tanzania among the elephants, impalas, zebras, giraffes, lions, leopards, rhinoceroses, and baboons. The rain had let up and the clouds had started to clear. He had to give Noah Blackwood credit. The guy knew how to display animals. They looked like they were all wandering across the same grassy savannah. There had to be barriers, but for the life of him Marty couldn't see where they were. It looked like the lions and leopards could pounce on the other animals, which would make for an interesting zoo-going experience.

But it would be kind of expensive, he thought. *And totally unfair to the prey. They wouldn't have a prayer of getting away. . . .*

His Gizmo vibrated. Another text from Luther.

Dylan's in. I'll keep you posted on our positions. Out.

Marty shook his head. Apparently, Luther had forgotten that they were all wearing tracking tags. All he had to do was look at the Gizmo to find out where they were. Dylan was in Sumatra near the orangutans, and Luther was in South America near the jaguars. Wolfe's jet was in Manaus, Brazil, presumably parked on an airport ramp, because Phil and Phyllis weren't moving. Ana and Laurel were about ten miles west, heading up the Amazon River toward the Lansas' jaguar preserve. They weren't wasting any time, which he was glad to see. Marty wished he was in the *real* South America with Laurel Lee and Ana Mika.

He put the Gizmo in his pocket and decided to loop back around to the Congo again. The path was shadowy and thick with green foliage, but that's where the resemblance to Central Africa ended. There were no swarms of bloodsucking, stinging, biting insects. No venomous snakes dangling from the branches or slithering over his sneakers. No razor-sharp thorns slicing through his skin. No heat and humidity. No sour scent of rotting vegetation. It was a completely sanitized Congo.

Kind of like the public image of the lovable Noah Blackwood, Marty thought as he looked overhead at the colorful chattering parrots. He couldn't see a net or glass, and wondered what kept them from flying away.

"Do you work here?" a woman's voice asked from around the corner in front of him.

"No!" a man's voice answered gruffly. "Get your kids out of the way. I'm in a hurry."

Marty nearly fainted.

"I was just asking," the woman said indignantly. "There's no reason to be so rude."

"Whatever."

Marty would have recognized that voice anywhere. Mr. Whatever was none other than Butch McCall, and he was coming Marty's way.

Marty tugged down the brim of his baseball cap and looked back down the path in panic. The next nearest bend was twenty yards away. He'd never make it before Butch rounded the corner, and Butch would recognize him whether he was coming or going. He dove over the short fence into the bushes and immediately clamped his hand over his mouth to muffle his scream. He had just discovered one of the ways Blackwood kept his animals in. Electrified wires! He scrambled away from the hot strand and hunkered down just as Butch came walking by.

Butch's black beard was back, as was some of the weight he had lost when they stranded him and Blackwood in the Congo. He looked to be in a hurry, but when he got parallel to Marty's pitiful hiding place he paused, as if he sensed something wasn't right. He looked up at the parrots in the trees. Marty held his breath. His heart was in his throat. He was afraid that Butch could hear it pounding. If Butch looked down, he'd see him. There was no place to go. Butch would grab him and try to finish what he'd started aboard the *Coelacanth*.

Butch's cell phone rang. He reached into his pocket, looked at the screen, and shook his head in disgust.

"Yeah . . . I'm in Africa. I was just about to go out and run some errands. . . . These aren't the kind of errands someone else can do. . . . I get it, but I babysat her all morning. . . . Okay, okay . . . I'll be right down."

Marty knew there was only one person Butch would submit to like that. But was the baby he was complaining about Grace?

Butch put the cell phone back in his pocket.

Marty continued to hold his breath.

Butch didn't move.

Apparently, *right down* did not mean right then. Butch looked back up at the parrots. Marty knew from experience that Butch was not a parrot lover. Parrots didn't like him, either. He was missing a part of one earlobe, torn off by Wolfe's African gray parrot, Congo. Butch reached up and touched the torn lobe with a frown. The woman and kids came around the corner. Butch glanced at them, glowered, then hurried away.

Marty let his breath out and waited a moment before getting slowly to his feet, trying to avoid the wires and another jolt of electricity.

The woman and the three children, twin boys maybe two years old and an older girl, watched him emerge from the bushes.

"Do you work here?" the woman asked.

"No," Marty answered, brushing the dirt off his pants.

"Then what were you doing in the bushes?"

Marty climbed over the fence. "Uh . . ." He looked in the direction Butch had gone. "I was just coming up the path and some guy pushed me."

"With a black beard? Big?"

"That's the guy."

"We saw him, too!" the woman said.

"I told you we should have gone and seen that giant squid," the girl complained.

"We need to find security," the woman said. "This needs to be reported."

Marty wished he'd told a different lie. The last thing he needed was to attract attention to himself with Ark security. For all he knew, Butch could be in charge of security.

"It's no big deal. He was in a hurry. I just got in his way. It was my fault."

"That's ridiculous!" the woman said. "And that's the other thing about this place. The only staff members I've seen have been in the concession stands and gift shops. Where are the keepers and grounds people?"

"They're probably at Northwest Zoo and Aquarium looking at the giant squid," the girl said.

"Would you just let it go!" the woman snapped. "You've been whining about that stupid octopus all morning. This was the absolute perfect day to visit the Ark until we ran into that bully."

"It's a squid, not an octopus," the girl said quietly.

One of the twins started crying. The other twin looked happy to see his brother's tears.

"Now see what you've done?"

The girl hadn't done anything as far as Marty could see. He was beginning to understand why Butch didn't want to stop and chat with them, not that he would have, even if they'd been the nicest people on earth.

The happy twin pointed up into one of the trees. "The tree is taking our picture."

Marty looked up. He was right. A video camera panned to the right. A second camera panned to the left. He pulled his baseball cap even farther down on his forehead.

"My parents are in South America," Marty said. "I'm going to catch up with them."

"What about the creep who knocked you down?"

"I'll tell my dad about it. He's a cop. He'll know what to do."

His dad was actually a journalist, but he *would* know what to do, and so would his photographer mother, if only they weren't hopelessly lost somewhere along the real Amazon.

Marty ran into the nearest restroom, found an open stall, and closed himself in. It was the only place he could think of where there wouldn't be a camera. He launched the dragonspy. He wanted to find out where Butch was going. He wanted to find out if he had been talking about Grace.

He flew the bot over the mom, the squid girl, and the twins. He flew over Asia, past tigers, gaurs, and elephants. Butch wasn't there. He flew across South America, past tapirs, three-toed sloths, jaguars, ocelots, butterflies, vultures, and a rather aggressive hyacinth macaw who tried to bite the bot in two with its massive black beak. He ditched the bird by diving underground into the Amazon River exhibit, where a big crowd was gathered, watching a giant anaconda swallowing a rabbit. Among the faces staring through the glass was a pale bald head with nicks and scabs. Luther was scarfing down a hot dog with one hand and had a spare clutched in his other hand. Marty called him.

"What's up, doc?" Luther asked with a bun-filled mouth.

"What are you doing?"

"Watching an anaconda eat Bugs Bunny. You can't believe how long it's taking."

"A lot longer than it takes you to eat a hot dog."

Luther's head whipped around, looking for him.

"Look, Mommy, a dragonfly!" the little girl standing next to him said.

Luther looked up and grinned, then started in on his spare hot dog.

“We’re supposed to be looking for Grace, not watching snakes eat rabbits,” Marty said.

“I get that. But she could come through here at any time.”

“Not likely. Crawling animals make her skin crawl.”

“I can’t blame her. It is kind of creepy.”

“Butch McCall is creepy, too,” Marty said.

Luther stopped chewing. “What do you mean?”

“I just saw him.”

“Where?”

“Africa.”

“Where is he now?”

“Out of Africa.”

“How’d he look?”

“Homicidal. His beard is back. I overheard him talking on his phone. He had to be talking to Blackwood. And he didn’t mention her by name, but I’m pretty sure they were talking about Grace.”

“What about her?”

Marty was about to tell him about the babysitting remark when on the screen of the Gizmo he saw something that turned his blood to ice.

“Don’t turn around,” he said.

Luther started to turn his head.

“DO! NOT! TURN! AROUND!”

Luther froze.

“Butch McCall is standing ten feet behind you.”

Grace ran up the stairs to her bedroom, wondering what had just happened.

Or what is still happening.

One of the strange design features of the mansion was that all of the windows were five feet off the ground. She supposed it was for privacy, but blinds would have been cheaper, and a lot more convenient. She pulled a chair over so she could see out. It looked like a normal late afternoon at a zoo. Families walking along the paths, or sitting at tables outside the concession stands, eating; people heading through the front gate to their cars, nobody coming in.

The pitiful tour had ended on Level Three, with Noah insisting that there was nothing to see on the other levels. They took an elevator up to Level One, where Noah disappeared into an office for a minute, then came out saying he would walk her back to the mansion. They got up to the ground level, and by sheer *coincidence* they ran into Butch McCall. Noah asked Grace what time it was, even though he was wearing a perfectly fine watch on his wrist. She looked at her expensive watch with a fake expression of pleasure and told him it was 3:45.

"I had no idea it had gotten so late," Noah said. "I have an appointment." He locked eyes with Butch. "Do you mind walking Grace back to the mansion?"

"Sure," Butch said flatly.

Grace had seen this dance before. She was being handed off. When Noah had slipped into the office on Level One, he had called Butch to intercept her.

"I know the way," Grace said. "I'm sure Butch has other things to do."

"Nonsense," Noah said. "Butch is here to —" His phone chimed. He pulled it out of his pocket and read the message on the screen. A look of alarm crossed his face, but just as quickly went away. "We're in luck. My appointment has been canceled. I'll walk back with you."

Grace could not imagine anyone canceling an appointment with Noah Blackwood.

Noah handed his phone to Butch. "Can you take care of this for me?"

Butch read the message on the screen. "Oh yeah," he said with a slight smile. "I can take care of that. Where do you want me to put . . . uh . . ." He glanced at Grace. "Where do you want me to put it?"

"Someplace safe. Give me a call when you have it stored away. I'll take care of the coverage."

On the way to the house, Grace had asked Noah what *it* was.

"Nothing to concern you," he had answered, sliding his key card through the front door lock. "I have some calls to make. I'll see you for dinner." Then he'd walked into the library and closed the door behind him.

Grace continued to look out her bedroom window. She had an odd feeling. A feeling she hadn't felt since she thought Marty was her twin. Back then, she could feel Marty's presence. There were times when she felt they could communicate with something like telepathy.

She was tempted to use the secret passage to try to sneak out and find out what was going on, but she couldn't. Not with all of the surveillance cameras on the grounds. If she went out during the day, someone was sure to spot her and report back to Noah. Then he would know that she knew about the passages.

Were they talking about Marty? she wondered, searching the Ark. *Is he out there?*

CONSTRICTION

"Is he still there?" Luther asked.

"Yeah."

"Is he looking at me?"

It was hard for Marty to tell in the dimly lit underground exhibit, but one thing was clear. Butch was not watching the snake swallowing the rabbit. He was staring in the general direction of Luther's nicked head like a snake himself, getting ready to strike.

"I think so," Marty said.

"Is he alone?"

"There are so many people jammed in there, I can't tell."

"Should I go left or right?" Luther asked.

There were two ways in and out of the exhibit, and Luther and Butch were standing about dead center between them.

"Go to your right," Marty said. "I'll try to distract him. When you get out, you need to avoid the surveillance cameras and find a place to hide out."

"Where you are hiding?"

"In a toilet stall."

"You're kidding."

"You need to go!" Marty said. "Ready?"

"I guess."

Luther put his phone into his pocket and moved his head and shoulders like he was loosening them up.

Marty dove the dragonspy into Butch's left ear. Butch turned and swatted at it. People yelled as Luther pushed his way through the crowd. Butch dove for him and missed, but the burly security guard waiting outside the exhibit didn't. By the time Marty got the dragonspy past the angry zoo visitors and outside, Luther was being half dragged, half trotted down the path between Butch and the guard. He thought about trying another dive-bomb attack, but worried it wouldn't work, and in the light Butch might figure out that the annoying bug was actually a high-tech bot.

Luther was yelling his head off about civil liberties, lawsuits, mistaken identity, kidnapping, assault, and rich, powerful parents. Butch and the guard ignored him. The handful of zoo visitors weren't paying much attention, either. It looked like security was escorting a crazy boy out of the zoo.

Which is completely believable, Marty thought. *Luther doesn't look like Luther. Maybe Butch had been sent to the anaconda exhibit to check out a potential crazy. Maybe I made a mistake in having him run. Does Butch recognize him now that he has him in hand?*

They stopped in the middle of the path. Butch said something to the guard, which the dragonfly was too far away to pick up. Marty flew it in closer.

"You're sure?" the security guard said.

"Yeah, I got this," Butch said, holding on to Luther's arm. "Shove off."

"Don't!" Luther yelled. "He's going to kill me!"

"Not likely," Butch said. "But I am going to call your mother and tell her you're back at the Ark causing trouble again. *She* might kill you." Butch gave the guard his best smile, which looked more like a grimace. "His mom's a big donor. Dr. Blackwood asked me to come up and take care of this personally, and quietly . . . if you know what I mean."

"What he means is that he's going to murder me!" Luther shouted.

The security guard laughed and walked away.

"You got a big mouth," Butch said.

"You ain't seen nothing yet."

"Where's your friend Marty?"

"Who?"

"That's what I thought you'd say." Butch reached into his pocket with his free hand. "Don't worry, we'll find him, Luther."

"My name isn't Luther."

Butch plunged something into Luther's arm.

"Ouch!"

"Good night, Luther Smyth."

"Huh? You're craz . . ."

As Marty watched the Gizmo's screen, helpless, Luther's eyes rolled up in his head. Butch caught him as he slumped to the ground, threw him over his shoulder like a sack of grain, and started walking down the path.

Marty slammed open the stall door, ready to run to South America and save his friend, but he only took a couple of steps before stopping.

By the time I get down there, Butch will be gone. If I start running through the Ark like a maniac, the cameras will pick me up and I'll be captured, too. What good would that do?

He looked again at the video stream. Butch had stopped in the middle of the path between South America and Antarctica, with Luther still slung over his shoulder like a corpse. Butch glanced up and down the path, then reached into his pocket and pulled out what looked like a credit card.

What's he doing?

Marty zoomed the dragonspy camera in for a closer look.

Butch slid the card into a slot concealed in the low metal rail running along the path. A second later, the earth opened up and an elevator rose silently out of the ground. Butch opened the door and stepped inside with Luther. The door slid closed and the elevator disappeared back into the ground as if it had never been there.

Marty cursed. He was so stunned to see the elevator appear out of nowhere that he didn't even think about flying the dragonspy inside with them. He checked Luther's tracking tag. It dropped sixty feet, then stopped. The tag started to move to the west quickly. Marty stared down at the Gizmo screen. Ten miles an hour . . . Fifteen miles an hour . . .

Butch sure isn't sprinting with Luther over his shoulder. No one's that fast. They're in some kind of vehicle.

The blinking icon came to a stop a quarter mile away. Marty watched for a full five minutes. It didn't move.

Dylan was in North America in front of the mountain lion exhibit when Marty called.

"What's happening?"

"We have a problem," Marty answered.

"Don't tell me Luther is hungry again."

"Luther's been kidnapped."

Dylan wasn't sure he'd heard him correctly, but there weren't too many words that sounded like *kidnapped*. In fact, there were none he could think of.

"By who?" he asked.

"Butch McCall."

"He recognized him?"

"I guess."

Dylan found that hard to believe. The Luther that had gone into his bedroom looked nothing like the Luther that had come out.

"How long ago?"

"Five minutes."

Dylan had dropped off the two hot dogs not ten minutes earlier.

"Where?"

"South America."

"Where are you?"

"Hiding in a restroom between Africa and South America."

"Butch saw you, too?"

"No, but there are cameras everywhere. I watched Butch grab Luther with the dragonspy. Before he took him underground, he asked him where I was."

"Underground?"

Dylan listened as Marty explained what he had seen. He had wondered where all the holding areas, service roads, and zookeepers were.

"We should call the police," Dylan said.

Marty laughed. "What a joke. They aren't going to take our word over Noah Blackwood's. We'd just be tipping our hand. He'll move Grace out of here. Who knows what he'd do to Luther. He's certainly not going to let him blab about being kidnapped."

"Wolfe?" Dylan asked.

"He's on his way to DC."

"We should call Ted, then."

"I already tried. His tag doesn't even show up on the Gizmo."

"What do you want to do?" Dylan asked, but he already knew the answer.

WATCHERS

Marty flew the dragonspy from the spot where Luther went underground back to the restroom. On the way he counted eight cameras. It wouldn't take Butch and Blackwood long to review the surveillance video and figure out where he was hiding. Even if they missed him on the video, security would find him during their sweep.

Dylan had talked to the ticket woman about Ark security. He had learned that the park had only one entrance and one exit. When the Ark first opened years earlier, they tried to keep track of how many people entered and exited, but they could never reconcile the numbers. Now security did a sweep through the park at closing with cameras, and on foot, to find stragglers. Dylan had found a good place to hide next to the Antarctica concession stand. Marty needed to find a good hiding place, too, and the restroom wasn't it.

He flew the dragonspy around to the back of the building. There were no cameras he could see. A row of narrow windows ran across the back of the stalls. He climbed onto a toilet and found, to his relief, that the window opened.

• • •

There were four tiers of video surveillance at the Ark. The first was for the zookeepers located on Level One. It was called AnimalCam, or AC for short. Each keeper had a station where he or she could monitor every move the animals under their care made. Noah Blackwood did not believe in having zookeepers wander around the grounds or the exhibits when visitors were there. He felt that the human presence took away from the natural beauty of the animals people came to see. The keepers arrived at the Ark early in the morning. All cleaning had to be finished and the animals let back into their exhibits an hour before the gate opened in order to let the animals settle in. Feeding was done with automatic feeders throughout the day. The feeders were in different places in each exhibit and programed randomly so the animals never knew where, or when, the food would appear. This kept the animals active and gave the visitors a decent chance of seeing them in the large exhibits.

The second surveillance tier was for human surveillance, known as PEDS. It was also located on Level One. The six people watching the monitors were responsible for observing zoo visitors as well as staff members.

The third surveillance tier was located on Level Four. It was called PI. Noah Blackwood and Butch McCall were the only ones who knew it existed. The surveillance room was twice as big as PEDS, but only one person sat in front of the wall of high-definition monitors. His name was Paul Ivy. As far as Butch knew, Paul hadn't been out of his surveillance room since the Ark was built. He had a small apartment connected to the surveillance room and lived on food lowered down from the concession stands on dumbwaiters. Paul weighed at least five hundred pounds, although it was difficult to tell because he never got out of the wheeled office chair he scooted around in.

It was Paul who had identified Luther Smyth. He used the same facial recognition software used by casinos around the world to track and identify cheaters. Paul had nothing better to do than run the software on random visitors coming through the gate. Over the years he had caught several people wanted by the police, but instead of turning them in, Noah Blackwood had hired them to do his bidding, threatening them with exposure if they balked.

Blackwood had given Paul the names and photos of everyone on Cryptos Island and aboard the *Coelacanth* and told him to keep an eye out for them. Paul had zoomed in on the boy with the newly shaved head and had gotten a positive identification. People could change their outward appearance, but they could not change the bone structure of their face. The software Paul used could see through all disguises.

Butch walked into PI's dim domain and grimaced. It didn't smell much better than Lab 251 with the farting dinosaurs.

"Did you find Marty O'Hara?" Butch asked.

"Of course," Paul said. He scooted over to a control board and hit some buttons. The video showed a kid wearing a baseball cap and sunglasses coming through the gate. Paul zoomed in on his face.

"Yeah, that's him," Butch said. "Where is he?"

Paul hit another button that followed Marty through the Ark in fast motion, ending with Marty hurrying into a restroom.

"That's it?"

"He hasn't left the restroom." Paul looked at the time stamp at the bottom of the frame. "He's been in there for twenty-nine minutes. I told Dr. Blackwood that we should put cameras inside the —"

"Get ahold of Blackwood!" Butch shouted as he ran out of the room. "Tell him I'm on my way and to shut the area down."

Noah Blackwood did not need to be gotten ahold of. He had watched the entire exchange from the *fourth* surveillance tier located on his snakewood desk on the top floor of the mansion. He switched off the cameras around the restroom and told foot security to stay clear of the area. No one questioned him. He often asked for a section of the Ark to be closed down so he could wander among his animals alone and unobserved. If a staff member made the mistake of violating his solitary walks, they were summarily fired.

Noah watched Butch sprinting up the path toward the restroom. As always, he was amazed at how quickly the big man moved.

The grace and speed of a major predator.

No one had come out of the restroom since Butch had left PI. And Paul had reviewed every face coming through the gate before and after Marty and Luther. None of them were associated with Travis Wolfe.

The question is, what do I do with them now that I've captured them?

He doubted Wolfe knew the boys were there. His spies had told him that Wolfe was on his way to Washington, DC, in a military jet. Noah had people waiting to follow him and find out what he was doing there. If the boys disappeared, the first place Wolfe's crew would look would be the Ark. The police would have to have probable cause to get a search warrant, and Paul would erase any video with the boys in it. The woman taking the tickets could be a problem. She might not remember Marty, but Luther was unforgettable. Luckily, the woman had a past that she would prefer to keep to herself. She had broken out of a low-security prison farm with five years still left on her sentence.

Be a shame if she had to go back to the farm.

Noah smiled. He started moving the pieces on his mental chessboard.

They won't be looking for a skinhead, they'll be looking for a boy with flaming red hair. Judging from the scabs, Luther shaved his head just this afternoon. Something will have to be done about Grace, though. I don't want her here with Marty and Luther so close. It might be time to jump on the jet and tour the other Arks. Perhaps take her to . . .

Noah's chess match was interrupted by Butch reaching the restroom. He watched him run inside without breaking stride. A few seconds later, he came back out. Alone. Butch glanced up at the camera, shook his head, then hurried around to the back of the restroom, out of camera view. He returned a couple of minutes later . . . alone.

Noah swore, then hit Butch's number.

"He climbed out through one of the windows," Butch said.

"Where'd he go from there?"

"He crawled off into the bushes, from what I can tell. I called Paul. The brat hasn't shown up on any of the videos since he went into the can. Paul's going to keep scanning for him."

"Marty has figured out where the cameras are," Noah said flatly.

"*I* don't even know where all the cameras are," Butch said. "He's just stupid lucky. I'll find him. He's probably holed up in some —"

"No." Noah cut him off.

"What are you talking about? I'll talk to security and —"

"Great idea, Butch," Noah said sarcastically. "Let's call security and have them help us kidnap a child. Use your head. The Ark closes in fifteen minutes. Go down to the front gate and make sure he doesn't leave. Once we're in night lockdown, there's no way out. We'll look for him at our leisure when everyone is gone. I'll jam the cell and satellite signals. Use the two-way. We're going dark."

Noah hung up and watched Butch stomp down the path toward the entrance. Marty O'Hara *was* lucky, but he was also smart. If he knew about the cameras, then he knew they were coming after him. Marty was well aware of Butch's tracking ability. He would not stay *holed up*. He'd move when it got dark.

But does he know we've taken Luther?

Noah assumed that he did.

"You'll be off the grid soon, Marty," Noah whispered. "Trapped inside the Ark like all my other animals."

CRASH

Marty was lying on his belly near a crash of rhinoceroses. He had learned they were called a crash of rhinos from watching an episode of Noah Blackwood's *Wildlife First*. There were three of them. He was close enough to see the bristly tufts of hair on their ears, the toenails on their three toes, their black eyelashes, and the mud caked on their enormous horns. The biggest of the armored beasts snorted, pawed the ground with his foot, then dug a deep furrow in the mud with his sharp horn.

I'm definitely not crossing that line.

Marty wasn't scooting backward, either, having learned from *Wildlife First* that rhinoceroses were nearsighted and sensed movement before they saw what was in front of them.

It could have been worse. I could have ended up in the middle of a pride of lions rather than a crash of rhinos.

The rhinos were definitely eyeballing him, but he didn't think they knew what he was. He had crawled from the back of the restroom through thorny bushes, across wet and dry moats, and under electric wires. He was covered from head to toe in bruises, scratches, and slimy muck.

The biggest rhino plowed another furrow in the ground, snorted, then swung around in a huff and trotted off with the other two rhinos following. Marty breathed a sigh of relief but stayed where he was. It would be dark soon, and he'd be able to move around without having to worry about the cameras. Belly and face to the ground, he called Dylan.

"Hello?" Dylan whispered.

"Where are you?"

"In a Dumpster behind the concession stand. I had a better place, but the security guards started to do their sweep and I had to move. Where are you?"

"Don't ask," Marty said.

"Any word from Luther?"

"No. Butch gave him some kind of shot that knocked him out cold. We won't be hearing from him. We have to find him."

"I overheard a couple of the concession workers talking about that."

"About Luther?" Marty asked a little too loudly. The big rhino turned around and faced him.

"No," Dylan said. "About how the Ark operates. The concession people are obviously low on the food chain, pun intended, but even Noah Blackwood can't stop staff from seeing what's going on here and talking to each other about it. One of the guys was a new hire. The other guy had been here for a while, hoping to become a zookeeper one day. . . ."

The boss rhino took a couple of steps toward Marty and scraped his horn along the ground like he was sharpening it. Marty glanced behind himself, wondering how long it would take for him to reach the moat and dive in.

"After they dumped a load of garbage on me," Dylan continued, "they hung around outside talking. The guy that's been here for a while said there are at least three levels beneath the Ark. The first level is for the keepers and operations staff. The second and third levels are for the research staff. He didn't know how many more levels there might be, or what might be on them. Nothing is above ground. All staff comes and goes through the front gate. The food and supplies for the animals are trucked in during the night and loaded onto freight elevators outside the perimeter. In the morning, the supplies are distributed on some huge underground conveyor belt. . . ."

The rhino charged. Marty wanted to get up and run for his life, but he knew better than to move. Noah Blackwood had said that most rhino charges were bluffs.

Most, he thought.

The rhino put on the brakes and snorted, close enough for Marty to see strings of snot come out of his nose.

"Are you listening?" Dylan asked.

Marty didn't answer.

"What was that noise?"

Marty didn't answer. The rhino turned around and peed in a waterfall-like gush, a biological phenomenon Blackwood had not covered on his television show.

"Are you there?"

"I'm here," Marty whispered, watching the rhino trot away again. "I just got boogered and peed on by a rhinoceros."

Dylan laughed. "Right."

"It wasn't funny," Marty said. "And I'm not kidding. But back to what you were saying. I lost track after 'conveyor belt.' "

"Everything is delivered from outside the perimeter at night. Blackwood has the place pretty much to himself after the Ark closes. No one's allowed inside unless you have his express permission. If you're caught arriving early or leaving late without his permission, you're fired."

"How does he manage that when he's not here?" Marty asked, keeping his eye on the rhino, who appeared to have forgotten all about him.

"That's the other weird thing I overheard. The old worker told the new guy that Noah Blackwood was *always* here."

"He doesn't know what he's talking about," Marty said quietly. "Blackwood was definitely off the coast of New Zealand and in the Congo, which is a long way from Seattle."

"I'm just telling you what he said. What do you want to do?"

"I'll come and get you after it gets dark."

"So you just want me to stay here in the Dumpster," Dylan said.

"I guess."

"You know, when I woke up this morning, I didn't think I'd end the day in a Dumpster."

"I didn't think I'd end my day getting peed on by a rhino, either."

Marty ended the call, hoping the rhino didn't come back for seconds.

Grace walked into the bathroom and closed the door. She rubbed her jaw, shocked at how badly it ached from wearing a fake smile all day. The bathroom was the only place she could be herself. She pulled the Moleskine out of the tank and jotted down some more smiley words about her . . .

. . . wonderful grandfather who took time out of his busy day to give me a fascinating and informative tour of his magnificent Ark, which he sacrificed so much to create . . .

Blah . . . blah . . . blah . . .

When she finished, she slipped the journal back into the tank, careful to note the exact position, then left the bathroom with the painful smile back on her face. She decided to head down to dinner a little early in order to give herself time to do some more exploring. Her bedroom was on the second floor along with seven other bedrooms — all beautifully decorated, and all completely unused. She wandered into a couple of rooms and looked around with an expression of . . . *wonder and happiness at how lucky I am to live in such a posh mansion. . . .* But her real reason for the side tour was to solve a mystery that had bothered her since the day she had arrived.

From the outside, the mansion was clearly three stories tall, but inside there were only two stories, with no access to a third floor. She had asked her grandfather about this, and he told her that the third story was a facade, which he intended to finish sometime in the future. This of course was a lie.

Who would build an entire floor without any access to it? How would you even build an upper floor without a way to get up there?

Grace opened a closet in one of the guest rooms, turned on the light, and smiled with delight as if she were marveling at its size and imagining it filled with expensive clothes for her to wear. What she was really doing was looking for a secret entrance to the floor above. She didn't find one. She closed the door and wandered down the long hallway to the next bedroom.

The room was much like all of the others — beautifully decorated and completely unused, which brought up the other mystery she was trying to solve.

Where does Noah Blackwood sleep?

She had been into every room in the mansion, upstairs and down, and not one of them belonged to Noah Blackwood, unless he had no clothes except the ones he was wearing and he didn't use a toothbrush.

Grace pulled a chair over to the window.

She climbed up on it and looked outside. The sun had gone down and fog was rolling in from Puget Sound. She looked at her ridiculously luxurious wristwatch.

Time for dinner.

FOOD FOR THOUGHT

Time to get out of the rhino poop, Marty thought.

He crawled backward through the muck, keeping a watchful eye on the silhouettes of the three rhinos until his ankle hit an electrified wire. The jolt through his wet pants was enough to lift him off the ground. He screamed, which was a huge mistake, but he couldn't help himself.

The rhinos charged.

He scrambled to his feet, stepped backward, slipped, and stumbled over a log, ending up on his back in the bottom of a moat, in two feet of slimy water. He looked up. The rhinos stared down at him, snorting, which he felt certain was how rhinos laughed when they saw something funny. He crawled out on the other side of the moat and found a place to dump his pack and unload his pockets to check his stuff for water damage. To his relief, the Gizmo appeared to be undamaged. The same could not be said for the Moleskines. They had swollen to twice their normal size.

Grace will kill me if Butch doesn't beat her to it.

He stripped out of his clothes, wrung them out, then draped them over bushes to dry out a little. He looked at his watch. He didn't know how long it would take the security guards to do their sweep, but he wanted to give them plenty of time to get it over with. Shivering, he started to check tag locations on the Gizmo.

Luther was in the same spot he had been in a couple of hours earlier. On the screen it looked like he was in the middle of the orangutan exhibit, but Marty knew he was beneath it somewhere. Phil and Phyllis were flying north and were halfway back to the States. Wolfe was in McLean, Virginia, across the Potomac River and a few miles west of Washington, DC. Marty zoomed in closer and saw that Wolfe was at the Central Intelligence Agency Headquarters. It didn't surprise him.

Spooks will love the technology he and Ted have developed.

He checked Ted next and found that he was still off the grid. He unbuckled a side pocket on his pack and found an energy bar that didn't look too contaminated. He unwrapped it carefully and started to eat.

Grace was eating, too. Carrots — steamed and slathered with butter and garlic. She was eating them slowly because she didn't want to eat the only other thing on her plate, which was a huge slab of rare beef. She was afraid it would moo if she cut into it. Her grandfather had no such reservations. He was carving his meat and forking it into his mouth like a hungry butcher. He hadn't even glanced at his carrots.

To her surprise, Noah Blackwood had been waiting for her when she arrived for dinner.

"You're not eating," he said now.

"I'm not a big meat eater," Grace said, wondering how someone who allegedly spent every waking moment protecting animals could devour animals at every meal.

"Vegetarian?"

Grace gave him the smile. "No, just a picky eater, I guess."

Blackwood forked another hunk of rare muscle into his mouth. The bottom of his plate was bloody. He dabbed away a spot of beef fat on his white beard with a napkin and gave her a teasing smile.

"Tomorrow night the cuisine may be more to your liking," he said.

"What do you mean?" Grace asked, returning his smile. But inside she was worried.

"It was supposed to be a surprise, but it occurred to me that maybe you don't like surprises. Some people don't."

"I love surprises!" Grace lied.

"I'm glad, but I'll tell you anyway, since I've already let the cat out of the bag. Tomorrow, you and I will be dining at the Michelin-starred Alain Déclassé au Plaza Athena restaurant in Paris."

"France?" Grace knew exactly where the restaurant was. She had dined there with Sylvia and Timothy O'Hara when she and Marty were little kids. Thanks to Marty, the meal had been unforgettable. It had started with a platter of escargot. Marty had complained to the waiter that the snails were overcooked and tasted like tainted slugs. The angry chef had come out of the kitchen and yelled at them. Marty insisted he had cooked them for too long at too high a temperature. The dinner had gone downhill from there, and they left long before dessert — to the waiter's and the other diners' delight. Timothy and Sylvia swore they would never take Marty to another restaurant ever again. Of course, they didn't keep their promise. Two days later they were at another famous Parisian eatery, which the eight-year-old Marty claimed was one of the best restaurants in the world. After dinner he had spent two hours in the kitchen with the chef talking food.

"If I get all of my work done tonight," Noah continued, "we'll leave tomorrow morning in my private jet. I haven't visited my Paris Ark in several weeks, so this will be a working holiday, but we'll definitely make some time to take in some sights. What do you say?"

What Grace wanted to say was no, but that would have been out of character for the adoring granddaughter.

What young girl would pass up a chance to go to Paris with her wealthy grandfather?

She broadened her smile, which really hurt, and said, "That's fantastic!"

Noah beamed back at her, apparently feeling no jaw strain at all, and said, "I thought you'd feel that way."

What Grace was really feeling was fear.

Why does Noah want to get out of town now? Out of the country? What happened today that made him want to leave?

"What about the hatchlings?" Grace asked.

"Chip off the old block," Noah said, still smiling. "Wildlife first. We'll take them with us, of course."

"On your jet?"

"Just like we flew them in here."

"But they're a lot bigger now."

"We have plenty of room. It will be just you and me and Yvonne. Maybe even Butch." Noah's smile faded and his blue eyes narrowed. "Do you not want to go to Paris?"

It was the last place Grace wanted to go. "Are you kidding?" she asked. "Of course I want to go! I'm just worried about the hatchlings. Moving them could be stressful."

"And not taking them with us could be dangerous," Noah said.

"What do you mean?"

"Travis Wolfe," he stated.

This was the first time he had mentioned her father's name since she had gotten to the Ark.

"I don't understand," she said, although she understood perfectly.

"He is going to try to get the hatchlings back," Noah answered, locking his blue eyes on hers. "He will try to get you back."

Grace met his gaze and did not blink. "I came here voluntarily."

"I don't think that matters to Travis," Noah said.

"Are you saying he'll try to kidnap me?"

"That's definitely a possibility," Noah said.

"Is that why we're going to Paris?"

"No," Noah insisted. "We are going to Paris to take care of Ark business and have some fun. I'm not worried about Travis Wolfe, and you shouldn't be, either."

The only worry Grace had about Wolfe was what Noah Blackwood might do to him if he caught him trying to take the hatchlings back, which she was certain he was going to attempt at some point. It would be a lot more difficult to retrieve them if they were in France.

"Will we bring the hatchlings back here?" she asked.

Noah wiped his hands with a napkin and stood up from the table. "Eventually, but I'm not sure when. We have wonderful facilities in Paris. . . ." He paused, then added, "And in other countries. I know you're attached to the hatchlings, Grace. By jet, regardless of where they are, they will only ever be a few hours away, and you can visit them whenever you like." He looked at his watch. "I have some work to do and you need to pack. I'm hoping to get an early start tomorrow." He started to walk away, then stopped and turned back. "I almost forgot. Don't leave the mansion tonight for any reason. We're sanitizing the Ark."

"You mean cleaning it?" Grace asked.

"In a sense. We're located in a very urban area. Periodically we have to search the Ark for homeless people and pests. It's a health and legal issue."

Grace knew this was not true. She had done a perimeter tour with the resentful Butch the second day she was there. Nothing bigger than an opossum could squeeze through the security fence surrounding the Ark. And even if it did, it wouldn't be able to avoid the cameras that seemed to track every move every visitor made.

"How do you find them?" she asked.

"We have specially trained dogs, which is why I don't want you to leave the mansion." He smiled. "And don't worry, the dogs are aggressive, but no harm comes to anyone. They simply round the people and pests up. The rodents are humanely euthanized. Larger animals like raccoons are relocated. And the people are taken to a shelter, which I pay for, where they are fed and given a helping hand." He gave her a charming chuckle. "*Wildlife first* is certainly my first priority, but helping people in need is a close second. My staff thinks I'm insane. They say that people sneak into the Ark intentionally so that they can gain entry into the shelter. There might be some truth to that, but I'm not going to change my ways. The shelter is my way of giving back. I've actually gone so far as to hire a few of the people we've picked up over the years. I've even paid for some of their educations."

He must think I'm incredibly dense to believe this hogwash, Grace thought, barely able to keep her fake smile in place. She wanted to ask him how dogs go about picking up rodents without harming them, but she didn't.

"I bet the people you help are grateful," she said.

"Very," Noah said.

"Perhaps I could volunteer at the shelter," Grace said.

"What a wonderful idea! I'll set it up as soon as we get back from Paris. I'll see you tomorrow morning. Stay inside."

"No problem," she said cheerfully. "I'm tired. I was planning on going to sleep early anyway."

Noah left her alone in the dining room with her uneaten dinner.

Grace had no intention of sleeping or staying inside.

NIGHT SHIFT

Luther's dinner was all over the floor. He puked again, then crawled away on his hands and knees to get away from the sour puddle.

His head hurt. He grabbed it with two hands, trying to stop the pounding, thinking that it was going to fall off his neck. It didn't help.

He put his hand in front of his face. He couldn't see it.

I'm blind! he thought. *Or maybe I'm dead!* Then he realized that dead people don't puke, have headaches, or worry about being blind. He remembered the anaconda slow-eating the rabbit, the dragonspy, talking to Marty, and Butch McCall. After that everything was a blank.

He felt the floor. It was cool to the touch.

Linoleum or cement.

He put out his hands and felt for a wall.

I'm in a room. Rooms have light switches.

He followed the wall on his knees, afraid that his legs wouldn't hold him up.

A lot of wall. Big room.

He came to what felt like a door frame. And that's when he smelled it. Unmistakable.

The hatchlings.

The stench was coming from beneath the door, faint, but they were definitely near. He sniffed again. It smelled worse than his vomit, but as bad as it smelled, he found himself leaning forward for a second helping. He wouldn't admit it to Marty, or anyone else, but he actually missed the prehistoric gasbags. He liked how they went nuts when they saw him and followed him around like very ugly puppies. He took yet another sniff, and strangely, the killer headache seemed to get better.

Maybe there's something magic in their gas. I could make millions.

Using the wall to brace himself, he got to his feet. He was still a little unsteady, but he was definitely getting better. He felt around the door frame, found the switch, and flipped it on. For a second he was blinded by the bright light. When his eyes adjusted to the blast, he saw that he was in a laboratory of some kind. Stainless steel work benches, sinks with shelves and cabinets above and below. But the cabinets and shelves were bare. In fact, the whole room was bare, as if it had never been used. There were no windows. The walls were made out of concrete. The door was made out of steel. He tried the handle.

Locked.

He caught a movement out of the corner of his eye. He looked up at the ceiling and saw a camera following him.

He stuck his tongue out at it.

Marty put his clothes back on. They were still damp and a little itchy. Using the light from the Gizmo screen, he found his way out of the bushes, carefully avoiding the strands of electrified wire. When he reached the path, he launched the dragonspy to scout ahead for security guards, keepers . . .

Or whoever wanders around the Ark at night.

His first task was to get Dylan out of the Dumpster. His second was to find a way underground and find Luther, which was going to be much harder than the first task. The plan to find Grace and talk to her was way down the list now. He flew the dragonspy a hundred feet ahead, tracking its tiny camera eyes back and forth, then catching up with it and sending it forward again. There weren't too many lights along the paths. When he came to one, he walked in the shadows around it. The night was cooling down, and thick fog was rolling in from Puget Sound. The fog would help to conceal them, but it would also make it harder for the dragonspy to see what lay ahead.

When the tiny bot reached the concession stand, Marty flew it around the building twice before making his approach. He walked around back and opened a gate. The Dumpster was closed. He tapped on the metal side. The tap was not returned.

"You in there, Dylan?" Marty whispered.

The lid flipped open with a bang and Dylan popped up like a jack-in-the-box, scaring Marty half to death.

"Why didn't you tap back?"

"How was I supposed to know it was you tapping on the outside?"

"You smell like hot dogs," Marty said.

Dylan sniffed. "And you smell like . . . What is that smell?"

"Rhino pee, among other things," Marty answered.

Dylan wrinkled his nose and climbed out, wiping what looked like a smear of mustard off his pants. "I was about ready to come out on my own. I thought you must have gotten nabbed. What took you so long?"

"I wasn't kidding about the rhino pee," Marty said. "I was hiding from Butch McCall." He brushed his own pants, but the stuff on his leg wasn't going to come off as easily as the mustard.

"What do we do now?" Dylan asked, looking around the foggy darkness nervously.

"We go underground," Marty said. "We stay clear of Butch McCall so he doesn't kill us."

"Great plan," Dylan said.

Grace came out of her bathroom in her expensive silk pajamas and gave an exaggerated yawn for the benefit of the camera. She climbed under her silk sheets, gave her pillow a fluff, yawned again for effect, then reached over and switched off the light. She lay still and concentrated on her breathing. The dark room had knocked the cameras out, but she assumed they could hear her. She wondered if she should try a light snore, but decided against it because she didn't think she was a snorer. Marty would have certainly told her if she had been.

Noah Blackwood looked at the dark screen, listening to Grace breathe. He wondered if she was for real, or if she was like her mother, Rose. After all of these years, his daughter's deceit still stung. She and Travis Wolfe had completely duped him. They had eloped and disappeared before he even suspected they were a couple. If he had known, he would have done something to stop it. Something that would have separated Travis Wolfe from his daughter forever.

When Travis returned from the Congo without Rose, Butch offered to kill him. Noah was tempted, but there were problems. One was that Wolfe had become prosperous during his absence. A man of means insulated by a private island, a loyal crew, and the backing of the federal government was not easy to get rid of quietly.

A second problem was that as much as Noah hated Wolfe, he needed him. Noah flipped on the lights of his diorama and looked at his collection, frozen in time in all their glory. Travis Wolfe was the greatest cryptozoologist there ever was — the only man on earth who could find animals that were not supposed to exist.

The animals I need.

He listened to his granddaughter's breathing for a few more seconds. Satisfied that she was asleep, he clicked another icon, then started to fast-forward through his new episode of *Wildlife First*. It was a brilliant twenty-two minutes — eight minutes for very expensive commercials. It was certain to get a lot of attention, especially the teaser at the end. He was tempted to send it to his television affiliates around the world right then, but decided against it. He preferred to send the episodes to the affiliates at the last minute.

There will be plenty of time to upload it in the morning before we head to Paris.

He took out his cell phone. He had a couple of quick calls to make before he jammed the satellite and cell signals and headed below in his secret elevator. He hit Yvonne's speed dial.

PASSAGES

Grace slipped out of bed and walked quietly into the bathroom. Once inside, she closed the door and put on her clothes in the dark. Earlier in the day she had gathered a few things she thought she would need for her night prowl and put them in her backpack. She felt to make sure everything was there. She pulled out her flashlight and looked at herself in the mirror.

Black jeans. Black sweater. Black sneakers. All I'm missing to complete the ninja-cat-burglar look is a black stocking cap and black gloves.

She popped the hidden latch in the shower stall, stepped through the opening, and closed the secret panel behind her. She used her flashlight to guide her. There were lights in the passage, but she didn't want to use them, afraid someone might notice.

Someone?

The only person she had seen in the house was Noah Blackwood. But he had to have people working inside. And they had to be working at night, because she hadn't seen anyone during the day. She hoped to get to the bottom of that tonight, but her real goal was to find a way up to the third floor. She felt all her questions would be answered there.

As she made her way along the passage, one thing was obvious: The mansion was built around it. The passage was not an afterthought. She had wondered why the mansion looked so big from the outside but seemed a little cramped inside. She thought it was because of the fake third floor, but it wasn't. The passage ran around the exterior of the house and was at least four feet wide. It also explained why the windows were so small and high. She was able to walk under the frames without ducking. Wires ran along the ceiling — thick video cable and smaller wires that could be, and probably were, connected to microphones.

All the bedrooms and bathrooms had a secret door leading into them. Every twenty feet there was a peephole drilled into the wall. The constant camera surveillance was bad enough; now she wondered if Noah had been watching her through the holes. The thought grossed her out. When she got back to her bedroom, she was definitely going to find the peephole and figure out a subtle way to cover it up.

At the far end of the house, the corridor made a hard right turn, then dead-ended about halfway down the passage.

Odd. Why doesn't it go all the way around to the bedrooms on the other side?

She reversed course, walking back past her bedroom and rounding two more turns, where she found a ladder built into the wall, leading to the first floor. She climbed down and found a secret door that opened into the library. She looked through the peephole and didn't see anyone wandering around. A little farther on she found a door to the outside. This door she did crack open. It led to the swimming pool behind the mansion, and beyond it was the helipad, which was empty. Noah's helicopter was kept at a nearby private airport, with pilots standing by 24/7 to whisk him away at a moment's notice.

Grace was tempted to slip outside but decided to finish searching the passage first. She found another secret door in a bathroom near the kitchen and yet another leading outside, hidden inside a closet near the front door. Then she ran into the same dead end as she had above. She was about to turn around when she heard a humming noise. She had heard it before in bed at night and assumed it was the furnace or air-conditioning. But here it was louder . . . a lot louder. She put her hands on the wall in front of her and felt it vibrating. Overhead was a large vent. She looked up at it just in time to see a shadow pass by on the other side, going down.

There were only two buttons on the elevator. UP and DOWN. Noah Blackwood pushed the DOWN button. The car dropped a hundred feet beneath the Ark. The doors slid open onto Level Four. Butch was waiting for him in an electric cart.

"Well?" Noah asked, climbing into the cart.

Butch shook his head. "Nothing. I was just about to check in with Paul."

"Let's go," Noah said.

Butch put the electric cart into gear and headed down the circular corridor. There were several rooms, but only three of them were occupied. They passed the taxidermy workshop where Noah's mounts were lovingly crafted by Henrico.

"How's Mitch Merton doing?" Noah asked.

"Mitch the Snitch?"

Noah nodded.

"According to Henrico, not too well," Butch said. "He's found him wandering around the corridor trying to escape."

"Fruitless," Noah said.

"We know that, but Mitch hasn't figured it out yet. Henrico's about ready to stuff *him*."

Noah smiled. "He'll adjust. Henrico was the same when he got here twenty years ago. Eventually, he gave up and got to work because there was absolutely nothing else for him to do."

"Kind of like Paul Ivy," Butch said.

"Paul is totally different," Noah said. "He never wanted to leave. He was a wanted man when he first came down here, but the statute of limitations expired long ago on that charge, yet he stayed."

"Probably because he can't fit through the door anymore," Butch said.

Noah nodded. "I am a little worried about his health. But if something happens to him, we always have Mitch. He might like staring at the monitors better than stuffing animals."

"I doubt it," Butch said.

"You're probably right," Noah agreed. "I have something else in mind for our friend Mitch, something that should keep him under control. I was talking to Strand about it just this afternoon."

"What is it?" Butch asked.

"Never mind," Noah said. "We have other things to take care of first."

Butch stopped outside Paul Ivy's domain, pulled his key card out of his coat pocket, and swiped through the lock. The door hissed open. Paul was scanning the monitors as he ate a hamburger. There were four more hamburgers lined up on his desk. Noah wondered how many he had already eaten. At the end of the day, the concession staff sent the leftover food down a dumbwaiter, thinking it was going off-grounds to Noah's homeless shelter.

Paul glanced at them when they walked in, then refocused on the monitors. "It's like a graveyard out there," he said, unwrapping another burger. "I told you we should have invested in thermal imaging cameras. A mouse wouldn't get past us. If your intruder stays out of the light, we won't see him at all. And the fog's making it worse."

Noah ignored the complaint. "What about Luther?"

Paul pointed at a black screen. "He came to a few minutes ago and it sounded like he puked. Then the lights came on for about five minutes. He stumbled around, then it looked like the lights were bothering him and he turned them off again. I haven't heard anything since. I figure maybe he passed out again. What did you give him?"

"Concession food," Butch said.

"Very funny," Paul said. "You should do stand-up."

Noah stared at the black screen. He didn't like it. "Did we get those remote lights installed yet?"

Paul shook his head. "Nope. We're still waiting for parts."

Noah cursed.

After peering through the peephole into the kitchen to make sure no one was there, Grace popped open the secret door. The kitchen was bright compared to the passage, and it took a second or two for her eyes to adjust.

She searched the drawers for a screwdriver but didn't find one. She did find a butter knife, though, that she thought might work.

In the center of the kitchen was a small table with four chairs. She picked up one, took it back through the secret doorway, and carried it down the passage. She had to stand on her toes with the flashlight in her mouth to reach the vent. The butter knife was not the ideal tool for loosening the screws, but she managed to get them out after several tries. She lowered the vent plate to the ground, then peered through the opening. As she suspected, it was an elevator shaft. High above her was another door that must have opened onto the third floor. Oddly, there didn't appear to be a stop on the first or second floors.

She shined her light around the shaft. There was a ladder built into the wall that reached all the way up to the third floor. She pushed herself through the opening and grabbed the nearest rung.

Noah and Butch left Paul to his burgers and monitors and got back into the cart. Noah glanced to his right and smiled as they passed the door marked 400.

Butch glanced at the door, too. "How's he doing?" he asked.

"I suspect he's a little bored, but he's used to that. If all goes well tonight, I'll activate him tomorrow and he'll have plenty to do over the next few days."

Butch stopped the cart outside another elevator. They climbed out and Noah swiped his card through the electronic lock. They stepped in and went up to Level Two.

"How do you want to handle this?" Butch asked as they walked toward the room where Luther was locked up.

"How about you opening the door, turning on the light, and putting him into a choke hold until he tells us who he came here with," Noah answered impatiently.

"I get that part," Butch said. "I meant after I get the information out of him."

"What do you think we should do with him?" Noah asked.

"How about pushing him out of an airplane over Lake Télé in the Congo and letting him try to thrash his way out of the jungle like we had to?"

Noah smiled. "I like how you think, but the Atlantic Ocean somewhere over the Bermuda Triangle would be better."

Butch opened the door marked 222. The light was on.

"I thought Paul said Luther turned off the light," Butch said.

"Where is Luther?" Noah asked.

Grace was one kick away from the third floor, but opening elevator doors from the inside while dangling from a ladder was proving impossible. Her legs weren't long enough to kick the emergency latch open. Frustrated and angry, she climbed back down to the vent and managed to drop her flashlight as she was trying to squeeze back through the opening. She watched it spin like a baton, its light growing smaller by the second, as it fell. At last it landed on what she imagined had to be the top of the elevator, with a bang loud enough to be heard all over the Ark. She held her breath, waiting for the sound of the lower elevator door opening and watching to see if the cables started to move. But everything remained quiet and perfectly normal except for the flashlight beam pointing accusingly up the shaft at her.

She thought about leaving the flashlight where it lay, then decided she should climb down and retrieve it. If it was caught in a cable or a gear, Noah would investigate and know she had been there.

The climb down the shaft in the dark was terrifying. She thought that at any moment the motor would fire up and the car would start to rise. She'd be scraped off the wall. If she jumped on top of the car to save herself, Noah would hear her.

If he didn't hear me land, he would certainly hear my screams as I was being crushed against the ceiling when the car reached the third floor. Of course, then it wouldn't matter. I'd be dead.

After what seemed like an eternity, she reached the top of the car and grabbed the flashlight, which was not anywhere near a cable or a gear. She was about ready to start the long climb back up when she noticed a thin line of light leaking from the top. She knelt down for a closer look. There was a trapdoor built into the elevator's roof, outlined by the fluorescent light of the car beneath it.

Why climb when I can ride? All I have to do is jump down inside and push the UP *button.*

But there were risks. The elevator could be under camera surveillance, of course. And how long would Noah be gone? What if he came back while she was on the third floor? He'd certainly notice the delay if the car wasn't waiting for him on whatever level this was. Which was the other strange thing about the shaft. There were only two elevator openings: one on the third floor, and one where the car had stopped.

She opened the trapdoor. The floor was at least a ten-foot drop below. If she decided to lower herself down, she'd have no choice but to use the elevator to get back up. She wasn't tall enough to pull herself back through the trapdoor.

But if I ever want to see what's inside Noah's third-floor "facade" . . .

She dropped her pack through the opening, then followed it into the waiting elevator.

HIDE-AND-SEEK

Butch had torn open every cabinet door in Lab 222. Luther was not there.

"Are you sure this is the right room?" Noah asked.

Butch pointed to the puddle on the floor. "Unless somebody else came in here and puked, yeah."

Noah walked over to the keypad next to the door. He hit a series of numbers that only he knew and looked at the readout. It told him exactly when and how many times the door had been opened in the past month. It had been opened three times: when Butch walked in carrying Luther slung over his shoulder; fourteen seconds later, when Butch left without Luther slung over his shoulder; and a few minutes earlier, when they walked in expecting to find Luther.

Noah looked around the room. He had designed and built thousands of animal exhibits. The laboratory was not an exhibit, but it was a cage of sorts. The human occupants didn't know it, but he controlled everything inside of it, including the humans to a large extent. One thing he had learned is that you design an exhibit as best as you can, but when you put the animal inside, it tells you what you did wrong.

"Sometimes it takes years," he said aloud.

"What?" Butch asked.

Noah pointed to the surveillance camera. The cable had been pulled out. He then pointed at the air duct. The cover was loose.

"Luther didn't turn the light off," Noah said. "He disabled the camera."

There were sneaker tracks on the counter. The Ark was honeycombed with air ducts. Luther Smyth had access to every room in the complex, and there were no cameras where he was crawling.

Marty showed Dylan the kidnapping video on the Gizmo.

"This is serious," Dylan said.

"You think?"

They were still standing next to the Dumpster, trying to figure out what they should do.

"Does that dragonspy thing see at night?" Dylan asked.

"Not as well as it does during the day, and the fog is not its friend, but yeah, it's pretty good in the dark. It helped me get to your Dumpster hideout."

"Then you should launch it and see what kind of security they have at night."

"I didn't see anybody on my way here."

"You could have missed them. It wouldn't hurt to double check. We're no good to Luther if someone sticks a needle in our arms, too."

Staying still was not Marty's best skill. He wanted to get underground and find Luther. But Dylan had a good point. Running around and risking a run-in with one of Noah Blackwood's goons didn't make sense.

He relaunched the dragonspy.

• • •

The second after Grace pushed the UP button inside the elevator, she realized she had made a mistake. The passenger who had last taken the elevator down might not have been Noah Blackwood after all. It could have been Butch, or Yvonne, or someone else. Which meant that Noah Blackwood might be up on the third floor waiting for her. She hit the DOWN button over and over, trying to stop the car, but nothing happened. Her stomach dropped as the elevator continued to rise, until it came to a gentle stop.

The door slid open. She wasn't sure how she was going to get back down to the mansion's second or first floor, but there had to be another way aside from the elevator.

What if the power went out? What if there was a fire?

The third floor was nothing like the mansion's other floors. It actually looked like someone lived there. It drew her in like a magnet. The elevator door slid closed behind her before she could turn around and stop it.

How many stupid things can I do in a row? I should have jammed it open!

Every door in the Ark, including the elevator doors, was accessed via a magnetic key card. But not every key card opened every door. Not even Butch's and Yvonne's cards opened every door. There had been a couple of times when they had swiped their cards and a door that had previously opened without a problem didn't anymore. Grace assumed that Noah controlled all of the cards, which was another way of controlling his staff, even those closest to him.

She swiped her card through the elevator slot and got exactly what she expected. Nothing. The door didn't move. Unless she found another way down, she would be trapped on the third floor until Noah Blackwood showed up.

Unless he's already here.

Grace held her breath and listened.

Luther was listening, too, because there wasn't much to see where he was. He felt like a sardine trying to escape from a very long tin can. Butch had taken Luther's backpack and emptied his pockets, but hadn't found the cell phone in his sock. There was no signal, but at least it worked reasonably well as a flashlight as he pulled himself forward one foot at a time.

Lucky I'm not claustrophobic.

He immediately regretted thinking this because instantly he *did* feel claustrophobic and began to wonder how long it would take them to start smelling his decomposing body after he died in the ductwork. He shook off the thought, pulled himself forward, and hit his head on something sharp.

"Ouch!"

He touched his head and felt something warm and wet.

What's another nick? I have a thousand of them. But what nicked me?

He twisted around with his cell phone and found a square box with sharp corners sticking out from the top side of the duct. Video cable wires were running in from one side of the box and coming out the other.

"Good night, Butch McCall," Luther whispered, then plucked the cables out one at a time.

THE CUBE

It looked like one gigantic room with a large black cube in the middle. The elevator had opened up into a large office area. Grace decided to forgo the office for now and circle the cube to get her bearings. Her first stop was her grandfather's sleeping area, and one thing was clear to her. There were no secret passages on the third floor. The perimeter walls had floor-to-ceiling windows covered with heavy blackout curtains. No hollow walls. No passages.

But there has to be another way out of here!

She looked around the bedroom. There was a king-sized bed, perfectly made, with red silk bedding. Next to it was a simple night table with a lamp made out of a large rhinoceros horn.

She had watched the *Wildlife First* episode at the Ark's Africa exhibit that showed Noah Blackwood tearing across the savannah in pursuit of rhino poachers. Poachers slaughtered the animals, then sawed off their horns and left the carcasses to rot in the hot African sun. The horns were ground up and sold on the black market for so-called medicinal purposes. A single horn could sell for as much as eighty thousand dollars.

Yet my grandfather uses one to read by.

The headboard was against the window curtains. When her grandfather woke up in the morning, he would be able to see his reflection in the wall of the black cube. On one side of the bed was a huge freestanding wardrobe and two dressers. She hesitated to open them, then thought about what Marty would do in the same circumstances. She laughed. *By now he'd have been through absolutely everything. And it's not as if Noah hasn't been invading my privacy and spying on me.*

She opened the wardrobe. A long row of safari shirts and pants in different colors were hanging with the plastic still on them from the dry cleaner's. She wondered if he sent them out, or if the Ark laundry did dry cleaning as well as the wash. Lined up neatly beneath the clothes were five pairs of perfectly polished shoes, identical — three brown pairs and two black. There was a space in the row of black shoes.

Which means he's wearing a black pair tonight.

She went over to the dresser and started opening drawers, discovering nothing except that Noah liked his socks, T-shirts, and briefs perfectly folded and stacked.

On the other side of the bed was a bathroom without walls. A glass shower stall, a freestanding vanity with a huge mirror, a clothes hamper, and a heated toilet. Noah Blackwood liked his reflection and his comforts, but Grace already knew that. What the wall-less bathroom told her was that Noah Blackwood never had guests up on the third floor.

She moved around the cube to the next section, which was an exercise area. Treadmill, elliptical machine, stair stepper, recumbent bicycle, weights, punching bag . . . every kind of apparatus imaginable, which was why her grandfather was in such good shape for a man in his fifties — although she didn't know exactly how old he was.

What lay around the next corner shocked her. Instead of curtains, the windows were covered by a solid green screen. In front of it was a junkyard minus the junkyard dog. There was a snowmobile, a dirt-encrusted four-wheeler, the cockpit of a small airplane, camping gear, and so many other things it was difficult for her to find her way through the incredible clutter.

She stopped next to a small pitched tent. Outside the opening were the ashes of an old campfire with pots and pans and cooking utensils scattered around it. She opened the flap and looked inside. There was an air mattress, an old sleeping bag, and a backpack. She opened the pack and found it was stuffed with newspapers. She wondered if all the junk was mementos from past expeditions. But even if they were, why would they be stored in such a haphazard way? Noah Blackwood was very precise in everything that he did. It was unthinkable that he could live with this kind of chaos on his private floor.

Why?

She moved on to his office to try to find the answer.

Marty was trying to find answers, too, and not having much luck. His thinking was that if he found a staff member wandering around the Ark, he might be able to follow them underground with the dragonspy and find Luther. But there was no one to follow. The Ark was like an eerie ghost ship drifting in a sea of fog.

"I'm getting a little creeped out," Dylan said.

"Me too," Marty admitted. "Maybe we should call Wolfe."

"In DC?"

"He won't be able to help us from there, but he may know how to get ahold of Ted or someone else who can." He flew the dragonspy back to the Dumpster and parked it under a light so it could recharge, then switched to the Gizmo's phone function. "Weird, I'm not getting a signal."

Dylan fished his phone out of his pocket and looked at it. "Me neither."

"I'll switch to satellite." Marty hit the icon. "Uh-oh."

"Dead?"

Marty enabled the tracking icon to make sure. *No Satellite Signal . . .* flashed across the screen. "As a doornail," he said. "I guess the dragonspy doesn't depend on sat signals to fly. You didn't happen to see any pay phones when you were wandering around, did you?"

"What's a pay phone?"

"Funny. So we're on our own . . . again."

"Just the way you and Luther like it," Dylan said. "Think about all the great scenes in your next graphic novel."

"Yeah," Marty said. "Like this scene: two guys squatting next to a Dumpster at night with fog swirling around them, debating about their next step and with no idea of what it's going to be."

Dylan grinned. "Point well taken. I guess we should do something, even if it's stupid."

"Exactly! Let's head over to where Butch snatched Luther and see if we can figure out how to call that elevator back up."

Marty parked the dragonspy in the Gizmo. They grabbed their packs and headed toward South America, staying in the shadows away from the lights.

"There are three cameras up ahead where the path forks," Marty explained as they walked. "Two on the right, one on the left. There are also spotlights at the fork and smaller lights embedded in the rails along both paths. We'll have to go around the spotlights, but we might be able to sneak past the cameras covering the path to the right because seven of the rail lights are out. The cameras aren't infrared. They won't be able to pick us up if we stay in the center of the path. I hope. There aren't any lights where Butch went down the rabbit hole, so we should be safe there unless —"

"Wait a second!" Dylan interrupted. "How do you know so much about the lights and the cameras?"

"The dragonspy."

"It counts cameras and lights?"

"No, I counted the cameras and lights, or more accurately, I've memorized them. I have an eidetic memory."

"Huh?"

"Perfect recall, photographic memory."

"That's awesome."

Marty shrugged. "It is and it isn't. What I see stays in my brain forever. Twenty years from now, providing we live through the night, I'll remember the lights and cameras and fog and this conversation in perfect brain-clogging detail." He pointed to his head. "I'm afraid that someday the tank's going to explode with too much useless information."

"But it's kind of handy tonight," Dylan said.

"I guess," Marty admitted. "We better head overland until we're past the spotlights. But watch out for the hot wires. They really hurt."

"Huh?"

Marty explained how Noah managed to keep the animals in without barriers as he led the way. He hadn't been into this area of the Ark before, but he had a pretty good idea of where the hot wires would be from his previous painful experience. As he picked his way through the bushes, whispering hot-wire warnings to Dylan, he thought about Luther. He was kicking himself for not listening to Dylan. He should have called for help when they still had reception. The cell and satellite signals being out at the same time could only mean one thing: Noah Blackwood knew he was there and had jammed the signals so he couldn't call for help.

"Wire," he whispered, pointing his flashlight app so Dylan could see it.

"Where are all the security guards?" Dylan asked, carefully stepping over the wire.

"I was wondering that myself. I think Blackwood got rid of them just like Butch got rid of the security guy who helped him nab Luther."

"That could work to our advantage," Dylan said. "Two against two."

"Hopefully two against three," Marty said. "Hopefully Luther's okay."

Noah and Butch were back with Paul Ivy in the surveillance room. The hamburgers were gone and Paul was frantic. His world was being shut down one screen at a time.

"There goes another one!" Paul shouted. "A third of the cameras are already down. If he keeps this up, we'll be totally blind in less than an hour."

Noah scanned the remaining camera feeds. There were a few cameras left on every level, but coverage was very spotty. "Are the cameras working in 251?"

Paul hit a button on his console and a close-up of the hatchlings appeared on the central monitor. The young dinosaurs were wrapped around each other, sleeping.

"Pan back," Noah said.

Paul toggled a switch and a panoramic view of the makeshift nursery appeared on the screen. Yvonne was lying on a cot twenty feet away from the hatchlings and looked to be as sound asleep as they were.

Noah was pleased. The newest member of his very small inner circle was turning out to be a very dedicated and loyal employee. He had spoken to her earlier from the mansion, knowing that she had been awake for thirty-six hours straight. He had suggested that she get some sleep because he needed her alert for something he had in mind for later that night.

"She's a team player," Noah said.

"By sleeping," Butch said resentfully.

"That's exactly what I told her to do," Noah said, suppressing a smile. He liked it when his lieutenants were jealous of each other. The competition for his approval kept them in line. "She could have gone up to the keeper level to sleep," Noah continued. "Which would have been a lot more comfortable for her, and it certainly would have smelled better. But instead she chose to sleep near her charges regardless of the discomfort. Impressive."

Butch frowned.

Paul shrugged.

The central monitor went blank.

"What am I going to do when all the cameras are out?" Paul whined.

"How about some exercise?" Butch said.

"Shut up, Butch."

"Both of you shut up," Noah said. "Is there a way to figure out where Smyth is by the cameras he's taking out?"

Paul shook his head. "I already thought of that. It's a spaghetti pile of cables and wires up there. Twenty years' worth. The only thing we can hope for is that he pops out on top before he yanks all of the camera connections."

"What do you mean by 'pops out on top'?" Butch asked.

"The surface. Air vents. If we didn't have them, we'd suffocate. There are three of them, and as far as I know they aren't locked."

"I don't want Luther on the surface," Noah said. "I want him contained down here."

"What about the cameras?" Paul whined again.

"Forget about them. Where are the surface vents?"

Reluctantly, Paul brought up a schematic of the Ark on the central monitor and pointed them out.

"If I recall," Noah said, "the vents are latched from the inside. There is no lock on the outside."

Paul nodded.

Noah looked at Butch. "Get up top and secure the vents. After you're done, I want you to find Marty. He's up on top someplace. We need to get him in hand."

Butch nodded.

Noah turned to Paul. "I want you to continue monitoring the cameras that still work. If you see anything remotely suspicious, let me and Butch know immediately on the two-way radio. I've jammed the cell and satellite signals."

"What do you mean by 'anything remotely suspicious'?" Paul asked.

Noah tried to control his anger. Could Paul possibly be this dense? "For instance, Paul," he answered slowly and deliberately, "if the cameras stop going out, I want to know because it probably means that Luther has found a way out of the vents. Right now our best hope is to catch him inside them, where he's vulnerable. We can't afford to have him running around seeing things he's not supposed to see. While Butch is up top, I'm going to conduct a room-by-room search below, paying particular attention to *suspicious* noises like a boy crawling through our ductwork. If I hear something, I will call you. You will look at the schematic and tell me where Luther is going so we can head him off and catch him. Does that clear it up for you, Paul?"

Paul gulped, then nodded. "I'll stay right here at my desk until I hear from you."

"Good idea," Noah said.

NO MORE MISTAKES

Grace sat down behind Noah's massive wooden desk. She didn't know what kind of wood it was, but it was beautiful.

And knowing him, she thought, *expensive.*

It was also impeccably neat. The only things on the polished surface were a phone, a computer monitor, a track pad, and a slim keyboard. She hit the computer's ON button, thinking that the computer would be password protected. But to her surprise the screen came to life with dozens of files, folders, and icons. She scanned their titles, then moved the cursor to a large icon marked COLLECTION. She clicked it, expecting something to appear on the screen. Instead, the lights above the desk started to dim and the black cube began to glow. She stood and approached the glass. By the time she reached it, the cube was fully illuminated. And what Grace saw was both beautiful and horrible. She was suddenly reminded of a conversation between Wolfe and Laurel Lee back on Cryptos Island. It seemed like a lifetime ago but had really only been a few weeks. She remembered every word of the exchange:

"Noah Blackwood is a collector," Wolfe had told Laurel Lee. "His parks are nothing more than holding areas so he can make money off the animals before he harvests them."

At the time, Grace thought Wolfe was exaggerating. Looking at what lay beyond the smoky glass, she knew she had been wrong. She was standing face-to-face with her grandfather's sick harvest. She circled the cube with revulsion and a certain amount of fascination. It was filled with dozens of extinct and endangered animals — all of them beautifully preserved, all of them extremely dead. She paused in front of the Tasmanian wolf, or thylacine, which she had overheard Wolfe telling Laurel Lee about. The species had been extinct for more than seventy years. She was staring at the last one that had ever drawn breath. In the diorama next to it was a Caspian tiger pouncing on an ibex.

Sickened by what she'd already seen yet unable to look away, she quickened her pace around the cube, but the display of the giant panda stopped her cold. Something bothered her about it, and it wasn't that it had been harvested in its prime. There was something strange about how the taxidermist had posed the panda. It was looking down at its chest, holding its paws up as if . . .

"Oh no!" Grace gasped.

As if the panda is holding a cub up to nurse it.

There were three panda cubs, two males and one female, at the Ark. Grace had wondered what would happen to the "extra" male. Now she knew. The odd male would be harvested and added to Noah Blackwood's twisted collection.

She hurried back around to Noah's desk and clicked the COLLECTION icon. The lights came back on in the office and the cube went dark.

Out of sight, out of mind, she thought, then realized this wasn't true. There are things that, once seen, cannot be unseen.

Noah Blackwood's collection was one of these. Grace promised herself that the baby boy panda would not be added to Noah's black cube. But before figuring out how to accomplish that, she needed to find out what else was on his computer.

She opened the *Wildlife First* folder, then a subfolder with the current date. Inside was a video called *Kaikoura Canyon (Final)*. The Kaikoura Canyon off the coast of New Zealand was where they had captured the giant squid. She started fast-forwarding through the video, slowing it down when she saw something she wanted to take a closer look at or hear. The gist of the show was about evil pirates trying to hijack his research ship, with Noah Blackwood seemingly repelling them all by himself. There was no video, or mention, of Wolfe's *Coelacanth* being attacked, or even of it being in the same area as Noah's beleaguered ship. At the end of the episode, a tearful Noah Blackwood dedicated the show to two crew members who supposedly died during the pirate attack.

The show was entertaining, dramatic, and a complete lie. The video made it look like the pirate attack had lasted for hours. The real attack on Noah's ship had lasted less than five minutes, then the pirates broke off and attacked the *Coelacanth*. While the *Coelacanth* was fighting off the pirates, Noah sent divers down through the Moon Pool with bombs to blow up the ship.

Thinking the video was over, Grace was about to close it out when Noah Blackwood appeared on the screen in torn and filthy clothes looking like death warmed over. The camera zoomed in for a close-up of his haggard face. He spoke in a raspy, weak voice. . . .

"I'm recording this from somewhere deep in the Congo, and it very well may be the last time you see me . . ."

He gave the camera his trademark grin tinged with a little sadness and regret.

". . . but don't despair. I've had a good run, and I've managed to save some animals along the way, for which I'm grateful. I came out here to rescue a dear colleague and I may have killed myself in the attempt, but looking back on my life I have no regrets — except one: that I won't be alive to see the impact of this, my greatest discovery ever . . ."

The camera moved jerkily to his right. A close-up of the two Mokélé-mbembé hatchlings appeared.

"Dinosaurs exist!"

The camera returned to Noah's feverish face.

"Two of them, anyway. The last of their breed. I will try to get them to safety, but if I can't, the last thing I do before I die will be to let them go . . ."

The scene switched to a close-up of a now well-groomed and healthy-looking Noah Blackwood.

"To quote Mark Twain, the reports of my death have been greatly exaggerated. But what has not been exaggerated are the dinosaur hatchlings I showed you while I was lost in the Congo. I managed to get my friend and the hatchlings to safety. Right now, for security reasons, we are keeping the hatchlings at an undisclosed location. They are thriving, but they need a little more time to adjust to their new circumstances. I will have more information for you on next week's show. Until then . . . Wildlife First!"

The camera panned back. Noah was sitting on a log near a small tent with a beautiful lake behind him.

Grace had seen the tent and the log before. On the other

side of the cube. The green screen covering the windows was used to project backgrounds like the placid lake, or the hideous jungles of the Congo. Noah wasn't in the Congo when he told his millions of viewers about the baby dinosaurs. He was right around the corner from his king-sized bed!

Probably admiring his collection of dead animals between takes, Grace thought, disgusted.

She was about to close the folder when she noticed another video marked *Outtakes*. She fast-forwarded through the video clips. . . .

Noah jumping over a rail on his ship to save someone and landing on an inflated pad instead of splashing into a cold sea . . . Noah unwrapping and chomping down on an Ark cheeseburger and drinking a soda with ice in the "Congolese jungle" . . . Noah standing with "the pirates" that attacked him and the *Coelacanth*, laughing at something one of the pirates was telling him . . .

He should change the name of his show to Wild Lies First*!*

Grace felt her lips curl into a smile, but this time it was genuine and it didn't hurt. The outtake file was about the same size as the final file. She selected *Outtakes* and changed its title, typing in *Kaikoura Canyon (Final)*; then she selected *Kaikoura Canyon (Final)* and typed in *Outtakes*.

If it works, the next Wildlife First *episode might turn out to be* Wildlife Last*!*

Her smile broadened and she considered hitting the SEND button right then, but thought better of it. If Noah discovered it had been sent early, he'd still have time to pull it before it aired. There was a risk that he would take one last look before sending it, but she had a backup plan in case he did. She opened Noah's email account.

Subject: This is not from Noah Blackwood
From: nbPhd@ark.org
To: marty@ewolfe.com

Marty,

You'll find the attached very interesting, and so will Wolfe. I'm at the Seattle Ark, but we may be leaving for Paris tomorrow with the hatchlings. I have a lot to tell you, but I'm not sure when I'll get another chance to contact you. NB keeps a very close eye on me. I'm using his computer to send this to you so DO NOT EMAIL ME BACK. As soon as this uploads I'll delete this email from his server so he won't know I've contacted you. Don't worry about me. I'm safe. I miss you and Wolfe and Laurel Lee and everyone.

Grace

She read over the email a couple of times, thinking she should say more, but there wasn't time. With the attached video it would take several minutes to send.

If Noah comes while it's uploading . . .

She hit the SEND button.

To avoid staring at the file's painfully slow progress, she double clicked the surveillance folder. It was divided into geographical subfolders. *South America . . . North America . . . Africa . . .* She clicked on *North America*. The screen filled with dozens of video thumbnails, some of which were blank, as if the cameras had been shut down for the night. She clicked on the *Mountain Lion Holding* camera. The thumbnail enlarged, showing three of the tawny-colored cats sleeping on an elevated platform. There were controls beneath the video. She played with them and found she could zoom in and out, move up and down, and pan left and right. There was even an audio button. She turned the volume up, but the cats were silent.

She switched to the *Mansion* cameras and clicked on a thumbnail called *Grace Bedroom*. To her relief it was too dark to make out any details even when she zoomed in on the bed where she was supposed to be sleeping. She turned up the volume to maximum and was able to pick up ambient room noise. If someone were talking, Noah would be able to hear it loud and clear. It was good to know, but she had a strong premonition that she would never be setting foot in that bedroom again.

She quickly checked through the cameras on the mansion's first and second floors, relieved to see no one was there.

She checked on the email to Marty. Frustratingly, it was only about halfway through being sent. She turned her attention back to the surveillance videos and discovered a folder called *Archived Videos*. She opened it and found a subfolder with her name on it.

If she'd had any doubts that her grandfather was watching her every move, they were gone now. He had video of her from the moment she'd stepped out of the helicopter days earlier to when she climbed into bed that evening, and everything in between.

But not everything after. He doesn't have me sneaking into the secret passage, or climbing up the elevator shaft.

There were videos of her playing with the panda cubs; feeding the hatchlings; shoveling elephant poop with the elephant keepers; walking around the Ark with her shadows, Butch and Yvonne; and hours of video of her in her room with that ridiculous, blissful smile on her face, which she had to admit looked relatively genuine, and nothing like Grace O'Hara. . . .

Or Grace Wolfe, or whoever I really am. All I know is that the smiling girl in the video is not really me.

Watching herself, she couldn't help but feel a certain amount of pride in how she'd been able to pull this off. Prior to falling into the Congo with Marty and discovering who she really was, she would have never tried such a deceit.

The email program finally made the swishing noise indicating the email had been sent. She trashed the email and scanned the computer for other files she might want to send. That's when she saw a folder marked *Luther.*

It can't be . . .

She opened the folder and clicked on the video clip, which was time-stamped for that very day. Grace had known Luther Smyth most of her life, and the gangly skinhead paying his money at the entrance to the Ark could not possibly be him. Luther would never shave his oddly colored hair. It was like his own personal national flag.

He's a country unto himself with a population of one.

As she watched the kid make a beeline for the nearest concession stand, totally ignoring the animals along the way . . . she started to change her mind. Where he was going, and how he was moving, was very Luther Smyth–like. The video of him at the concession stand was much clearer. She slowed down the video and her heart leaped up into her throat. She had watched Luther consume junk food a thousand times. It wasn't a pretty sight, but the skinhead boy eating the double cheeseburger in two gigantic bites could only be one person. Luther Smyth IV.

And Noah Blackwood knows he's here.

It looked like Noah had videoed every step and bite of food Luther had taken from the moment he came through the gate. She fast-forwarded through the video, pausing when Luther was near other people, and scanning the faces around him. She didn't see Marty, but she knew he had to be in the Ark, too. Luther and Marty were inseparable.

The cameras followed Luther into the Amazon River exhibit, where he swallowed a hot dog while he watched a gigantic anaconda swallow a rabbit. If she'd had any lingering doubt that it was Luther, the doubt was gone now. None of the other peds watching the snake had the stomach to eat.

Luther fished his cell phone out of his sock with his hot dog–less hand, put it to his ear, smiled, then looked at something above his head. The smile was replaced by a look of alarm, then terror. He was talking, but there was no audio in the exhibit.

He has to be talking to Marty. Where is he? What's Marty telling him?

Whatever it was had scared Luther. His eyes went wide and it looked like he was going to faint as he slipped the phone back into his sock. A second later he bolted out of the exhibit, causing a minor riot as he pushed his way through the startled snake watchers. The cameras followed him outside, where a burly security guard was waiting. Luther tried to get around him, but the guard was faster than he looked. He grabbed him around the waist and pulled him down. A glowering Butch McCall came into view. He jerked Luther to his feet, then he and the guard marched him down the path away from the crowd.

Butch had a short conversation with the guard. The guard shrugged and walked away, leaving them alone.

Grace glanced at the time stamp. This had all happened as Noah was walking her back to the mansion, which explained the strange exchange she'd overheard with Butch and Noah in the keeper area.

Luther was yelling at Butch, but she couldn't hear what he was saying. Butch looked like a grizzly bear contemplating homicide. He reached into his pocket, pulled out a syringe, wrapped his arm around Luther's skinny neck, and plunged the needle into Luther's arm. Luther went limp almost immediately. Grace's eyes flew open in shock as an elevator popped out of the ground from nowhere. Butch threw Luther over his shoulder and stepped inside. A few seconds later the door opened again. Butch dumped Luther into the back of a golf cart and drove down the same corridor she'd been in with Noah that afternoon. He stopped outside a door marked 222, set Luther on the floor inside, then left, locking the door behind him.

The video ended. She stared at the blank screen for a full minute, trying to calm herself and piece together what was going on.

Marty was in the Ark. She was convinced of that now. And he had somehow eluded Ark security. Noah's night sweep had nothing to do with homeless people or pests. *Although a lot of people consider Marty a pest of the first order.*

The sweep was all about Marty. So was the sudden trip to Paris. Noah wanted her and the hatchlings out of there. He didn't want her, or the dinosaurs, anywhere near Marty, or anyone else from Cryptos Island.

She rewound the video to the place where Luther got the cell phone call and played it back, pausing it when he looked up and grinned. She couldn't see what he was looking at, but she knew what it was.

The dragonspy. Which means Marty has seen what I just saw.

She hoped he had called Wolfe, or the police, but knowing Marty, she doubted he had called anyone. The boy she once believed was her twin brother wasn't big on asking for help even when he needed it.

She reached into her pack, opened a cleverly concealed pocket inside, and pulled out the dragonspy Luther had flown to her aboard the *Coelacanth*. She hadn't even looked at it since she had arrived at the Ark. Without light, the solar batteries had gone dead, and without a Gizmo, there was no way to fly it, but as soon as it charged up they would be able to track her. They would know where she was. She laid the little bot on the desk beneath the light, wondering how long it would take for it to come to life. While she waited for it to charge, she began searching through the live video feeds for Noah Blackwood and Butch McCall.

If I'm going to help Marty and Luther out of the Ark, I need to know where Noah and Butch are and what they're doing. I need to know if Luther is still in Lab 222. I need to know where Marty is. I need to get off the third floor. I need to . . .

She closed her eyes and took several deep breaths, having learned that panic destroys all hope of useful thought.

Marty's and Luther's lives are at risk. My life is at risk, or it will be soon. The one thing I need to do right now, above all else, is to think. No more mistakes.

CH-9

When Grace opened her eyes, the panic was gone, but the sense of urgency was still there. She thought about her reasons for coming to the Ark. The first reason had been to stop Butch McCall from killing Laurel Lee.

Mission accomplished.

As far as she knew, Laurel and everyone else who had been aboard the *Coelacanth* were alive and well.

Her second reason for coming to the Ark was to find out about her mother, Rose Blackwood.

Mission definitely not *accomplished.*

She'd discovered virtually nothing about her mother. She stared at Noah's computer screen and realized the answers might be in one of the thousands of files on his hard drive. But there wasn't time to look.

She selected several folders and dragged them into another email to Marty.

Subject: This is not from Noah Blackwood #2

From: nbPhd@ark.org

To: marty@ewolfe.com

Marty,

Again DO NOT REPLY to this. Attached are a bunch of files from NB's computer. I have no idea what they are because I don't have time to look at them right now. I just saw a video of Luther's abduction. I assume you're in the Ark someplace as well and I hope you haven't been taken, too. Luther is in Lab 222. It's on the second level beneath the Ark. I'll be heading that way soon to see what I can do about getting him out. Blackwood is looking for you. You need to get out of the Ark as quickly as you can. Don't worry about Luther. I'll find him. LEAVE THE ARK NOW!

Grace

She hit the SEND button. While she waited for the files to load, she continued her video search for Noah Blackwood and Butch McCall. There were hundreds of cameras, but the thumbnail feature made it easy to scan for people because of Noah's rule of emptying the Ark at night. It was likely that anyone she saw would be in on Luther's abduction and the search for Marty. At least she hoped they were still searching for Marty and hadn't caught him. Better yet, she hoped he had already left the Ark and was miles away, although she knew this was highly unlikely. He would never leave the Ark without Luther.

She clicked the thumbnail for Lab 251. The hatchlings were asleep, as was Yvonne on a cot not ten feet away from the snoring, farting duo. She was about to move on to another thumbnail when Yvonne started to stir and opened her eyes. A moment later, Noah Blackwood came into view. Grace turned up the audio.

"Sorry to wake you," Noah said, not looking at all sorry.

Yvonne sat up. "No problem. What's up?"

"Marty O'Hara and Luther Smyth are here."

"Where?"

"We're not exactly sure. I think Marty's up top. Luther is in the ductwork."

Yvonne looked up at the ceiling and frowned. Grace smiled.

"We've locked the Ark down," Noah continued. "So there's no place for them to go. The problem is that Luther is taking out our surveillance cameras one by one."

That explained why some of the cameras weren't working. Grace almost cheered. It was so Luther. She could just picture him pulling himself along, wreaking havoc for what Butch did to him.

"We need to flush him out," Yvonne said.

"We'll get to that in a minute." Noah looked over at the hatchlings, seemingly unaffected by the terrible odor Grace knew was there. "How are they doing?"

"I did a complete blood panel this morning and everything appeared to be normal."

"Since they are the only two in existence, we have nothing to compare 'normal' to," Noah pointed out.

"Normal unto themselves, then," Yvonne said. "There have been no changes since they arrived. Their appetites are good. They are alert when they are awake and almost comatose when they are asleep. Their behavior is consistent and predictable."

"Can they be trained?"

"Any animal with a food drive like theirs can be trained. But at this point they're food stupid. When they're hungry, which is basically any time their eyes are open, a starvation panic mode sets in. We may want to separate them to see if the competition is contributing to the panic. I suspect it is. I can't start any training until we get rid of their codependence and imprinting on each other. I think —"

"I understand the theory," Noah said impatiently, cutting her off.

Grace had spent a good deal of time in her grandfather's library reading about developmental behavior in animals, and she could not have disagreed more with Yvonne. The hatchlings were only a few weeks old.

In spite of their size, they're just babies, Grace thought. *Yvonne wasn't in the Mokélé-mbembé nest in the Congo. She didn't see the dead mother with the vultures feeding on her. It was more of a lair than a nest . . . a secret nursery carved in the jungle thousands of years before and occupied by generations of Mokélé-mbembé. From the layers of bones covering the lair, it was obvious that Mokélé-mbembé carried its kills back to the nest to be eaten. The hatchlings were not separated at feeding time.*

"You're the trainer," Noah continued. "And we will have a perfect opportunity tomorrow to begin the separation."

"Another lab?" Yvonne asked.

"Another country," Noah answered. "I'm flying them to Paris in the morning. After tonight, I have a feeling that our current location is going to become too hot for our sleeping friends here. Which brings me to the real purpose of my visit. I need your help getting Luther out of the ventilation system before he completely blinds us."

"What do you want me to do?"

Noah glanced over at the hatchlings. "How long will they be asleep?"

"Unless they're disturbed, several hours. Maybe a little longer this time of night."

"It shouldn't take that long," Noah said. "I want you to put CH-9 in the ventilation system and get that kid out of there."

"I have limited control over Nine. I can't guarantee Luther's safety."

"I'm not concerned about what happens to Luther Smyth," Noah said angrily. "If he dies, he dies. As soon as he's taken care of, we'll send CH-9 after Marty O'Hara."

"Sounds like fun," Yvonne said with a smile. "I'll just grab my gea —"

The camera went dead.

Luther! Grace thought, staring at the abruptly blank screen. *Bad timing!* She could just imagine him crouched inside the Ark's underground ventilation system, gleefully yanking out cables and cords. But Noah's last words terrified her. What kind of weapon was CH-9?

Grace got out of the surveillance program and quickly scanned the desktop. She found the folder marked *CH-9*, clicked it open, and stifled a scream. A video of a snarling, vicious animal appeared on the screen. It was lunging at the camera with its long white fangs snapping. Its fierce malevolent eyes glowed like red-hot coals. She fumbled with the track pad, and after several attempts managed to shut the video down. The terrible image was replaced with several folders marked *Chupacabra*.

She'd heard the name before, but couldn't remember where.

She opened Noah's search engine and typed in the name. Hundreds of links appeared. She clicked on the top one.

The Chupacabra or Chupacabras (Spanish pronunciation: [tʃupa'kaβra], from chupar, *"to suck," and* cabra, *"goat," literally "goat sucker") is a legendary cryptid rumored to inhabit parts of the Americas. It is associated more recently with sightings of an allegedly unknown animal in Puerto Rico (where these sightings were first reported), Mexico, and the United States, especially in the latter's Latin American communities. The name comes from the animal's reported habit of attacking and drinking the blood of livestock, particularly goats.*

Physical descriptions of the creature vary. Eyewitness sightings have been claimed as early as 1995 in Puerto Rico, and have since been reported as far north as Maine and as far south as Chile, even being spotted outside the Americas in countries like Russia and the Philippines. It is supposedly a heavy creature, the size of a small bear, with a row of spines reaching from the neck to the base of the tail.

Sightings of the Chupacabra have been disregarded as uncorroborated or lacking evidence, with most reports in northern Mexico and the southern United States being verified as canids afflicted by mange. Biologists and wildlife management officials view the chupacabra as a contemporary legend.

The description triggered Grace's memory: She had first heard about the chupacabra in the same conversation she'd overheard between Wolfe and Laurel Lee back on Cryptos Island. Wolfe had told Laurel that he suspected Blackwood was not only fattening up animals for his private collection, he was genetically engineering animals to put on exhibit. . . .

"I wouldn't put it past him to make a chupacabra in his lab, let it go for a while to build the myth, then recapture it and put it on display in one of his Arks . . . ," Wolfe had said.

Wolfe had also expressed concern that Blackwood was going to clone Mokélé-mbembé so he could have them on display in all of his Arks.

The chupacabra is no longer a legend, Grace realized with a shudder. *Noah Blackwood has made one. Or maybe more than one . . .*

She opened a couple of the chupacabra files. It looked like CH-9 was the ninth version of the beast.

What do the others look like? Are they still alive? Are they hidden away somewhere on the third level?

There was no time to find the answers on Noah's computer. She needed to find a way off the third floor. She needed to get below and find Luther before the chupacabra found him!

She pulled several CH-9 files into a third email to Marty.

Subject: This is not from Noah Blackwood #3

From: nbPhd@ark.org

To: marty@ewolfe.com

Marty,

Again DO NOT REPLY to this. Noah Blackwood has a chupacabra and he's going to sic it on Luther and you!

It's a horrible animal with big teeth that will tear you apart. You NEED TO GET OUT OF THE ARK NOW. I'm in a better position to help Luther. I've attached more files for you to look at later. GET OUT OF THE ARK. NOW!

She doubted Marty would pay any attention to her warning, but she had to try. She hit the SEND button and got up from the desk. She didn't care if Noah Blackwood found out she had sent this email. There wasn't time to wait.

I'm going home. I'm going back to Cryptos Island.

Her eyes teared up at the thought and she caught a sob before it turned into an all-out cry. This was the first time she had allowed herself to think about the possibility of going back to Cryptos. She missed Marty and Wolfe and Laurel so badly that it hurt.

No time for that now. I have to get out of here.

She looked down at the dragonspy and touched it. It moved . . . a little. She smiled.

It's coming back to life just like I am.

She put it in her pack.

Noah's desk had only one drawer. She opened it and nearly jumped for joy. Sitting among the papers were three key cards. Next to it was a two-way radio. She snatched up both along with the papers, which she stuffed into her pack. She attached the key cards to the lanyard around her neck and turned on the two-way. Loud static came over the speaker, followed by the voice of Noah Blackwood.

"Butch?"

"Yeah."

"Where are you?"

"Headed up top."

"You haven't secured the vents yet?"

"It took me a while to find the chain and padlocks. Everything here is electronic."

"Well hurry. Meet me in Lab 222."

"Is the kid back in there?"

"No, but the thing that's going to ferret him out will be in a few minutes. Hurry. I'm going to head up to the mansion and take care of a couple of things in my office. I'll see you below."

Grace turned off the radio and put it back into the desk along with the papers she had put in her pack. The lanyard with the keys, she kept. She hoped that if Noah opened the drawer, he would see the radio and papers and not notice the key cards were missing.

She ran over to the elevator and tried one of the keys. Nothing happened. She quickly swiped the other two cards one after the other, then swiped all three of them again. The elevator door didn't budge.

BELOW

Marty and Dylan were on their knees with their flash-light apps.

"It's Astroturf. The same stuff they put on indoor football fields," Dylan said. "You wouldn't notice it among the real plants and grass."

"I see the crack where the sides flip open." Marty shined his light along the seam. "We need something to pry it open with, and a rope to climb down the shaft."

"Dang it," Dylan said, snapping his fingers. "I can't believe I forgot to bring my rope and crowbar."

"Ha," Marty said. "Some burglar you'd make." He tried to wedge his fingers into the seam, but it was too tight.

Dylan stood up. "I'll look around for a branch, or a stick, or a crowbar."

"Watch out for hot wires. They really hur — Wait!" Marty put both palms flat on the fake grass. "It's vibrating." He put his ear to the turf. "Something's definitely moving." The ground started to open. "Hide!"

Dylan dove behind a tree. Marty rolled under a bush and lay on his stomach, facing the rising elevator. He wished he'd picked a better place to hide.

Too late now.

The elevator door slid open. Butch McCall stepped out, chains dangling from his meaty hands. He was in a hurry. He jumped the fence, swiped his key card through the hidden slot in the rail, and started down the path without a glance in Marty's direction.

Marty scrambled forward on his hands and knees and thrust his arm between the doors just before they closed. The doors sprung back open. By the time he got to his feet, Dylan was at his side.

"Nice move," he said.

Marty grinned with pride.

They stepped inside and the doors closed. There were three buttons.

"What floor?" Dylan asked.

Marty thought about it for a second. He had no idea what level Luther was on. "Top to bottom, I guess."

Dylan hit the button for Level One.

Noah Blackwood stepped out of the elevator on Level Four. He had no idea how long it would take for the chupacabra to flush out Luther, or for them to find Marty, but he was preparing for a long night. Unlike Butch, he was not going to underestimate the two boys, or Travis Wolfe. They had bested him before, but he was not going to let them do it again. Whatever happened tonight, he was leaving the country in the morning with the hatchlings and Grace.

His first stop had been to check on Paul Ivy up on Level Three. The big Peeping Tom was sitting in front of his bank of monitors, half of which were out, drinking a soda. He was startled when Noah walked in, and slopped some soda onto his keyboard.

"I take it you didn't see me coming," Noah said.

Paul shook his head. "All the corridor cameras are out on every level. There are only a few cameras left."

To accent his point, a camera in the keeper kitchen blinked off.

"At least we know he's still up there," Noah said. "Keep monitoring the situation and let me know if the cameras stop going out." He put his hand on Paul's shoulder. His T-shirt was clammy with sweat. "And don't worry. We'll get your cameras back online soon. We were due for an upgrade anyway. I'll get together with you tomorrow to discuss what we need to do."

Noah walked back out into the corridor with no intention of meeting with Paul about the cameras, although a meeting would certainly take place. He pulled out a sanitary wipe and cleaned his hands, then climbed back into the cart and stopped outside of Lab 400. He hadn't been inside for several days, but had been in constant contact with the lone occupant. He swiped his key card through the lock and the door opened. If anyone else were to walk into room 400, they would see what he was looking at: yet another empty laboratory with counters, sinks, cabinets, and capped gas lines for Bunsen burners. But there was a secret room beyond the laboratory. He crossed to a closet on the far wall, opened the door, and swiped his card in a hidden slot beneath one of the shelves in back. A hidden door slid open, revealing an enormous room. Noah stepped in. The door slid closed behind him.

The room was similar to his quarters on the third floor of

the mansion. There was a bedroom, a study, an open bathroom, and a video studio scattered with props. There was no black cube. Mr. Zwilling was not a collector. He preferred his animals alive. He was sitting at a snakewood desk identical to the one in Noah Blackwood's study.

"Are you current?" Noah asked.

"I believe so," Mr. Zwilling said. "Luther is crawling around in our ductwork, Marty is above, Yvonne is readying CH-9 for a little adventure, Butch is doing Butch things, Paul is mourning his vision loss, and you are taking the hatchlings and Grace to Paris in the morning."

Noah smiled and gave him a nod. A perfect summary, which didn't surprise Noah in the least. Zwilling was the only person in the world that he trusted without reservation.

"What do you want me to do?" Zwilling asked.

"I want you to go out to dinner and enjoy yourself. Perhaps go to Canlis in Queen Anne."

"I love that restaurant," Mr. Zwilling said.

"Invite some of our friends," Noah said.

Zwilling looked at his watch. "Short notice."

"They'll go," Noah said confidently. He reached into his pocket and handed him an envelope. "After you finish, take your guests to the ballet. I have two boxes reserved. When the ballet is over, go to the Olympic Hotel for drinks. When you're finished, check into our suite and spend the night."

Zwilling nodded and put the tickets in his pocket.

"Come back tomorrow morning for rounds," Noah continued. "Then head over to Northwest Zoo and Aquarium to see the giant squid."

"That ought to be interesting."

Noah nodded in agreement. "Here's a list of things I need you to do at the mansion before you leave. I'll give you a lift to the elevator."

Zwilling ran a comb through his white hair and slipped into his jacket.

The elevator carrying Marty and Dylan came to a stop on Level One.

"You think they'll be waiting for us?" Dylan asked.

"Probably," Marty said. "You step out first."

"Very funny."

The elevator door slid open. No one was waiting for them. Marty stepped out, followed by Dylan, and looked up at the ceiling. "Cameras," he said.

"We're busted if anyone is watching," Dylan said.

"Let's see what happens." Marty waved and made a face at the closest camera.

"Are you insane?"

"Might as well find out if anyone's paying attention." Marty pointed down the corridor. "Too many cameras to avoid."

While he waited to be Tasered, tackled, and cuffed by a gang of NFL-sized security guards, he took in his surroundings. The underground warren appeared to be gigantic. There were numbered doors on both sides of the corridor for as far as he could see, which was only about a hundred feet in either direction because the corridor was curved.

"Quiet as a tomb," Dylan said.

"Bad choice of words," Marty said.

Dylan shrugged. "There are a lot of doors. Any idea which one Luther's behind?"

Marty shook his head. "How far do you think we dropped?"

Dylan shrugged. "Twenty, thirty feet. It's hard to tell in a closed elevator."

"Then I made a mistake. We're not deep enough." Marty punched the elevator button. Nothing happened. "And we're stuck here unless we can find a staircase or a key card. Luther is somewhere below Southeast Asia. Maybe beneath the orangutan exhibit." He pulled out the Gizmo and launched the dragonspy. "We'll have it scout ahead. My hands are going to be busy flying it and looking at the vid. You'll need to shake door handles and see if any of them open."

"What if there are people behind the door?"

"Close it quickly and run."

"That's your plan?"

"Unless you have a better one."

Dylan shook his head and tugged on the nearest door. It didn't open and he looked relieved. He went to the next door. It didn't open, either.

"This might not be such a bad plan after all," he said, pulling on the third door.

It opened.

Marty parked the dragonspy on the ceiling to keep an eye on things in the corridor. Then he walked into the room.

HAMPERED

Grace was on her third trip around the cube, trying to keep her desperation and panic at bay. She had looked everywhere and could not find a way down aside from the elevator. She had swiped the key cards several more times and had even tried to pry open the doors, to no avail.

There has to be a secret way into this hideous harvest . . . some way to get the dead animals into the cube.

She was examining the smoky glass inch by inch, trying to find a way in, which would hopefully lead to a way out, when she heard the elevator come to life. The car would have to drop before it came back up, which gave her maybe a minute before he arrived. She hoped she had put everything back in place exactly as it had been so he didn't know someone had been looking around his lair. She hoped Noah didn't get suspicious about having to wait for the elevator and start looking around for her.

Because Noah's lair was so open, there were few places to hide. Grace decided to use Blackwood's tent because it would give her a partial view of both his office and his bedroom. She did one last quick loop around the cube, then crawled into the weathered nylon television prop. She zipped herself into the musty sleeping bag just as the elevator door slid open, and peeked through the mesh opening. If Noah was disturbed, or suspicious, about the elevator, he wasn't showing it. In fact, he was whistling, which shocked her more than if he had stepped out of the elevator with a gun drawn, ready to shoot an intruder. Nobody whistled unless they were happy, and the only reason she could think of that would make him this happy was if he'd already let the chupacabra out and it had done its job. She was sick with worry.

He walked over to his desk and sat down in front of the computer. Grace held her breath. If the last email to Marty was still uploading, it was all over for her.

Noah continued to whistle as his manicured fingers danced across the keyboard. Grace let out her breath. The email must have finished uploading. He typed for at least five more minutes, whistling as he worked, as if he didn't have a care in the world. She was definitely seeing a different side to Noah Blackwood. Perhaps the third floor was the only place he let down his guard to be himself. He stood up and stretched, apparently finished with the computer, and walked right by her without a glance at the tent or anything else. She watched as he pulled his shirttail out of his pants and started to unbutton it. The whistle turned into a hum as he rounded the corner to his bedroom, where she couldn't see him. The shower came on. The humming stopped and he started to sing. Badly.

"Baby . . . baby . . . baby . . . ooh . . . Baby . . . baby . . . baby no . . ."

Grace would have burst into laughter if she didn't think that Noah would rush out of the shower and murder her. She considered sneaking into his bedroom and stealing his key card from his bedside table, or wherever he had tossed it.

It's probably sitting next to his rhino horn lamp!

"Baby . . . baby . . . baby . . . ooh . . ."

She was about to risk it when she remembered the promise she had made to herself about not making any more mistakes. There were no walls in Noah's bathroom. She couldn't possibly get the card without him seeing her.

"Baby . . . baby . . . baby . . . no . . ."

Her only hope of getting off the third floor was to wait and see what Noah was up to.

Why is he taking a shower?

"Baby . . . baby . . . baby . . . ooh . . ."

Doesn't he know any of the other words?

The shower stopped, but not the song — or the only two lines he knew from the song.

Maybe he's getting ready to go to bed.

That would mean he had already taken care of Luther and Marty, or he was going to leave it to Butch and Yvonne to do his dirty work. There was a chance that she might be able to lift the card while he slept. She'd had some experience as a pickpocket in the Congo under much worse circumstances than these. If Blackwood was a sound sleeper — and Grace thought he would be because he didn't appear to have a conscience to keep him awake — she'd have a good chance of getting her hands on the card. But it wasn't to be. Noah came back around the corner, scrubbed and wearing a fresh khaki safari suit. He was running a comb through his mane of white hair. He was whistling again. He walked right past her, once more without a glance, through the office, around the corner, and out of sight.

Grace heard the elevator door swish open and close. She stayed where she was, looking at her watch, waiting a full five minutes before crawling out of the tent just in case it was a trick. It wasn't. Noah was gone. She almost wished he had stayed. Her only way off the third floor might have just gone down the elevator. Shaking off her disappointment, she walked over to the computer and checked the sent emails. The last one she had sent to Marty had gone through. She dragged it into the trash, then emptied it to destroy the evidence. There were two other emails. One was to Noah's pilots, telling them to ready the jet for a flight to Paris and to pick them up at sunrise in the helicopter. The second email was to an alphabet of television stations. The large attachment was still uploading, and she had no intention of trashing it.

Subject: Wildlife First Episode #527
From: nbPhd@ark.org
To: Multiple Recipients

Attached you will find the latest 22-minute segment titled "Wildlife Pirates!" It is relatively violent. If the viewers in your region are sensitive to violence, you may want to include a warning prior to airing. I'm sending this a little earlier than normal, but as always the show is proprietary until your regular scheduled airtime. Any violation will result in legal action and cancellation of *Wildlife First* on your network or station.

I've added a brief teaser at the end of the show that I believe will shake the scientific community and the general public to its very core.

Dr. Noah Blackwood

It would be Noah Blackwood who would be shaken to his very core after the episode aired, but there was no time for Grace to gloat or celebrate. She still had to find a way off the third floor and find Luther or Marty.

If it isn't too late.

She hurried into Noah's bedroom. If it weren't for the wet shower floor, she wouldn't have known he had been there. She opened his wardrobe. A set of clothes was missing. A pair of brown shoes was gone, replaced by a pair of slightly scuffed black shoes. This wasn't surprising. Noah had changed clothes after his shower.

But something's missing.

She turned around and smiled. She had just found a way off the third floor. She started tearing the pillows, sheets, and blankets off Noah Blackwood's king-sized bed.

Marty and Dylan were standing in the middle of a massive room filled with industrial washers, dryers, dry-cleaning equipment, and commercial presses.

"It's a laundry," Dylan said.

"No kidding," Marty said, looking up at the ceiling, which had several large square chutes sticking out of it. On the floor below the chutes were laundry carts the size of Volkswagen Beetles. The carts were marked by area: *Keepers*, *Maintenance*,

Science, *Concession*, etc. A series of conveyor belts filled one wall and were marked like the carts so the laundry workers could send the cleaning back to where it belonged.

"Luther probably needs a good cleaning," Dylan said. "But I doubt they dumped him in here."

Marty smiled. "You know what this is?"

"Uh . . . yeah. It's where Ark laundry is done."

Marty pointed up at the chutes. "It's also our passage to every level beneath the Ark." He walked over to the cart marked *Dr. Noah Blackwood*. "And above the Ark."

"We'll need a tall ladder," Dylan said. The chutes were at least a dozen feet from the floor. "Must be a honeycomb of conveyor belts in the structure's guts to get the stuff to this one room."

"Exactly. We'll finish searching this level, then come back here and do a little belly-crawling through the guts."

Luther was still doing some belly-crawling of his own, and he was getting pretty sick of it. His cell phone was at 8 percent, which meant he'd have light, as pitiful as it was, for about five more minutes. Not that there was anything to see in the maze of dust-choking ductwork. He thought he might be on the level above the lab where he escaped, but he couldn't be certain. He might be a level below for all he knew. He'd passed several vents that opened into dark rooms, but the vents were secured from the room-side and he had been unable to get them open because of the awkward angle he was in. What he needed was a vent where he could use his feet to kick it open. So far he hadn't come across one. He was using his nose more than he was using his eyes or touch. He wasn't sure if Marty had seen

Butch snatch him, and even if he had, he was certain the dragonspy hadn't followed him below. Marty didn't know where he was.

But he's going to try to find me. He's not leaving the Ark until he does, because that's what I would do if he'd been snatched.

He felt that his best chance of finding Marty, or having Marty find him, was to bump into him. They had come to the Ark to find Grace and the hatchlings. If Marty found Grace, their next stop would be the hatchlings. Luther had made a few wrong turns in the vents and lost the sharp scent of the stinky dinos. He slithered backward until his nostrils had reacquired the stench.

Marty and Dylan were headed out of the laundry when they were stopped in their tracks by a loud mechanical squeak.

"It's just incoming laundry," Dylan said.

"Which means someone is in the Ark tossing their soiled underpants," Marty said, moving back into the middle of the room. "Let's find out who it is."

They cocked their heads back, staring up at the chutes as the hidden conveyors churned. Something large dropped from the chute over Blackwood's cart. They hurried over to see what it was.

"It's a blanket," Dylan said.

"Watch out!" Marty shouted.

Dylan wasn't quick enough. A pillow hit him in the head. He jerked backward.

Marty laughed.

"Yeah, real funny," Dylan said. "It could have been heavy."

Four more pillows plopped down in quick succession, followed by a thick comforter, another blanket, a silk top sheet, a silk bottom sheet, and a mattress pad. Marty leaned over the edge of the cart for a closer look. He dug out one of the pillows and saw the case was monogrammed with the initials *N.B.*

"Watch out!" Dylan shouted.

Marty turned his head to look at Dylan. "Ha. Like I'm falling for tha —" Something heavy slammed into his back and flipped him into the cart. He struggled to untangle himself from the blankets, and pillows, and . . .

"What are you doing here?" Grace shouted, then threw her arms around him and gave him a hug.

CONTAINMENT

"I think you might have broken my back," Marty said. "But I am pretty happy to see you, too."

Grace let him go and wiped her tears away. She wasn't sure what she was happier about: seeing him safe and in one piece, or surviving the horrifying plunge from the third floor of the mansion.

"How'd you get here?" he asked.

"Down Blackwood's clothes hamper."

"Scary," someone said.

Grace turned her head to the strange voice. She had been so focused on Marty she hadn't noticed that he wasn't alone.

"It was." Grace looked at him. "Who are you?"

"Dylan Hickock. You must be Grace."

"Duh *du jour*," Grace said.

Marty smiled and helped her out of the cart. "Sorry to cut the homecoming short, but they snatched Luther."

"I know."

"What do you mean you know? Do you know where he is?"

Grace told them about what she had found in Noah's lair.

"The guy sounds really twisted," Dylan said.

"Have they let this chupa . . . whatever you call it . . . loose on Luther yet?" Marty asked.

"Chupacabra," Grace said.

"Goat sucker," Dylan said. "It's a cryptid."

"Are you with the cryptid crew?" Grace asked.

"My mom and dad, mostly my dad, are the new caretakers on Cryptos Island. I just hooked up with Marty and Luther today."

"I'm so sorry," she said, and turned her attention back to Marty. "I don't think the chupacabra is a cryptid. I think Blackwood manufactured it in his genetics lab. I uploaded a bunch of Noah's private files to you. Didn't you get my emails?"

"No. I've been kind of busy, and there's no cell or Internet reception down here."

"Blackwood probably jammed the signal so you couldn't call out. Does anyone know you're here?"

Marty shook his head.

"What were you thinking?"

"I was thinking that someone ought to get you out of here."

"I was perfectly fine," Grace said, even though that wasn't exactly true.

"Okay, then," Marty said. "We'll just grab Luther and be on our way. Nice talking to you, cuz."

"Maybe I wasn't *perfectly* fine," Grace admitted.

Marty grinned.

"How'd you two get down here?" Grace asked.

"The same elevator Butch used to take Luther below," Marty said. "We snuck in after he got out of it and rode it down."

"Speaking of Butch," Dylan said. "We've been in here for a long time. You should probably check the dragonspy."

"Good idea." Marty fished the Gizmo out of his pocket and turned it on. His eyes went wide. "Actually, that was a great idea! Butch is coming. Blackwood's with him."

"What are the chances of him checking in here?" Grace asked.

"About a hundred percent. He's pulling on door handles as he's walking down the corridor. The laundry door's unlocked. He's about ten doors down. Eight now."

"Can't we just lock the door from the inside?" Dylan asked.

"Not without a key card," Grace said, tempted to try the four she had around her neck, but there wasn't time. "We need to turn off the lights and hide. Right now."

"I'll get the lights," Marty said, and ran toward the door.

"Use the laundry cart," Grace told Dylan. "You're bigger than me. There's plenty of bedding to hide under. I'll jump in one of the dryers."

The lights went out a second before she reached it. She climbed under the dry towels. Marty, using his Gizmo to find his way across the room, walked directly to her dryer. "This one's taken," she whispered.

"Scoot over. It's the only one that has clothes in it."

She made room for him. He crawled in and closed the circular glass door behind him. The room beyond the glass was pitch-dark.

"I'm glad you came here for me," she whispered.

"No sweat," Marty said. "Now all we have to do is grab Luther and get out of here."

"And the hatchlings," Grace said. "Noah is planning on taking them to Paris in the morning. If he gets them out of the country, we may never get them back."

"Yeah, okay. And the hatchlings, if we can manage it."

"And the three panda cubs," Grace added.

"What panda cubs?"

"They're adorable. And Noah is going to stuff one of them if we don't take them with us."

"If Noah catches us, we'll be the ones getting stuffed."

"They're small. We can each carry one."

"I don't have anything against adorable panda cubs," Marty said, "but it's going to be hard enough to get the hatchlings out of here. And if the hatchlings get their maws on the pandas, they'll stuff *themselves* with them."

Grace hadn't thought of that. It was a disturbing image. So was the crack of light on the other side of the room as the door opened. Butch was the first in. He switched the lights on. Noah followed. They were talking, but she couldn't hear what they were saying through the dryer door. Noah was definitely not whistling, humming, or singing now. He looked agitated and angry. He stood in the center of the room, peering up at the ceiling as if he were listening for something while Butch searched around. If she had jumped down the hamper five minutes later, she would have landed right in their laps. Butch walked over and looked into a couple of laundry carts, but not the one Dylan was hiding in, luckily. He peeked into a couple of dryers and a washing machine, then shrugged and said something to Noah, who nodded and started for the door. Butch followed him. He switched the light off on his way out, plunging the room into darkness again.

"Wow," Marty said. "That could have gone a different way." He took the Gizmo out of his pocket and switched it on. They both looked at the screen. Noah and Butch were walking down the hallway side by side, shaking doorknobs like security guards.

"What's Butch carrying in his hand?" Grace asked.

Marty zoomed in on it.

"It looks like a remote control," Marty said. "Like they use for flying those RC helicopters."

"What do you suppose that's for?" Grace asked.

Marty shook his head. "I don't know, but I don't like it." He continued following them down the corridor. "What I don't understand is why they aren't opening the doors. If Luther's in the vents, he could be in any one of those rooms."

"Because you have to have a key card to get into and out of the rooms," Grace said. "It's one of the ways Noah keeps track of everyone. I saw some data on his office computer."

"What else did you see up there?" Marty asked.

"I'll tell you everything once we're safely out of the Ark," Grace said, opening the dryer door. "I can say this, though. Noah Blackwood is going to have a very bad day tomorrow."

"I'm glad to hear it," Marty said. He walked over and switched on the light.

Dylan popped his head out of the cart.

"What were they talking about?" Grace asked.

"Blackwood was complaining about the laundry staff leaving the door unlocked, saying that he was going to fire all of them in the morning. I guess it wasn't the first time they've done it. Then he said that Luther was like any other escaped animal. The first priority was containment. The second priority was to catch him. The third priority was to kill him if he posed a threat."

"So we're still on containment," Grace said.

"Yeah," Marty said. "And we're the ones who are contained. They locked the door on us."

"Where are they?" Dylan asked.

"Getting into the elevator."

"Follow them," Grace said.

Marty shook his head. "No can do. They'll see the dragon-spy. I'm going to have to let them go."

PART THREE | CHUPACABRA

THE GEEKENSTEIN MONSTER

Butch stepped out of the elevator on Level Three behind Noah Blackwood. His right wrist ached from rattling every right-hand door handle on every level while Blackwood rattled the left handles. He thought it was a ridiculous precaution until they discovered three unlocked doors. So Dr. Blackwood had been right, again, which shouldn't have surprised him because Dr. Blackwood was always right, even when he wasn't.

They walked down the corridor, rounded a corner, and saw Yvonne Zloblinavech in the distance, standing outside the secret genetics lab. Butch wasn't happy to see her, but he was happy to see her outside the lab rather than inside. If she had been inside, it would have meant that Blackwood had upgraded her key card. No one was allowed inside the secret genetics lab without Blackwood or Dr. Strand, including Butch. Yvonne had made a meteoric rise into Blackwood's inner circle since she had been hired two years earlier. It used to be just him, Blackwood, and Mr. Zwilling. Now there appeared to be four people in the inner circle.

"Is Dr. Strand inside?" Butch asked.

Blackwood shook his head. "I told him to stay in his apartment and not to leave for any reason whatsoever. The fewer people who know about this the better. Yvonne and I are taking the hatchlings and Grace to the Paris Ark in the morning. I'll need you to stay here and tie up any loose ends."

Butch did not like the sound of this. The "loose ends" thing was fine. He had been tying up Blackwood's loose ends most of his life. What he didn't like was that Yvonne was joining Blackwood in Paris.

"Has Mr. Zwilling been apprised of the situation?"

"Of course he has!" Blackwood said.

What Butch really wanted to know is if Yvonne knew about Zwilling, but he knew better than to ask. There were times when he thought that Blackwood regretted telling him about Zwilling.

When they reached her, Yvonne gave them a dazzling smile, which was yet another thing Butch didn't like about her. Day or night, regardless of what she'd been through the previous twenty-four hours, she always looked like she had just stepped out of a spa appointment. Blackwood returned her smile with a dazzler of his own. Butch narrowed his eyes and frowned. He handed her the remote control, glad to be rid of it.

"How are the hatchlings?" Blackwood asked.

"Sleeping like babies."

"Perfect," Blackwood said. "This shouldn't take that long."

"The timing couldn't be better, either," Yvonne said, beaming. "It's exactly what we needed to test the training I've done with him the past several days."

Blackwood beamed back at her. Butch turned away so they couldn't see his humongous eyeball roll.

Blackwood slid his card through the lock. The door popped open with a slight hiss. The genetics lab was hermetically sealed, as were most of the other labs beneath the Ark.

"Ladies first," Blackwood said, waving Yvonne through.

Behind their backs, Butch shook his head in disgust, and thought he might be sick as he followed them into the vestibule and waited for the first door to seal and the second door to hiss open. On the other side of the lock was the most sophisticated genetics laboratory in the world, according to its creator, Dr. Strand, or Dr. Geekenstein, as Butch called him when Noah Blackwood wasn't around.

Before his alleged death six years ago, Dr. Strand was thought to have been the greatest geneticist in the world. He had gotten into some kind of trouble and Blackwood had gotten him out of it by making him disappear in a tragic accident, changing his appearance with plastic surgery, and resurrecting him under the name Dr. Strand. Normally Strand worked in another of Blackwood's secret genetics labs out of the country, but he had been brought to the Seattle Ark to run the Chupacabra trials, which were just about complete. Since coming to the Ark, Strand hadn't seen the light of day, and he was going a little stir-crazy confined to his lab on the third level and his small apartment on the fourth. Noah, Butch, and Yvonne were the only people who knew he was there. His laboratory was filled with millions of dollars' worth of equipment, the names of which Butch could not even pronounce, invented by Strand and patented by Blackwood.

Somehow the machines were capable of creating living creatures like Nine.

Butch had spent most of his life among animals. He didn't love animals. He didn't even like animals very much. But he was very comfortable around animals. Except for the freaks of nature pieced together by Dr. Geekenstein.

There had been nine versions of the chupacabra based on field research Butch had done over a two-year period in Puerto Rico, Mexico, and the southwestern U.S. He had interviewed hundreds of people, examined every photograph, footprint, scat, and bone. He had even captured a couple of live chupacabras, both of which turned out to be coyotes with severe cases of sarcoptic mange. After his exhaustive, and exhausting, investigation, he was convinced that *El Chupacabra* was an urban myth, not a true cryptid.

When he broke the news to Blackwood, he was afraid his boss would blow a gasket, but just the opposite had happened. Instead of being angry, Blackwood had been delighted. He had rubbed his manicured hands together in glee and said, "This gives us a chance to invent our own goat sucker. A beast much more terrifying than the myth, and therefore more commercial. We'll make millions."

They were scheduled to release Nine into the wild within the month. They had picked the small town of Glen Rose, Texas, as ground zero. The plan was to let Nine wreak havoc for six days, then have Noah step in on the seventh day and capture it alive just in time for that week's *Wildlife First* episode.

Save the day and put it on display, Butch thought. A philosophy that had made Noah one of the richest men in the world.

His new scheme, Release and Catch, was bound to make him even richer.

Noah slid his card through the lock leading to the animal room at the back of Strand's lab. They filed into another airlock and waited for the second door to open.

"Has Nine even been out of this room?" Butch asked.

"Twice in the last three nights," Yvonne said. "The trial runs went perfectly."

This was news to Butch . . . bad news. Noah hadn't told him anything about the trial runs. He was usually in on everything Noah did.

Why didn't he tell me about this?

The second door opened and the scent of urine punched Butch in the nose like a fist. Because of the secrecy of the project, Strand had no keepers to help him clean. Blackwood scowled and his eyes watered. Yvonne didn't seem to notice the stinging scent at all.

No doubt due to hanging with the hatchlings 24/7, Butch thought. *Probably smells like perfume to her.*

"Strand's husbandry skills need a little help," he said.

"I want you to talk to him about it first thing tomorrow morning, Butch," Blackwood said. "This is not acceptable. Show him how it's done. I won't have any of our animals living in squalor."

Butch had no problem showing people the proper way to clean a cage, even Geekenstein. What he didn't like was the idea of doing it while Yvonne and Blackwood were on a private jet sipping champagne on their way to Paris. He had to give Blackwood some credit, though. He took good care of his animals before they were sacrificed for his collection.

"I'll take care of it," Butch said.

Yvonne switched on the light in the animal room. There was only one resident now. Chupacabra versions One through Four had died of natural causes. Versions Five through Eight had been euthanized due to uncontrolled aggression. Butch had personally shot number Eight a second before it tore Geekenstein's throat out. All nine of the chupacabras had been genetically engineered from bits and pieces of other animals and incubated in jaguar wombs. It had taken Geekenstein and Blackwood nearly a decade to come up with one that might work.

Apparently, they had taken care of the aggression problem in chupacabra version 9.0 by implanting electrodes in its brain. Its every move, and *mood*, could be modified with the remote control Yvonne was now booting up. The remote looked like the controls used to direct unmanned drones. It had a five-inch high-definition monitor so Yvonne could see what the chupacabra was seeing.

"What's the range?" Blackwood asked.

"We haven't used it beyond the boundaries of the Ark," Yvonne answered. "Presumably miles, but we won't know for certain until we take Nine into the field for a complete environmental test." She looked at Blackwood and smiled again. "I'm ready."

Blackwood smiled back at her. "Let's see what our little friend can do."

They followed her down an aisle of small stainless steel cages. At the end was a much larger cage. Scattered around the concrete floor of the cage were a dozen doggy chew toys, each without a single tooth mark on them.

Guess Nine isn't into chew toys, Butch thought. *Unless they're made out of flesh.*

Inside the stainless steel cage was a wooden den box. Lying on top of the den box was an animal about the size of a coyote. It had dark brown fur, unusually long canine teeth, and disturbing orange catlike eyes. Running down its spine were knobby bones, as if its skeleton was trying to burst from the skin surrounding it. The muscular hind legs were longer than the front legs and built for speed. The front legs were designed for maneuverability. They were topped by three long claws that looked like they could gut an elephant. Nine was wearing a thick leather harness. Attached to the harness was the tiny camera Butch had stolen from the *Coelacanth*.

As always when looking at Nine, or when Nine was looking at him, the hair on the back of Butch's neck stood on end. Behind the blazing orange, the animal's eyes radiated an icy calm intelligence. They didn't just see, they evaluated.

Yvonne showed Nine the controller. The beast didn't seem overly impressed. Butch hoped the batteries were fully charged.

Attached to the outside of the cage was a stainless steel crate. Yvonne opened the sliding door between them.

"Crate," she said.

Nine didn't move.

"Crate," she repeated, and hit a button on the controller.

Nine jumped up from the top of the den as if he were on fire, hit the cement floor running, and disappeared into the metal crate on the other side of the slider with a loud bang.

"Better living through electrodes," Yvonne said with a smile.

She slid the door closed, unbolted the crate from the big cage, and looked at Butch.

"What?" Butch said, although he knew what she wanted.

"Just pick it up," Noah said. "We have a kid to catch."

Butch picked up the crate. He estimated the chupacabra weighed about forty pounds. It could kill Luther in two seconds flat. He wondered if Yvonne or Noah would allow that to happen, and he didn't care one way or the other.

DUCTWORK

"Let me see those key cards," Marty said. They were gathered around the laundry room door.

"They haven't been programed," Grace said. "They don't work."

"They didn't work on Noah's private elevator," Marty said. "That doesn't mean they won't work on the doors down here."

Grace slipped the lanyard over her head and gave them to him.

Marty slid the first card through the slot. Nothing happened.

"I told you," Grace said.

"If one of these other two don't work, we're going to be heading up through the chutes," Marty said. "How's that sound?"

Grace didn't even want to think about it. The slide down had been terrifying. Climbing back up would be worse. The sides of the chute had been like glass. She'd thought she was hurtling down a bottomless pit.

Marty swiped the second card and there was an audible *click*. He smiled.

"Lucky," Grace said.

"I'd rather be lucky than smart any day." He looked at the Gizmo to see if anyone was in the corridor. It was empty. He opened the door.

"What's the plan?" Grace asked.

"Dylan has never seen a dinosaur," Marty said. "If you can believe that. I thought we'd show him a couple. And if we bump into Luther on the way, I thought it might be good to save him from getting killed by a chupacabra if we get the chance."

"I see you haven't changed a bit since I saw you last."

"Why change perfection?"

Grace gave him an eye roll as they stepped out into the corridor.

"What room are the hatchlings in?" Dylan asked.

"Level Two," Grace said. "Lab 251. But before we try the elevator I want to go into the keeper area and see if the phone works. We're going to need help. I want to call Wolfe."

"He's at the CIA headquarters in McLean, Virginia," Marty said. "A lot of good that's going to do us."

"He'll send people over from Cryptos."

"She's right," Dylan said. "We need to call."

"We need to find Luther before that chupacabra thing does," Marty said.

"I want to find Luther, too," Grace said quietly. "But we need to do this smart. There is only one phone on this level. Except for Butch and Yvonne, Noah doesn't even allow people to carry cell phones."

"Kind of paranoid," Marty said.

"You don't know the half of it."

"Let's make it quick," Marty said.

Grace led them down the corridor. Marty had to swipe all four keys before he found one that worked on the keeper area door. Grace picked up the phone on the head keeper's desk. There was no dial tone. She slammed it back into the cradle in frustration.

"No dial tone?" Marty asked. "Big surprise. No point in cutting the cell and satellite signals, then leaving the landline active. We're on our own. Let's go."

"Wait a second," Dylan said.

"What?" Marty replied impatiently.

"How do the keepers and staff stay in touch with each other without phones?"

"Two-way radios." Grace pointed at a row of chargers and radios behind the head keeper's desk. "They check them out in the morning and check them in before they leave."

"Noah's a nutcase," Marty said.

"I think we should split up," Dylan said.

"Why?" Grace exclaimed.

"So we can cover more ground."

"Forget it," Marty said. "We have three key cards — four if we count yours." He took Grace's key off the lanyard and handed it to her. "Put that in your pocket so we don't get mixed up." He looked back at Dylan. "We don't know what doors these other three keys open. We don't even know if they'll work on the elevator."

"I'm not going to use the elevator."

"What are you talking about?" Grace asked.

Dylan walked over and plucked three radios from the chargers. He tossed one to her, one to Marty, then pointed at a vent in the ceiling over the head keeper's desk. "I'm going to take a more direct route to Luther. The ventilation ducts all have to be connected. We'll stay in touch with the radios."

"I don't know," Grace said, looking up at the narrow vent.

"I'm only a little bit bigger than Luther. I've been in some pretty tight spots, so I know I'm not claustrophobic."

"If you drop into a room, you'll be stuck there," Grace said. "You can't get out without a key card."

"Neither can Luther," Dylan said. "And he can't tell you where he is because he doesn't have a radio. He could be in the room right across from here and you wouldn't know it. He wouldn't pound on the door because he'd be afraid of who might answer. I think Blackwood and Butch were making sure the doors were locked so Luther wouldn't have a way out. I don't know much about this kind of thing, and I know you're in a hurry to find Luther, but I'd slow it down a little bit if I were you."

Grace looked at Marty.

"What do you have in mind?" Marty said.

"Blackwood and Butch have already been through this level. I don't think they're coming back. You need to unlock every door you can and prop it open so Luther has a way out. You also need to unhook the latches on the vents so he can get into the room. It will take time, but it will give Luther an escape route."

"How are you going to find him in the vents?" Grace asked.

Dylan went over to the toolroom and pulled out a stepladder and a flashlight. He set up the ladder, scrambled up to the vent, opened it, and put his hand inside. When he took it out, it was covered with dust.

"I'll follow his trail."

"What if *you* run into the chupacabra?" Grace asked. Dylan seemed like a nice boy. It would be a shame if he got mauled in the ductwork so soon after they'd met.

"I kind of hope I do before it runs into Luther. He doesn't know it's coming after him. I do, so I'll have a better chance." Dylan snapped his dusty fingers. "Here's another thing you can do. Turn the lights on in the rooms you've opened. That way I'll know which room to drop into if the chupacabra is on my tail. The vents are about eight feet off the ground. I doubt the chupacabra can jump eight feet straight up. If I can trap it in one of these rooms, Butch and Blackwood will have to open the door to get it out. It might slow them down long enough for us to find Luther and get out of here."

"I'm glad they talked you into coming with them," Grace said.

Dylan blushed, climbed down from the ladder, and changed the subject. "When Blackwood and Butch came into the laundry room, did you notice if they were wearing two-way radios?"

"I know they have radios," Grace said. "I heard them talking to each other when I was in Noah's office."

"Did you happen to notice what channel they were talking on?" Dylan asked.

"No," Grace said, now wishing she had grabbed the radio before she jumped down the chute.

Dylan walked over to the row of radios in their chargers. "These are all set on channel twelve. We'll just have to pick a number and hope Butch and Noah aren't on the same channel. We'll start with channel nine. If you hear anyone on nine, switch to channel three." He climbed back up the ladder.

"You sure you don't want me to do the crawling?" Marty asked.

Dylan shook his head and wriggled into the vent until his sneakers disappeared.

"Kind of reminds me of that anaconda eating the rabbit this afternoon," Marty said.

Grace shuddered. "Let's go open some doors."

HUNT

Yvonne followed Noah and Butch into Lab 222 on the second level, enjoying herself immensely. She was away from the hatchlings; she was about to show off her stuff for Noah Blackwood; she would be on her way to Paris in a few hours; and she was ordering the big jerk, Butch McCall, around. Life could not have been better.

Butch set the crate on a bench beneath the vent Luther had slithered into.

"You'll have to get Nine out of the crate," Yvonne said.

Butch pulled a large caliber pistol out of the back of his pants.

She gave him a derisive laugh. "You won't need that," she said. "I have complete control over Nine. You're safe, Butch."

"That's what Geekenst —" He gave Noah a nervous glance. "I mean Strand, said just before Eight went for his throat. He was pretty happy when I put a bullet in the chupacabra's brainpan."

"That bullet cost me millions of dollars and delayed Release and Catch by eight months and counting," Noah said angrily. "Your bullet is still costing me money."

Yvonne maintained her amused smile. Butch was so predictable. She knew he would pull his pistol out. Shaping behavior was all about knowing what the animal was going to do before the animal knew it was going to do it.

"You'll need both hands anyway," she said pleasantly.

"For what?" Butch asked.

"To give Nine a boost. You'll need to lift the crate up to the vent."

"You gotta be kidding me."

Yvonne shook her head. "Nine can't get up to the vent by himself. I'll need both hands for the controller. If you're afraid, maybe Dr. Blackwood could —"

Butch opened the crate door right where it sat. Yvonne had not anticipated this. She jumped back as Nine skittered out onto the slick bench, snarling. Butch had holstered his gun and stood his ground.

"Didn't mean to startle you," he said with a smile — or what passed for one through his black beard.

Noah appeared to be amused as well, although he did take a half step away from the bench, out of reach of Nine's claws, which were clacking on the cold stainless steel.

"I'd be focusing on the little monster rather than looking at us," Butch said. "You have complete control? Show us what you got."

Yvonne had badly underestimated Butch McCall. Not only had he just proven that he wasn't a coward, he had taken complete control of the situation by giving *her* complete control of the situation. It was brilliant and dangerous. Nine's fiery, malevolent eyes were fixed on her as if she were the only person in the room. She felt sweat trickling down beneath her arms.

"Funny thing about animals," Butch continued. "Even genetically engineered animals like this mutant. They remember the people who hurt them. Years ago, we had a lion escape here at the Ark. We had it cornered in the concession area. Me, seven keepers, and one veterinarian. He went directly for the vet because the vet was the one who had given him all the painful shots over the years. Mauled the man pretty bad. Never even looked at me or the keepers."

Yvonne listened, but didn't dare take her eyes off Nine. With a few button strokes she could make him move forward, backward, sideways; jump; sleep, wake, or attack; but she wasn't sure she could type in the right combination before Nine tore her head off.

"I'd put the little fella to sleep if I were you," Butch said. "And I'd do it pretty quick. Looks like he's just about made up his mind about something, and I don't think it has anything to do with me or Dr. Blackwood. When he's asleep I'll give him that boost you were talking about. We'll lock the vent behind him in case he gets any ideas about doubling back to kill you. After he's secure, you can send him on his way. It's up to you, though. You're the one in control."

Yvonne quickly typed in a command, then hit the SEND button. Nine's orange eyes went wide, then rolled up into his head. A second later he was slumped on the bench, sound asleep.

"Impressive," Noah said.

She wasn't sure if he was referring to Butch, her, or the slumbering Nine. She suspected it was Butch he was impressed with, and wondered if she was still going to Paris in the morning.

Butch jumped up on the bench with more agility than she would have guessed. He grabbed Nine by the scruff of the neck, stuffed him through the vent opening, then closed and latched the grate.

"You should be safe now," he said, jumping down.

Yvonne wanted to say something that would undo all the damage Butch had just caused her, but it was obvious words wouldn't be enough. The only way to fix this was by action. She woke Nine up. Noah stepped closer so he could see the controller's monitor. Butch remained on the other side of the bench as if he couldn't care less.

There wasn't much to see. The infrared camera showed a long, dust-covered tunnel.

"I assume there's GPS?" Noah asked.

"Of course, but we'll need points of reference to make sense of where he is."

Noah unclipped the two-way radio from his belt. "Are you getting the video feed?"

"Yeah," Paul's voice crackled back. "There's nothing else to watch. That little juvenile delinquent just took out the last camera. We're blind."

"We'll have your delinquent soon," Noah said. "Keep track of the feed. I'll be in touch."

"Is that some kind of animal up there?" Paul asked.

"You don't need to know." Noah clipped the radio back on his belt.

"Who was that?" Yvonne asked. She thought she and Butch were the only two staff members in on this.

"You don't need to know," Noah said.

She glanced at Butch. He was smiling. He knew who Noah had been talking to.

Noah pointed at the monitor. "Is it going to just sit there?"

Yvonne typed in a command, then shouted up at the vent, "Hunt!" When possible, she liked to pair verbal commands with the electronic commands.

The chupacabra started to move.

LADDERS, DOORS, AND LAUNDRY

Marty popped his head out the door and called across to Grace, "Did you hear that?"

"They're on channel nine!" Grace said, coming out of the room opposite him. "It's lucky we weren't talking on the radio before we found out."

Marty had been thinking about luck and being smart as he propped open doors, mostly because propping open doors was turning out to be the most boring thing he had ever done. He was reevaluating his "I'd rather be lucky than smart" quip, thinking that it would be better to be smart *and* lucky.

"I think you should switch your radio to channel three so we can stay in touch with Dylan," he said. "I'll keep my radio on channel nine so we can listen in on what they're saying."

"Smart thinking, Marty," Grace said.

He could count on one hand the number of times Grace had used his name and the word *smart* in the same sentence. It felt pretty good.

Grace unclipped her radio, fiddled with the dial, then depressed the TALK button. "Dylan, are you there?"

They waited. Dylan didn't answer.

"Maybe he hasn't switched channels yet," Grace said.

Yeah, and maybe he's being devoured by the chupacabra, which they obviously just put into the ventilation system, he thought, but didn't share this with Grace.

"Try him again," he said.

"Dylan?" Grace repeated.

No answer.

"We almost have all the doors open on this level," Marty said. "Let's keep going while we wait for him to answer. We need to get down to Level Two."

He swiped a card through the lock of the nearest door. It didn't work. He swiped the second card and the lock clicked open. He handed the lanyard to Grace, stepped into the room, and switched on the light. In the first two rooms they had both made the mistake of letting the doors close before they could grab something to prop them open. Grace had to let herself out, then had to let Marty out. It would have been funny if the situation wasn't so deadly. Grace had the idea of using dirty laundry to block the doors. It had worked well, except for the wasted time running back and forth to the laundry room to grab more laundry. Marty stuffed a lab coat under the door, hauled his stepladder in, set it on the bench, clambered up to the vent, and hesitated.

What if the chupacabra is waiting on the other side of the vent, looking at me right now?

He answered his own question.

I hope it is waiting so I can trap it in here.

He undid the latches, the vent flopped open, and nothing scary jumped out at him. He was almost disappointed.

Almost.

He jumped down and did a quick search of the room for anything they might be able to use. So far, in the other rooms, he'd found a couple of flashlights; a length of rope; a folding knife; and two cans of soda, which he drank. The Ark workers didn't leave much hanging around when they went home for the night. What he was hoping to find was a sawed-off shotgun, a box of grenades, or a machine gun. So far, no such luck.

He grabbed the stepladder and was reaching for his stack of laundry when Grace came in with a big smile on her face. She was holding the radio in her hand.

"I'm with Marty now," she said.

Dylan's scratchy voice came over the speaker. "Sorry I didn't answer the first time you called. I had the radio in my pocket and I couldn't get to it. It's kind of tight in here. I actually got stuck for a while, which was a little nerve-racking. Anyway, I'm carrying the radio in my hand now. I heard Noah talking to that other guy. Was that Butch?"

Grace clicked the TALK button. "No. I don't know who that was. It definitely wasn't Butch."

"So it's three against four, or three against five if you count the chupacabra. That's not good."

"Are you okay?" Grace asked.

"It was a little hard, until I got the hang of it, but I'm okay now. The only tracks I've seen belong to mice and rats. If Luther was on this level, I think I would have seen his drag marks by now. I just passed a shaft or duct that goes down. I'm going to backtrack and try to get to the second level. Are you just about done with the doors? I've seen some of the lights. Believe me, it's a welcome sight in this dank place."

"We have three rooms to go," Grace said.

"Have you checked if the keys open the elevator?"

"One of them does. The other two are for the doors."

"That's a relief. I wouldn't want to go to Level Two without you being there. Hey, Marty, Grace told me about keeping channel nine open so we can listen to the bad guys. Smart."

Marty tried not to blush, but failed. "Let me talk to him," he said. Grace handed the radio to him.

"You sound kind of tired," Marty said. "Why don't you drop down into one of the rooms here and I'll take your place. I'm a little smaller than you, and I'm rested."

"I appreciate the offer, and I might take you up on it after I've crawled around the second level for a while. There's sort of a weird logic to the duct and vent layout. I suspect it's going to be the same on every level. I don't know if I could explain it to you. It's kind of an intuitive thing. If we switched places now, you'd have to waste a lot of time figuring out what I've already figured out. Just get down to Level Two and get those lights on and vents open. I can't tell you how uplifting those lights are. It's like a Christmas tree on Christmas morning. Knowing you can jump into that lit room anytime you want is good for a hundred more feet of crawling."

Marty was about to argue the point, but thought better of it. "See you on Level Two," he said.

Grace was staring at him with those robin's-egg-blue eyes, as if she were reading his thoughts. There was a time when they could read each other's thoughts. He wondered if she could still do it.

"He's right," she said quietly.

"I know," Marty said, handing the radio back to her. "I'm just worried. For all we know, the chupacabra might be heading right for him. This isn't really his fight."

"It is now," Grace said.

Nine smelled the musky scent of rats and mice, the sharp sweat of a human, and something else he had never smelled before. Something powerful and strange. Repugnant yet compelling. Delicious. Dangerous. But not nearly as dangerous as the woman with the box he had left behind. But she was never behind. She lived in his head. In his fur. She was buried deep in his muscle and bone. No amount of scratching and licking could rid him of her. He dreamed about her when his eyes closed. Fearful dreams . . . *Stop!* He would stop when he wanted to go. *Go!* He would go when he wanted to stop. *Sleep!* He would sleep when he wasn't tired. *Wake! Right! Left! Fast! Slow! Dig! Climb! Hide!* She was slow and weak, but she had the box. She watched him, but not nearly as much as he watched her. He knew her better than she knew him. In the room he had smelled her fear. The sour scent of her terror overwhelmed the fear of the other two humans. He was about to move when — *Sleep!* — it went dark. He awoke in another steel crate that seemed to have no end. The sweating human seemed to be traveling in the direction of the dangerous smell. Trails of loose wires lined the path. Nine tasted the coppery ends. The human had bled. Nine licked the dried salty blood. *Hunt! Fast!* The commands shouted in his head. He hated the woman. He hated the box. He wanted to kill the woman. He wanted to drink the woman's blood. But he could not. She was commanding him. She was inside his head. *Hunt! Fast! Hunt! Hunt!*

SMOKE AND MIRRORS

Noah, Butch, and Yvonne had gone down to Yvonne's office on Level Three to watch the hunt on a bigger screen. She had a way of hooking the box up to her twenty-one-inch computer monitor. Butch had stayed with them for about thirty seconds, then left them there. He had no desire to *watch* a hunt. He needed fresh air, he needed to get away from Yvonne Zloblinavech and her little freak show. But mostly, *he* needed to hunt, not watch something else hunt.

Luther's going to meet a grisly end. Glad I won't be there to see it. If I didn't despise him so much, I might feel sorry for the kid.

Butch shook off the thoughts. He had more important things to think about. Namely, Marty O'Hara. If he could tie up that *loose end* for Noah, there was a good chance he would be on his way to Paris in a few hours. He wasn't looking forward to spending any more time than he had to with Yvonne, but anything was better than spending time with Mr. Zwilling. He felt a chill go down his spine at the thought of it. Zwilling creeped him out even more than the chupacabra.

The elevator door opened and he stepped out into a thick fog. A cold, steady breeze was pushing it in from Puget Sound. It would delay Noah's flight if it didn't clear by sunrise.

Marty O'Hara is somewhere in this fog. Confused, cold, vulnerable, and all mine.

The elevator disappeared back into the ground. Butch stood in the swirling fog, letting his eyes adjust to the dark, listening for noises that didn't belong. He knew the sounds of the Ark so well. The lion's roar, the chuff of the tiger, the grunt of the hippo, the crocodile's bellow. Marty had gotten the better of him twice now. In the Congo, he had snuck up behind him and split his head open with a tree branch.

A tree branch!

Butch still couldn't believe the kid had gotten the drop on him like that.

And then aboard the Coelacanth . . .

Butch shook his head in wonder. He had tossed Marty over the side of the ship. He had seen the terrified expression on his face when he dropped. Then a few hours later he saw Marty on deck, goofing around with Luther as if nothing had happened.

I'll have to ask him how that happened before I kill him. Professional curiosity.

He climbed over the rail, deciding that the best hunting technique under these conditions would be *walk, stop, listen, and stalk.* By now Marty would be moving. He wouldn't have seen anyone in hours. His guard would be completely down. He would have already searched the perimeter and realized there was no way out.

He'll be back probing the center by now, wondering if Luther was hiding inside the Ark or had left when it closed, thinking that Marty had split. Gets confusing when you hunt with others.

Butch smiled. This was exactly why he preferred to hunt

alone. Friends and partners always got you in trouble. You spent more time thinking about them than your prey.

He walked fifty paces down the path, stopped, and lis —

"Butch?"

The radio! He cursed himself. He should have turned it off, or at least plugged in the earpiece. He fumbled to get it off his belt before the impatient and loud Noah Blackwood started to shout —

"Pick up, Butch!"

The shout was loud enough to wake every animal in the park. Noah might have just as well announced over the Ark's loudspeakers that Butch was hunting Marty.

"I'm here," Butch said quietly, hoping Noah would get the hint.

He didn't.

"Where?" Noah shouted.

Butch turned the volume down as low as it would go. "Up top. Southeast Asia. Have you finished the . . . uh . . . experiment?" They were careful when they used the two-ways, just in case some ped outside the park was scanning radio frequencies.

"We're working on it. What are you doing up top?"

"Looking for . . . uh . . . intruders."

"I want you to go to the mansion."

"Why?"

"Check on my girl."

"You said she was asleep."

"I want you to make sure everything is . . . uh . . . secure."

Meaning Noah wanted to make sure she was still in bed and probably had a bad feeling that she wasn't. Butch had a bad feeling, too, but it had nothing to do with Grace Wolfe. It had to do with Marty. He could cause them a lot more trouble than his cousin, who seemed perfectly content to be with her rich grandfather while he showered her with gifts and spoiled her rotten.

"You want me to go into her . . . uh . . . room?"

"How else would you make sure?"

"She's probably asleep."

"If she wakes up, say something about the sweep."

"The sweep?"

"This is getting tedious, Butch. Just check and get back to me."

"Why don't you just send —"

"He's not here. Just check on Grace!"

Butch wasn't going to actually say *Mr. Zwilling* over the radio, which he and Noah commonly did, because nobody knew who Mr. Zwilling was. It was a test to see if Yvonne, who was no doubt standing right next to Noah, knew about Zwilling. Noah cutting him off meant that she didn't.

She doesn't know about Paul. She doesn't know about Zwilling. Noah doesn't trust her. Yet.

"I'll check on Grace," Butch said.

"I have to go," Grace said, pulling the door keys off the lanyard and handing them to Marty. They had just gotten to Level Two.

"Wait a second!" Marty said.

"There's no time," Grace said, slipping the lanyard over her head. "I have to be in bed when Butch gets there." She started for the elevator. Marty followed her.

"This is a bad idea," he said. "He'll beat you to the mansion."

"I know a shortcut," she said.

"Who cares if they know you're there or not? They're going to find out in a few hours anyway."

Grace slid the key through the elevator lock. "Timing," she said, stepping into the car. "If I don't get back, everything will be ruined. It has to do with the emails. I'll explain later. Turn on the Christmas lights for Dylan." She tossed her radio to him. "I won't need this. I'll be back."

The elevator door slid closed on a stunned and angry-faced Marty O'Hara. Grace regretted leaving him like that, but there really hadn't been time to explain. If she wasn't in her bed, Noah would wonder where she was. He'd return to the mansion. He would go to the third floor and find the bedding gone. He would check his computer and know that someone had tampered with it. He might discover that he had sent the episode of *Wildlife First* that would turn into *Wildlife Last* if it aired. The elevator stopped on the first level. She sprinted down the corridor to the animal service elevator, hoping the key card worked. It did. She stepped out into the fog on the keeper service road. The road was cleverly hidden from public view, and provided a much quicker route to just about everywhere in the park, including the mansion. Butch was on the public path, which twisted and turned and switched back on itself, giving the illusion that the Ark and the animal exhibits were much bigger than they actually were.

Illusion, she thought as she sprinted down the road toward the mansion. *Noah Blackwood is an illusionist. A wolf in sheep's skin. A shape-shifter. The Ark is a mirage. It's all smoke and mirrors. . . .*

She reached the restricted path leading up to the mansion. It was blocked by a heavy gate, opened by the same key card that opened the mansion. She pulled the card from her pocket, swiped it through the slot, and squeezed through as soon as it was wide enough. She sprinted up the path and came around the corner just in time to see Butch lumbering up the steps to the porch. At the top he paused and turned around, almost as if he could sense her. She dove behind a statue of Noah Blackwood surrounded by a dozen adoring endangered species. She had never been this close to the sculpture before. In the dim light, she saw that the animals looking up at him could all be found in the cube on the third floor. There was a bronze plaque on the bottom that read: WILDLIFE FIRST! COMMISSIONED BY DOCTOR NOAH BLACKWOOD TO HONOR ALL CREATURES GREAT AND SMALL.

Great and small, and stuffed up on the third floor, Grace thought. *Who commissions a statue of themselves?*

Butch continued to stare out into the night, then turned around and walked through the front door. Grace hesitated, then sprinted across the manicured lawn.

Butch switched on the light in the foyer. He didn't know how Noah could stand this place. It looked more like a movie set of a home rather than a real home. Nothing was out of place. There wasn't a speck of dust anywhere.

A cockroach would starve to death in here.

Of course, Noah's private quarters on the third floor were a different story. By the looks of them, Noah did the cleaning up there himself. It actually looked lived-in. Butch had never had this verified, but he thought that Noah's private taxidermist, Henrico, was a frequent guest. The cube where Noah kept his beloved collection didn't have a fingerprint on it. There had to be a secret door for Henrico to get the animals into the cube from below. And if there was a secret door inside the cube, there was bound to be a door in the cube leading to the private quarters. Butch suspected Henrico was invited up to discuss future projects while Noah had him polish the glass.

Butch had been up on the third floor many times. He wondered if Yvonne had been invited up there. He hoped not. He turned on the light over the antiseptic staircase, which looked like no one had ever tread on the carpeted risers.

This time of night, the mansion was usually crawling with house cleaners. Noah didn't like to see them, so he had them come in when he was asleep. Same for the cooks. Meals were prepared the night before and set out in the dining room by the concession manager just before Noah wanted to eat. If the manager made the mistake of being seen by Noah, there would be a new concession manager serving up the next meal.

Butch was halfway up the stairs when he realized he didn't know which room Grace was using. There were several bedrooms on the second floor. This was going to slow down the ridiculous errand unless he got lucky.

He did not get lucky. The first two bedrooms were empty, as was the third, but it wasn't enough that they were empty. In order to determine that Grace wasn't using the rooms, he had to search the closets and dressers for her things.

Why am I wasting my time opening empty drawers? Marty's outside, not in here!

By the time he got to the fourth bedroom, he was thoroughly disgusted. He threw the door open and flicked on the lights.

Grace let out a bloodcurdling scream. Butch stumbled back through the door in shock.

"Sorry . . . I . . . uh . . . sorry . . . I . . ."

"What are you doing in here?" Grace shouted.

"I . . . uh . . . Dr. Blackwood . . . uh . . ."

"What?"

"He . . . uh . . . he . . . the sweep."

"The sweep? What about it?"

She spit the two questions out. He had never seen her angry. If he'd ever had any doubt that Grace was related to Noah Blackwood, that was gone now. Her rage was just like her grandfather's.

"We're . . . uh . . . still in the middle of our . . . uh . . . sweep," he said, managing to string out a partial sentence. "He wanted to make sure you were inside."

"And you thought kicking open the door and turning on the lights would be the best way to do that? Are you insane?"

"I didn't know which room was yours."

"So why not kick all the doors open until you found the right one? Why not scare Grace half to death? I'm going to talk to my grandfather about this in the morning. Get out! And turn out the light when you go!"

Butch turned out the light and quietly closed the door. When he got outside again, he unclipped his radio, surprised to find his hand was shaking. His hands never shook. He took a couple of deep breaths before clicking the TALK button.

"She was asleep," he said.

"Good," Noah said. "I hope you didn't wake her."

Butch glanced up at Grace's window. It was dark. "She's asleep," he said, which probably wasn't true.

Hard to fall asleep when you're mad.

"Fine," Noah said. "I'll let you know when our experiment down here has run its course. Over and out."

Butch continued to look up at Grace's window, wondering if she was watching him. He had a strong sense that she was. He thought back over the exchange in her bedroom. Something wasn't quite right. In fact, something was wrong. The girl in the bedroom was not the Grace Blackwood that he knew. He'd never seen her really frightened, which could explain her reaction, but he didn't think so.

He turned the radio off and clipped it to his belt. He walked away from the mansion. He did not look back. He did not go very far.

THE MOTHMAN

"Over and out to you, too, Noah," Marty said without depressing the TALK button — although he was tempted to, just to rattle both Blackwood and Butch.

He was glad Grace had beaten Butch to the mansion and apparently saved the day — but from what, he didn't know. He was happy Dylan was up in the vents trying to save his best friend. He was extremely pleased that Luther and Dylan hadn't been eaten by the chupacabra, as far as he knew. What he wasn't happy about was his role in this whole thing. As critical as opening doors and turning on lights was, it wasn't doing much for him personally. He felt useless and underutilized. He had spoken to Dylan twice since Grace had run off, offering to switch places with him. Both times Dylan had passed, saying that the vents were actually wider on the second level and that he was making good progress.

The only interesting room Marty had been into was what he decided to call the pig room. He wasn't sure what they were being used for, but three miniature potbellied pigs were in it. He thought about letting them go so the chupacabra wouldn't get them, but figured they were probably safer in their stainless steel cages than they'd be wandering around the corridor.

Marty walked down the corridor, opened yet another door, kicked yet another towel into the jamb, flipped on yet another light switch, set up the ladder on yet another bench, opened yet another vent, climbed down, gathered his things, walked to the next door, slid the key card through yet another lock, opened yet another door, and started the whole boring routine again.

Except this one ended with the chupacabra sticking its ugly face in Marty's as soon as the vent dropped open.

Marty fell backward off the ladder, sending a half-dozen beakers of chemicals flying across the lab. He tried to get up and run, but his legs were tangled in the ladder and a stack of towels and rags. The chupacabra continued to slither out of the vent as Marty struggled to free himself. It was gray, and horrible-looking, and much bigger than he thought it would be. In fact, as Marty stared in horror, it looked like the ceiling was giving birth to The Mummy, which was somehow more frightening than a genetically engineered monster. Marty finally got his legs untangled and managed to pull himself to his feet. He wondered if he should knock the chupacabra senseless with the ladder while it was wiggling out and vulnerable, or simply run out of the lab and slam the door behind him.

"Are you just going to stand there, or are you going to help me out of here?"

Marty stared up at the ceiling in complete shock. The Mummy, or chupacabra, could talk, and it sounded a lot like Luther Percival Smyth IV.

"Jeez! Hurry up, you nose-picker. Get me down from here."

Marty was relieved on several levels, but he was not about to show it. That wasn't how things worked between him and Luther. "You look like you're decomposing," he said.

"Yeah?" Luther said. "You look like a custodian."

Marty grinned. The joke was kind of lame, but not bad under the circumstances. With all the rags stuffed in his pockets, he *did* look a little like a custodian. He climbed up on the bench and helped Luther out of the vent. The gray matter was dust sprinkled with rodent pellets, some of which got into Marty's mouth, causing him to gag, to Luther's delight.

"Tell me about it," Luther said. "My lungs are filled with that toxic sludge. It's disgusting up there."

"I take back what I said about decomposing," Marty said, choking. "You look like the Mothman."

"You know the rules," Luther said. "You get one insult shot. There are no take backs. What's a Mothman?"

"It's a cryptid," Marty said. "I wouldn't be surprised if Noah had a couple of them in storage down here."

"Cool," Luther said. "We'll put the Mothman in our next book." He went over to the sink and rinsed the dust off his head.

"Now you look like a vulture," Marty said.

Luther ignored him. "You know I got kidnapped and drugged."

Marty nodded. "Got it on film."

Luther grinned. "It'll go viral."

"They also sent a chupacabra after you."

"Why would they send a candelabra after me? That doesn't make sense."

"*Choo-pah-cah-brah,*" Marty said slowly. "It means *goat sucker.*"

"Coat sucker? What's the matter with you?"

"Clean out your ears," Marty said.

"Huh?"

Marty pointed at Luther's ears, which were still the color of ash.

"Oh." Luther put his head back under the faucet and scooped half a teaspoon of gray goop out of each ear with his index finger. "Say something."

"I'm glad you're okay," Marty said.

"Say that again," Luther said, grinning.

"Forget it," Marty said.

"So what have you been doing since I got abducted, heroically escaped, took out several of Blackwood's cameras, and found you completely on my own?" Luther asked.

Marty began to tell him, but he didn't get very far. Dylan's voice came over the radio.

"Marty, do you copy?"

In his excitement at seeing Luther, Marty had completely forgotten about Dylan. Before he could answer, Dylan started talking again.

"I've found Luther's track. He's definitely been here. I think I can hear him crawling in front of me. I haven't seen him yet, but he's not too far ahead. Keep opening those vents."

"Don't move," Marty said into the radio.

"What?"

"Luther's with me."

There was a long pause, then Dylan said quietly, "I guess that's one of those good news, bad news things."

"Yeah," Marty said. "Can you still hear it?"

"Yep."

"Coming or going?"

"I can't tell."

"Do you have any idea where you are?"

"Nope. I passed an open vent about a hundred feet back. I don't see any light up ahead."

"Then you need to move backward."

"Easier said than done."

Marty looked at Luther.

Luther nodded. "He's right. It's kind of a one-way street up there. It's a lot easier to pull yourself forward than it is to push yourself backward. He can do it, but it's going to be slow, and going backward makes a lot more noise."

"So you've seen only one lighted vent?" Marty asked.

"One," Dylan confirmed.

"Give me a second."

"I'll give you all the time you want if you can get me out of this pickle without getting me mauled."

"I love that guy," Luther said.

"You ought to," Marty said. "He was trying to save your life. Now shut up for a second while I figure this out."

Marty closed his eyes and walked . . . well, ran . . . through the rooms he'd been in, with his eidetic memory. Even though he hadn't been up in the ductwork, he had a pretty good idea of how the vents ran from opening all the grates on Level One and a half dozen on Level Two. When he opened his eyes, he knew the direction Dylan needed to go.

"You need to crawl forward," he said into the radio.

"That's kind of counterintuitive," Dylan said.

"I know," Marty admitted. "We're going to get in front of you and draw the chupacabra away. Just ahead of where you are, you're going to come to a junction. You need to go right.

With luck, the chupacabra is going to double back and go left, toward us."

"And you know this how?"

"That memory thing of mine."

Luther gave him an eye roll.

"You'll take another right," Marty said, ignoring him. "You'll see a light. Drop down into the room and get out of there. We'll find you in the corridor after we trap the chupacabra. Oh . . . and turn off your flashlight."

"Okay," Dylan whispered. "Over and out."

Marty grabbed his ladder and rags and ran out of the room. The Mothman followed.

LIAR, LIAR, PANTS ON FIRE

Grace was standing on a chair.

She had watched Butch walk away from the mansion from her bedroom window, wanting to flee as soon as he disappeared in the swirling fog, but resisting the urge. She was making herself wait for ten minutes before stepping off the chair. She wanted to make sure Butch was well clear of the mansion before she left and headed down below again. She looked at the expensive watch Noah had given her. The second hand had one more lap to go. She wondered if she should leave the watch behind as a message for Noah that she couldn't be bought. That was the kind of thing the heroine always did in movies.

I'm not a heroine and this isn't a movie. I like the watch. I'm keeping it.

She stepped off the chair.

She had used the secret passage next to the pool and helipad to get into the mansion, and decided to leave the same way. It was closer to the service road than the front door, and there was more cover in case some of the surveillance had been fixed, or was will working. She hoped Butch would head down below right away. The thought made her quicken her pace. Noah, Yvonne, and the chupacabra were still hunting for Luther. At least she hoped they were. She had to get back below and help Marty. She ran by the pool and the helipad to the service road gate. Once again she swiped her key and squeezed through before it was fully open, then swiped her key on the other side to close it behind her. The gate was unclimbable. Like the levels below, the service area ran in a circle along the back side of every exhibit in the Ark. This way, the keepers could access the animal exhibits for maintenance and cleaning without the public seeing them. If an animal escaped from the back of one of the exhibits, or a holding area, the service road acted like a second cage, allowing keepers to wrangle the escapee before it got out into the public areas. It was a clever design. Because of the winding public paths, hidden moats, and electrified wires, the public thought the animals were running free in gigantic exhibits, but of course that was a lie like everything else Noah Blackwood was involved with.

No matter how pretty you make it, a cage is a cage.

She looked at the watch, glad she had kept it now. It would remind her of Noah's cages for the rest of her life.

"Where do you think you're going?"

Grace nearly jumped out of her shoes. Butch had appeared out of nowhere.

"What?" he said. "No spitting rage? Nice performance at the mansion. A little overplayed, but —"

"I don't know what you're talking about," Grace said, kicking herself for doing exactly what he was accusing her of. She *had* overplayed the role, and she should have realized it. "I tried to call my grandfather after you broke into my room, but there was no signal. Where is he?"

"Busy."

"Take me to him." She couldn't very well use the elevator key around her neck that she wasn't supposed to have in front of Butch. Once she got below she would figure out how to get away from him.

"What are you really doing out here?" Butch asked.

"I already told you."

"I think you're lying," Butch said. "I think you've been lying since the moment you got to the Ark. I saw you leave by the secret door near the pool. So Noah has secret passages in the house?"

Grace said nothing, surprised that Butch didn't know about the passages.

Butch gave her his version of a smile. "You used the passage to your room before I got up there," he said. "Where were you? How did you know I was going to the mansion to check on you?"

"You've really lost it, Butch," she said, and started to walk away.

Butch grabbed her by the arm and yanked her back. She tried to get away, but it was useless.

"You're hurting me," Grace said.

Butch's smile broadened and he tightened his grip.

"My grandfather will fire you," Grace said.

Butch laughed, then said, "Your grandfather might have me killed, but he would never fire me. I'm much too valuable of an employee to be fired. And I'm about to get more valuable. Where's Marty?"

Grace was reevaluating her idea of going below with Butch. If she could keep him up top, Marty and Dylan would have one less person to deal with down below.

She gave Butch a defeated look. "He's waiting for me at the orangutan exhibit in Southeast Asia."

Butch loosened his grip, but he didn't let her go. "That's better," he said. "Who else is here?"

Grace didn't answer. Butch increased the pressure on her arm.

"Okay, okay," she whined. "Luther was with him, but I think he must have left when the Ark closed, because we can't find him anywhere. Marty just wants to find him and leave, but he can't get out."

"How did you know Marty was here?"

"He told one of the concession workers and she told me when I went in to get something to eat. I snuck out and met him a couple of hours ago."

Butch let up on his grip, but his eyes narrowed. "How'd you know I was going to the mansion to check on you?"

"We overheard you and my grandfather talking on the path in Southeast Asia. We were hiding a few feet away when you got the radio call."

Butch let her go. Grace was surprised. She rubbed her arm.

"Let's go find him," Butch said.

"What are you going to do to him?"

"I'm going to let him out of the Ark. What do you think I'm going to do with him?"

"You tried to kill him aboard the *Coelacanth*," Grace said.

"Is that what he told you? No wonder you're so paranoid. I didn't do anything to him aboard that ship. All we were trying to do was get the hatchlings and you. We have nothing against Marty, or any of Wolfe's crew. Not anymore."

"We still have to find Luther," Grace said.

Butch shook his head. "He left just before the Ark closed. You were right. We have it on the surveillance video. We were surprised Marty wasn't with him."

Liar, liar, pants on fire, Grace thought. *You weren't surprised at all, and you have no intention of letting Marty or Luther go. But first you have to find Marty. And I'm not going to let that happen.*

Butch stared at her as if he were waiting for something. The problem was that Grace didn't know what that something was.

"Why did Luther shave his head?"

This was a test question. He was trying to figure out if she had seen Luther, which she had — on the surveillance video. But she wasn't about to let Butch know that. "Luther shaved his head?" she said.

"Like a cue ball with scabs."

"Maybe it wasn't Luther."

"It was Luther," Butch said, continuing to stare.

Grace met his gaze. "Maybe we should call my grandfather and tell him what we're doing," she said.

She was pretty sure he wouldn't call him. Butch wanted Marty, and he was using her to find him. Blackwood wouldn't want her anywhere near Marty O'Hara under any circumstances.

"He knows what we're doing," Butch said. "Well, at least what I'm doing. He doesn't know you're looking for Marty, too." He unclipped his radio. "You sure you want me to tell him?"

He was bluffing. Grace was tempted to call him on it, but decided it was too big a risk. "I guess not," she said, smiling shyly. "We're going to Paris tomorrow. I'm sure he's busy getting ready."

"Yeah," Butch said. "There are a lot of loose ends to tie up before he leaves."

"What's the deal with the phones?" Grace asked. It seemed like a logical question, and one that he might be waiting for. "Marty tried to call Luther, but he couldn't get a signal."

"That's a problem here," Butch said. "It's a pain in the butt. I think it has something to do with the fog."

Like fog has anything to do with cell signals! It was all she could do not to give him a humongous eyeball roll.

"Let's go find Marty," Butch said. "I'm sure he's worried about what's taking you so long."

That was the only truthful thing Butch had said since he'd grabbed her. She was certain Marty was worried. She wished she could let him know what was going on.

HOOT AND HOLLER

The only thing Marty was worried about at the moment was not getting his face eaten off by the goat sucker. He was standing on the ladder with his head through the vent and flashlights pointing to his left and right so he could see it coming. The plan was to hoot and holler until he saw the chupacabra speeding down the duct like a bullet, jump off the ladder without breaking his leg, run to the door, and trap the slathering beast in the room. Luther (a.k.a. Mothman) was manning the door and the radio. His job was to keep tabs on Dylan's progress via the two-way (Dylan was still crawling toward the light), and to slam the door closed, preferably with Marty in the corridor and the chupacabra locked in the room.

Marty had to admit that it wasn't the greatest plan he'd ever had, but it was all he could think of. He had also discovered a flaw in Dylan's original plan. It was true that by turning on the lights and opening the vents, someone would theoretically be able to get away from the chupacabra and trap it in the room. What was also true was that the chupacabra could use those same open hatches and open doors to get into the corridor. And that's exactly what he thought the chupacabra had done.

He felt that if the monster was still in the ductwork, it would have answered his taunts by now.

He popped his head out of the vent. Luther stood in the doorway with a radio in one hand and the Gizmo in the other. They had parked the dragonspy across from the elevator, which as far as they knew was the only way to get to the second level. The elevator was on the opposite side of the circle from them. If Blackwood or any of his people arrived, all Marty and Luther had to do was run out into the corridor and move in the same direction they were walking to lose them. If by chance Blackwood's people split up, there would be plenty of time to get into one of the rooms and hide. At least that was their theory.

"Any word from Dylan?" Marty asked.

"He's just about there," Luther said.

Marty stuck his head back into the vent and immediately started sneezing. This had happened every time he put his head back into the ceiling. He didn't mind. It saved him from having to call out: *Here, chupacabra! Come and get it! Nah-na-nah-nah-na!* Or whatever he thought would entice the chupacabra to try to kill him.

He was mid-sneeze when one of his flashlights caught the two orange eyes. They were two pinpoints at first, but getting larger very quickly. He had promised himself that as soon as he saw anything, he'd be out of there pronto, but he found himself staring at the eyes, unable to move. He'd always wondered why deer got frozen by car headlights. Now he knew.

"Fear!" he shouted.

He jumped off the ladder, ran down the bench, jumped to the floor, and ran for the door.

"What?" Luther shouted.

Marty risked a glance back at the vent. There was nothing there. He stopped and turned around.

"What?" Luther repeated, but a lot quieter this time.

"I saw . . ." Marty hesitated. Now he wasn't exactly sure what he had seen, or if he had seen anything at all. "I thought I saw oranges eyes."

"Orange?" Luther asked.

"Two of them."

"Are you sure?"

"I was."

They stared at the vent, which looked about as scary as . . . an open ceiling vent.

"Maybe your sneezing scared it off," Luther said.

"Give me the radio." Marty had left his radio out in the corridor with his backpack.

Luther stepped farther into the room and handed it to him. Marty pressed the TALK button.

"How's it going?" Marty asked.

"I got stuck," Dylan said. "Now I'm unstuck. I'm about twenty feet away." He sounded out of breath.

"Do you hear anything?"

"Just my heart pounding in my chest. It's pretty narrow through here. Hard going."

"Keep crawling," Marty said. "When you get into the room, get out, and close the door behind you. We're in Room 219. If you see any open doors on your way here, shut them. Hurry."

"What's going on?"

"Once you're safe, we don't want the chupacabra getting into the corridor where we are."

"Hadn't thought of that. Will do."

Marty handed the radio back to Luther.

"What are you going to do?" Luther asked.

"Guess I'm going to stick my head back through the ceiling."

Marty did not want to stick his head back through the ceiling, but he didn't know what else to do. He couldn't distract the chupacabra by staring at the vent.

"What about the orange eyes?" Luther asked.

"I hope I was hallucinating."

"Want me to stick my head up there?" Luther asked.

"We want to distract it, not have it die of fright."

"Ha-ha."

What happened next wasn't so funny. The chupacabra dropped out of the ceiling and landed on the bench like an agile cat.

"Marty!" Noah said. "How'd he get down here?"

He and Yvonne were staring at Yvonne's computer monitor. They had seen the flashlight beam and Nine barreling down the duct toward the light. They thought that was it; Luther was going to be mauled. Then Nine suddenly stopped. Yvonne frantically tapped in commands. *Hunt! Kill!* But the commands didn't work. Nine resisted everything she threw at him. The camera showed him simply staring through a vent in the ceiling at a stainless steel laboratory bench. Then he jumped, turned, and there was the wide-eyed Marty O'Hara, and just behind him an equally shocked Luther Smyth looking like a bald dust bunny.

"Do something!" Noah shouted.

Yvonne was frantically hitting buttons on her controller. "I'm trying!"

Then the monitor went blank.

Noah got on the radio. "Where is it, Paul?"

"Level Two, but the GPS went out before I could pinpoint the room."

"Keep trying," Noah said.

His next call was to Butch, but Butch didn't answer.

"Did it just die?" Luther asked.

"It's still breathing," Marty said. He was closer to the chupacabra than Luther and could see its dust-covered fur moving up and down with each breath.

Luther tiptoed up and peered over Marty's shoulder. "It's really cool-looking, in a horrible way."

Marty took a few steps closer but made sure he had a clear path to the door just in case. Luther was right, the chupacabra was pretty cool-looking. "Check out those fangs and claws," he said.

"You think it really eats goats?"

"I think it eats whatever it wants."

"Vicious, but kind of cute," Luther said. "I wonder if Blackwood designed it that way intentionally so people would pay to come and see it."

"Wouldn't put it past him," Marty said. "See that harness it's wearing?"

"Yeah," Luther said. "And the camera. Looks like a Ted Bronson special."

"Sure does," Marty said. "Must be one of the cameras he stole from the *Coelacanth*." Marty leaned a little closer but kept his feet exactly where they were. "When it jumped down, the light on the box was blinking. It's not blinking now."

"Uh-oh. So you think they saw us?"

"They saw me anyway," Marty said.

Dylan came on the radio. "I'm out. I'm closing doors."

"Keep your eyes open for Noah, Butch, and Yvonne," Marty said. "They're onto us. I'll explain when you get here." He turned to Luther. "Watch the elevator. Let me know if they show up."

"What are you going to do?"

"I'm going to blow their minds." Marty walked up to the chupacabra and touched it.

"Are you insane!" Luther shouted.

"Probably," Marty admitted, then touched the chupacabra again with a little more force. It didn't wake up, to his great relief. "I'm going to take the harness off Sleeping Beauty."

"You *are* nuts. Why?"

"Because without the elevator key card, we don't have a way out of here. We're going to have to play hide-and-seek until Grace shows up, which I hope is soon. The camera on the harness is just like the one on the dragonspy. It runs on solar. No light in the air ducts. It went dead, but it will charge back up now that it's back under the lights. My bet is that it has GPS, too, running off the same solar battery. I don't know how yet, but we might be able to use the harness to confuse them."

Luther pointed at the chupacabra. "So what made the fur ball go dead?"

"Good question. I just hope he stays dead long enough for me to get the harness off."

He started to undo the buckles, ready to run at the chupacabra's first twitch.

"Confuse them how?" Luther asked.

"Don't know yet," Marty said. "I'm working on it."

He got the last buckle undone. Very gently, he pulled the harness away from the chupacabra's dusty fur and took a closer look at the little box and camera.

"We'll need a screwdriver to get this open."

"Plus or minus?" Luther asked, pulling a multi-tool that he'd picked up in one of the labs out of his pocket.

"Plus," Marty said.

Luther opened the Phillips and handed it to him.

A couple of turns of the two screws and the panel came off.

"Yep," Marty said. "GPS." He turned the camera and the GPS off and screwed the panel back on. "Okay, I did the hard part getting that harness off. Your turn now."

"Sure," Luther said. "What do you need?"

"Pick up the chupacabra and put him in one of the cabinets," Marty said.

"Huh?"

Dylan walked into the room looking like Mothman Two. "Whoa! Is that the chupacabra?"

"Yep," Marty said.

Dylan hurried over for a closer look. "Is it dead?"

"Just taking a nap," Luther said.

Dylan stepped a little nearer. "Glad I didn't run into that thing up there."

"You and me both," Luther said. "By the way, thanks for crawling after me." He clapped Dylan on the shoulder, sending up a plume of dust.

"No problem," Dylan said. "Now let's get out of here."

"Easier said than done," Marty said. "And we have a couple of things to do before we leave."

"Like what?"

"Like we have to wait for Grace to get back down here with the elevator key," Marty answered.

"Yeah," Luther said. "And we have to put the chupacabra away." He walked over to a cabinet and opened the door. "Grab him, Dylan."

Dylan frowned. "Why don't we just lock it in the room?"

"I guess we could," Marty said. "But someone might open the door and let it out, and that could be a problem for them and us."

"I don't really care about *them*," Dylan said. "But I get your point." He reached out for the chupacabra.

Marty stopped him. "I'll do it," he said.

"I'm not going to argue," Dylan said. "I'll find something to secure the cabinet."

Marty gingerly picked up the chupacabra, hoping it didn't wake up in his arms and tear off his face. It was heavier than it looked. Dense. Powerful. It felt like it would be fast. Very fast. He wasn't sure he could have beaten it to the door if it hadn't passed out, or whatever had happened to it.

What had happened to it?

He put it into the cabinet. Dylan closed the door and wrapped the handles with a roll of copper wire he'd found.

"That'll hold," Luther stated.

"Now, where did Grace go?" Dylan asked. "When's she coming back?"

"She went up top to Noah's mansion," Marty answered. "I'm not sure why, but I hope she gets back soon."

"Securing the chupacabra is one thing, but you said we had a couple of things to do," Dylan said. "What's the other thing?"

"We still have to get the hatchlings out of here."

Dylan grinned. "You're kidding, right?"

Marty shook his head.

"I thought we bagged that part after Luther got kidnapped."

"We did," Marty said. "But now that he's back, we at least have to try to get them out of here."

"Do you even know where they are?"

"I do," Luther said.

"How?" Marty asked.

Luther pointed at his nose. "You may have that photographic memory thing, but I have the magic schnozzle. I was sniffing them out when I dropped in here. Follow me."

"We have one other stop to make on the way," Marty said.

"Where?" Dylan asked.

"We have to catch a pig," Marty answered.

REBOOT

"How much more time is this going to take?" Noah asked.

He and Yvonne were still in Yvonne's office, where Noah's mood had gone from glee at watching the hunt to absolute fury over the technological failure. Yvonne had plugged the control box into her computer and was desperately trying to reprogram it.

"It shouldn't be too long now," Yvonne said nervously.

Noah was glad she was nervous. He'd had people killed for a lot less than what she had done. To fail like this at the last moment was unforgivable. She was the only person who knew how to control the chupacabra. He would be taking care of that error in judgment at his earliest convenience. Right now was not the time. He still needed her.

But her time will come very soon. Perhaps I'll have Butch toss her into the Atlantic on our way to Paris. Butch would enjoy that.

The thought calmed him, but only for a moment.

Butch! Where is he? Why isn't he answering his radio? Maybe I should have him tossed into the Atlantic tied to Yvonne. He'd hate that. Up on top looking for Marty? I've got news for you, Butch. Marty is somewhere on Level Two with Luther, where we just were! He's opened doors. Somehow he's managed to get a key card and . . .

Noah stepped out into the corridor before he lost control. He didn't want Yvonne to see it if it happened. He didn't let anyone see him like that. This was his private mood, reserved for when he was by himself in his private quarters on the top of the mansion. He walked down the corridor to the restroom. He washed his face in cold water. He combed his hair and beard. He looked in the mirror at the ruggedly handsome Dr. Noah Blackwood, who was in remarkable shape for his age. He felt better. He thought of his options.

There was a good chance that the chupacabra had already taken care of the two boys. Marty had been standing close to Nine, and the chupacabra was lightning fast. That would be the best outcome. But he couldn't rely on that. Another possibility was that Butch had ended up on Level Two after discovering that Marty was not on top. If that was the case, and the boys had somehow gotten away from Nine, they would have to deal with Butch, and he was much worse than any chupacabra. This would be unfortunate for Nine as well, because Butch wouldn't hesitate to kill the chupacabra if he saw it on the loose and uncontrolled.

Unfortunate, but not the end of the world. We have more on the way. Two brood jaguars were carrying versions Ten and Eleven.

It would delay his Release and Catch program, which he had been dreaming about for years, but he had the hatchlings, which were going to make his fortune for decades to come.

This is just a glitch; it's only to be expected when you try to achieve great things.

He felt his blood pressure lowering, his heart slowing, his calculating calm returning. He reminded himself that there was no hurry. Even if Luther and Marty had managed by some miracle to get back up top, there was no place for them to go. He and Butch had the only key cards that opened the front gate. Without the card, there was no escape.

He had an office on every level beneath the Ark. This way he could meet with his people on that level without having them on levels where they were not wanted. The offices were unpretentious. Noah Blackwood did not like frills. A desk, a conference table, a computer with absolutely no compromising data on it, and a safe cleverly hidden behind a bookcase. The contents of the safes were identical. He found what he was looking for, then joined Yvonne back in her office and sat down across from her.

"How long?" he asked.

"A half an hour," Yvonne said. "Maybe a little longer. I'm really sorry about this, Dr. Blackwood. The camera and GPS are solar powered. I think in the dark ventilation system they simply ran out of juice. It's my fault. I should have anticipated that."

"And the electrodes inside Nine?" Noah asked mildly, knowing these had nothing to do with solar power.

"It's a software problem. This is all new technology. And all of the concrete and metal between us and Nine didn't help. The system works fine out in the open. We've never tested it inside what is essentially a bunker. It got overloaded."

"A glitch, then," Noah said.

"Several glitches."

"And this reboot will fix it?"

"Absolutely," Yvonne said. "As long as we're on the same level, we shouldn't have a problem. I wouldn't go up there if I didn't believe that. We don't know if Nine is contained in that room or not. If he's in the corridor, we'll need the box."

"I have complete confidence," Noah said.

Yvonne gave him a grateful smile. She had completely missed the fact that he had not said *in you*. People always filled in the words they wanted to hear, the words they were desperate to hear. Noah had no confidence in Yvonne Zloblinavech. Not anymore. But he did have confidence in himself and in the pistol he had retrieved from the safe, just in case the box didn't work. If he had to use the pistol on Nine, he would use it on Yvonne as well. He had realized that, as much as he would like to see Yvonne's terrified expression as she plummeted down to the Atlantic Ocean, it would be difficult to accomplish with Grace on board. Someday Grace might understand, but that wouldn't be for a long time, if ever. Grace's mother had never understood, which was why she ran away with Travis Wolfe. But he had hopes for Grace. She looked like her mother, but there was an edge to her that Rose never had. He was going to try to hone this edge beginning tomorrow. He was going to put Grace in charge of the hatchlings when they got to Paris. She would get a great deal of attention when the news of his discovery broke. The media would love her.

But will Grace love the fame?

He thought she might.

Most people do.

He returned Yvonne's grateful smile. She seemed to relax, as if everything was right in the world.

Just because you think it's right, Yvonne, doesn't make it so.

CARD TRICKS

Grace was not smiling, nor was Butch. They were standing outside the orangutan exhibit.

"So where is he?" Butch asked for the fiftieth time.

"I'm sure he's hiding here somewhere," Grace answered for the fiftieth time. "He's just afraid."

"I don't have all night," Butch said.

Neither did Grace. She had to get below, but there was no way to do it with Butch hanging around. She squatted down and crawled under a bush. "It's okay, Marty," she said, feeling ridiculous. "Butch isn't going to hurt you. All he wants to do is let you out of here. Luther has already left the park. It's on video. He's safe."

She crawled back out and brushed off her clothes.

"It might be helpful if you called for him, too," she said.

"He thinks I tried to throw him into the ocean. Why would he believe me?"

"I'm getting cold," Grace said.

"Oh, for crying out loud." Butch took off his jacket and gave it to her; then he did an odd thing. He untucked his shirt.

The jacket, which had hung just below his waist, hung down below her knees.

Why did he untuck his shirt?

"Just try talking to him," she begged. "What can it hurt?"

"Okay, okay," Butch said. "Marty . . . look man, I know you don't like me much. And you don't trust me, but I'm being honest here. All I want to do is unlock the gate and let you out. . . ."

He continued talking, but Grace was no longer listening to what he was saying. Butch's key card opened just about everything in the Ark, including the front gate. She looked at him. He wasn't wearing a lanyard with the key dangling around his neck like the other staff members.

"Your cousin is getting cold out here," Butch continued. "I'm getting cold. . . ."

She reached into the pockets of his jacket like she was trying to warm up. She felt a set of car keys, a wallet, and a piece of plastic the size of a credit card. She squatted down like she was looking under the bushes again, hoping the jacket would hide what she was about to do next. She clipped his key card onto her lanyard, and put the elevator card into his jacket. The cards all looked the same. He wouldn't know what she had done until he got below and discovered that his card didn't open anything but the main elevator.

Now what?

She stood and turned around.

Butch had his back to her. "I want to go to sleep, Marty," he was saying. "I'm sure you want to get home and go to sleep, too. . . ."

He bent over and his shirt rode up to his waist. He had a pistol tucked into the back of his pants.

"Come on, Marty, give us a break." Butch turned and looked at her. "How was that?"

Grace shrugged. "It didn't work."

"Are you sure this is where you left him?"

"Right where you're standing, actually," Grace said.

"You know what else didn't work?" Butch asked.

Grace shook her head. Butch's hand struck like a cobra, ripping the lanyard from her neck and knocking her to the ground. "Your little card trick," he said.

Grace sat on the ground, looking up at him in utter shock.

He reached back, pulled out his pistol, and pointed it at her. "And yes, this is a gun. You think I'm stupid?"

He pulled the trigger. The muzzle flash lit the night. The sound was deafening. An elephant trumpeted, and the lions began to roar.

"They're the only ones that heard that," Butch said. "We had to put up a special soundproof wall around the Ark to keep the neighborhood happy. What happens in the Ark stays in the Ark. Last chance. Where's Marty?"

DECK DITCHING

Marty stepped out of the pig lab, listening to Luther gripe, which he was happy about because it meant that Luther was alive.

"As if the rat and mouse pellets weren't bad enough, now I'm smeared with pork poop," Luther said.

"It's a good look on you," Dylan said.

"You have a clump of it in your hair," Luther said. "That's attractive."

"At least I have hair."

"I hate to interrupt this," Marty said. "But we're looking for dinosaurs."

"I'm on it," Luther said, skipping ahead and sniffing every doorjamb he encountered.

"Wow," Dylan said. "I can honestly say that's something I never thought I'd see."

"Stick with us and you'll see a lot of things you never thought you'd see," Marty said with one eye on Luther and the other on the Gizmo.

"Seriously, Marty, what *is* the plan?"

"Seriously, Dylan, we don't have a plan, which is why we're joking around. That's what we usually do when we're scared out of our wits and have run out of options. Without Grace and the key, we have no way out of here. I'm worried about her. Very worried. But there's nothing I can do about it, so we might as well find the hatchlings and see what's going on with them. The alternative is to find someplace to hide, or circle the ship."

"Circle the ship?"

"You ever been on a cruise?"

"No."

"These circular corridors down here are like the promenade decks on cruise ships. I used to drive my parents out of their minds by doing a thing I called deck ditching. I'd walk ahead of them in the same direction they were walking, but at a faster pace. After a couple of laps, I'd lose them . . ."

"What if one went clockwise and the other counterclockwise?" Dylan asked.

Marty felt his heart squeeze. "My parents were inseparable," he said quietly. "They always traveled in the same direction."

The squeeze must have shown on his face because Dylan put a dusty hand on Marty's shoulder and said, "Wolfe will find your parents. I'm sure of it."

Marty wished he was as certain as Dylan. His parents had been missing for a long time.

And the longer they're missing, the less likely they'll . . .

He shook off the squeeze. There was no time for that now. He needed to stay focused on the current horror.

"Back to deck ditching," he said. "It looks like Luther knocked out all of their cameras down here." He showed Dylan the live feed from the dragonspy. "We'll see the bad guys when they come out of the elevator. We'll be able to track them, but they won't be able to see us as long as we stay a curve ahead of them."

"What about the pig?" Dylan asked.

Marty gave him a grin. "I'm not sure why I did that. I guess I just wanted to mess with their heads. To let them know that the big bad chupacabra they sent after us didn't scare us."

"Is that true?"

"No," Marty admitted. "I nearly wet my pants when it dropped from the ceiling."

"So you really think they saw you before the chupacabra camera shut down?"

"If they were watching, they saw me. It was pointed right at . . ." Marty stopped walking.

"What?"

"Stupid!" Marty said. "I was having so much fun watching you and Luther with the pig, I forgot to turn the camera and GPS back on. I should go back and —"

"Bingo!" Luther shouted. He had stopped in front of a door marked 251. He turned to look at Marty. "Think they'll recognize me?"

The way Luther looked now, Marty doubted Luther's own mother would have recognized him. He swiped the key card through the lock. Luther yanked the door open and they were hit with a blast of dino gas.

Dylan staggered backward, gagging.

Marty's stomach lurched, and for a second he thought he might be sick.

Luther didn't seem affected in the least by the smell. If anything, he seemed to like it.

"Told you I could sniff them out," he said, smiling.

"There is something seriously wrong with your olfactory senses," Dylan said, trying to catch his breath.

"It's not that bad," Luther said, stepping inside.

Reluctantly, Marty and Dylan followed.

"Food prep!" Luther said.

"It looks like a butcher shop," Dylan said.

The room they'd stepped into had a long stainless steel table in the center of it strewn with chunks of red meat. Hanging on a hook above the table was a side of beef with a bloody meat cleaver buried in the muscle. Blood ran down the center of the table to a drain. Sitting on a wheeled cart beneath the drain was a five-gallon bucket filled with blood that needed to be dumped. Next to it were a half-dozen other buckets filled with animal entrails.

"Ghoulish," Marty said.

"You'd think they'd have a better setup at a zoo," Luther said. "We had a much better food prep system aboard the *Coelacanth*."

"Maybe Noah will hire you when this is all over," Marty said.

"He could do worse," Luther said.

"It looks like somebody left in a hurry," Dylan said. He pointed to a heavy door in the wall behind the table. "If I'm not mistaken, that's a cooler. They should have at least wheeled this stuff in there so it didn't go bad."

Marty thought back to the Mokélé-mbembé nest in the Congo. There certainly wasn't a cooler there, but Dylan had a good point. Why hadn't they cleaned up here before they left?

"Maybe the butcher's coming back soon," Luther said.

"Grace told me that the only people allowed in here are her, Yvonne, and Butch," Marty said.

"Maybe Butch is the Butcher," Luther said.

"Wouldn't surprise me." Marty stared at the meat and gore. There was something niggling at the back of his brain. Somehow all of this was important, but he couldn't put his finger on it.

"Let's check the hatchlings," Luther said.

There was another door to the right of the cooler. It was locked. The first key didn't work. Marty swiped the second key. The lock clicked. He opened the door and they were hit by another blast of choking stink, but it wasn't nearly as bad as the first cloud.

"Guess we're getting used to it," he said.

"Getting used to what?" Luther asked.

Marty shook his head and stepped back, letting Luther go through first, then waved Dylan in behind him. He took another look at the food prep area before following them in, wondering what it was about the butchery that bothered him.

"They're asleep," Luther whispered.

Marty joined them. The hatchlings were half buried under a pile of straw with their long necks, tails, and feet entangled. It was difficult to tell where one stopped and the other started, but it was clear they were dinosaurs, and more specifically, babies. Their skin was the color of green olives, dappled with purple splotches. Their tails were as long as their bodies, thick at the base, tapering down to a fist-sized nodule at the tip. Their legs were the size and shape of a baby elephant's, but on each foot, instead of toenails, the hatchlings had three large claws. Their necks were nearly as long as their tails, topped by a large skull with two rows of sharp teeth.

The hatchlings were snoring, and farting, and they were a lot bigger than they had been when Marty had last seen them.

He looked at Dylan and nearly laughed. His mouth was hanging open in mute shock, and his eyes were as big as pancakes. He looked like he might faint from shock.

"You weren't lying," he managed to whisper.

"Duh *du jour*," Luther said. "Getting them out of here isn't going to be easy. When Blackwood nabbed them, they fit into pillowcases. They're at least twice as big now. Guess they have better meat here than we had aboard the ship. Maybe we can walk them out. We'll need harnesses like the one you had us put on that pig, but bigger. Why did you have us put that harness on that pig anyway?"

Up until that very second, Marty didn't know. Now he did. He looked at the Gizmo. The elevator was still closed. He hoped he had enough time.

BUTCHERY

Butch fired another round into the bushes.

"Stop it!" Grace screamed.

"Tell me where Marty is."

"I don't know where Marty is!"

Butch fired a third round, closer this time.

"You're going to hurt one of the animals!"

"We can always get more animals." He fired a fourth shot. Grace felt it zing past her head.

"Close one," Butch said. "If you've lost count, that was four. The clip holds eighteen, and I have another clip in my jacket. In fact, hand over the jacket. The way this is going, I might need that clip." He laughed at his own joke.

The laugh triggered a fundamental shift inside of Grace. She saw herself cowering on the ground with the fog swirling all around her, and she did not like the picture. That was the old Grace. The Grace who was afraid of everything. She felt the fog of terror burning away as if the hot sun were rising inside of her. Butch was a thug and bully, but he wouldn't possibly be so reckless, so stupid, as to actually shoot his boss's granddaughter. And he wouldn't get any information out of her about Marty if she were dead!

"Give me the jacket," Butch ordered again.

Grace got to her feet and shrugged out of Butch's giant jacket, not in obedience, but because she didn't want it to get in her way. As the jacket dropped to the ground, she palmed the elevator card. Butch squatted down to pick up the jacket. That's when Grace kicked him in the face and ran.

"If you spill blood or gore in the corridor, you need to clean it up," Marty said. "It needs to look like we were never in the corridor." He shoved a pile of towels into Dylan's arms and ran from the dino nursery.

Dylan looked at Luther. "And I thought you were crazy."

Another shot rang out behind Grace, but she didn't look back. She knew the worst her kick had done to Butch was to startle him, but she allowed herself a small smile at the memory of his shocked expression. She sprinted all the way through Southeast Asia and didn't slow down until she reached Australia, stopping in the underground duck-billed platypus exhibit to catch her breath. Gasping, with her hands on her knees, she thought about her next move. She had to get back down to Level Two; she had the elevator key card in her back pocket. But how was she going to get below without leading Butch to Marty, Dylan, and Luther? Butch obviously didn't know Marty was down there, or he wouldn't be up top searching for him. And he hadn't mentioned Dylan, so there was a good chance he didn't know that Marty had brought a friend.

She started out of the platypus exhibit, then stopped. She knew the Ark well, but not as well as Butch, and not in the dark, although it was getting lighter and the fog seemed to be lifting. She wondered if Butch was stalking her . . .

Or circling around to ambush me?

She took a deep breath and told herself it didn't matter. She had to get below, and she wasn't going to let Butch, or anyone else, stop her.

Luther cautiously opened the door, just in case the chupacabra had broken out of the cabinet. It hadn't, but it was trying to. It was slamming its body into the door, and its claws were frantically slashing at the stainless steel. Dylan checked the wire he had tied around the handles.

"It'll hold," he said.

"Let's hurry anyway," Luther said, wheeling the cart into the center of the room. "That thing freaks me out."

When they finished their grim work, they stepped back out into the corridor and waited for Marty, as he had requested. It wasn't long before he appeared, sprinting down the corridor chasing a potbellied pig that was snorting and running with surprising speed.

"Stop him!" Marty shouted breathlessly.

The two pig wranglers sprang into action. Dylan dove and managed to snag the pig's hind leg. Luther wrapped his arms around its squealing head. Marty ran up and dropped to his knees and opened Luther's multi-tool.

"Nice grab." He unscrewed the panel on the harness. "Turn him around with the camera facing away from us, toward the lab door."

They swung the pig around.

"Hope that chupacabra doesn't get out while he's in there," Luther said. "This pig will be bacon."

Marty frowned.

"The chupacabra's not going anywhere," Dylan said. "He's locked in that cabinet until someone lets him out."

"Good," Marty said. "As soon as I turn on the GPS and the camera, shove Mr. Pig into the room and slam the door. I won't have time to replace the panel. Ready?"

Luther and Dylan nodded. Marty flipped the switches. They shoved the pig through the door.

"We're back online!" Yvonne said. "Oh my God!"

Noah hurried around the desk to look at the monitor. It wasn't a pretty sight, and he couldn't be happier. The lab looked like a slaughterhouse. Nine was rooting around in pools of blood and guts. He watched the carnage for a full minute, relishing the wave of relief washing over him, savoring the terrible end to Marty O'Hara and, judging by the immense amount of gore in the lab, Luther Smyth as well.

He gave Yvonne a smile. She didn't know it, but she had just dodged a bullet.

"Get up there and take care of the mess," he said. "Then get the hatchlings ready to be transported."

"They're due to wake up any minute now," she said. "I'll have to feed them before we go. Then I'll have to get Nine back to Strand's lab."

"And your point is?" Noah asked, knowing exactly what her point was, and not caring in the least.

"I thought maybe Butch could clean the lab," Yvonne said.

"Are you squeamish?"

"Not particularly. I just thought —"

"Butch didn't make this mess. You did. Now get to it. We have a flight to catch."

"Yes, sir."

Noah left her. As soon as he found Butch he *would* send him down to help, not as a reward to Yvonne, but as a punishment for Butch. It was a toss-up as to which one of them he was more angry with. The situation had been resolved in spite of their incompetence.

As he strolled down the corridor, he almost felt like whistling. It had turned out to be a good night.

Release and Catch still in place. Marty and Luther out of the way. Travis Wolfe will come looking for them, but he'll find nothing.

He smiled.

NIGHT HAND

Marty, Luther, and Dylan were walking down the corridor toward the nursery, pushing two carts with empty five-gallon buckets.

"So what was that all about?" Dylan asked.

"Hopefully, it was about our grisly death via the chupacabra camera," Marty said. "I started going over the sequence of events: The last thing they saw before the camera died was me probably looking . . . well, scared to death. Then I went back even further, to when Butch and Noah were checking doors."

"Your eidetic memory," Dylan said.

"Oh, brother," Luther said.

"It does come in handy sometimes," Marty admitted, ignoring Luther.

"Remember that remote Butch was carrying?"

Dylan nodded.

"I think that's how they were controlling the chupacabra and seeing everything it was seeing. The death of the camera and me being scared to death got me thinking about what death by chupacabra might look like after he had his way with us. I put it all together when I saw the blood and guts in the nursery. I don't know if it'll work, but it was worth a shot."

"So now we're ghosts," Luther said. "But we can't pass through concrete walls. We still have to figure out a way of getting out of here with two dinosaurs."

"You two *do* look kind of like ghosts," Marty said.

"Yeah," Dylan said. "There's a shower in the nursery. I get dibs on the first scrub."

"Are you nuts?" Marty said. "We don't have time for showers."

"Easy for you to say," Luther said. "You're not covered in dust and defecation."

Marty swiped the card through the nursery lock and opened the door. They walked in.

"How often do the hatchlings have to be fed?" Marty asked.

"Used to be every two hours," Luther said. "Like clockwork. And if you're late, they get a little crabby and grabby. Gotta count your fingers after the feed to make sure they didn't get an extra chunk of meat."

"So Yvonne should be coming down here to feed them soon," Marty said.

"Which means we need to get them out of here," Dylan said.

Marty shook his head. "Not necessarily."

"What do you mean?" Luther asked.

"Do you know what Yvonne has?" Marty asked.

"A bad attitude," Luther said.

Marty laughed. "You're right about that, but do you know what else she has?"

Luther grinned. "Duh *du jour*. She has an elevator key." He pulled the bloody meat cleaver out of the side of beef and brandished it like a mad butcher.

"I was thinking of something a little more subtle," Marty said. "And a lot more fun."

Grace was having no fun. Every shadow and bush looked like a homicidal Butch McCall, although she really wasn't worried about him killing her. She was worried about him intercepting her before she reached the elevator, or worse, him seeing her use the elevator, which would lead him to Marty and the others.

She was walking past the sleeping penguins in Antarctica when she heard the helicopter. She looked at her watch. It was still an hour before sunrise.

Why are they arriving so early? Noah must have called them. What's changed?

Grace quickened her pace, then heard something, or someone, coming up behind her. She jumped off the path and crawled beneath a bush.

Butch heard the chopper, too, but ignored it. Someone was coming his way and it could be only one of two people. One of them had once hit him in the head with a tree branch. The other had just kicked him in the face. If it was Marty, he would snap his neck. If it was Grace?

Outcome to be determined.

He did not like getting kicked in the face. He did not like nosebleeds. He would like to snap her neck, too, but that would be difficult to explain to her grandfather. And then there was Marty. Grace knew where he was. He was absolutely convinced of that. And if he snapped her neck, it would make it difficult for her to tell him.

The footsteps grew louder. He stepped off the path. It was perfect. Pitch-dark. No lights. He could tell by the way they were walking that they weren't afraid. There was no caution in the footfalls. He crouched like a tiger.

Surprise and overwhelming force.

He launched himself.

The surprise was all Butch's. His prey was bigger than Marty and Grace put together. There was a loud *Oomph!* Then something cold and hard slammed against the side of his head. Butch stopped himself from killing his attacker just in time.

"What the blazes do you think you're doing?" Noah Blackwood shouted.

There was just enough light to see the thing Noah had slammed into his head. It was a pistol. The barrel was pointed two inches from Butch's nose. It wasn't shaking, which frightened him more than the gun itself. There was no time to reach for his own pistol. All he could think was . . .

I'm going to die now.

But he didn't die. Noah allowed him to live. He lowered the pistol and stood stock-still.

"Explain," he said.

Butch got to his feet and swallowed, trying to get enough spit into his mouth to speak.

"Well?"

"I . . . uh . . . I thought you were Marty."

"Marty's dead!" Noah shouted. "That Luther kid, too. Nine did his job. Yvonne did her job. While you were up here having a stroll through the Ark with your radio off!" He raised the pistol and pointed it at him again.

"Grace," Butch said.

"What about her?" Noah growled.

"She's out here somewhere."

"You told me she was asleep in her bed."

"She was, then she came out through a secret passage. I didn't know you had secre —"

Noah's curse cut him off.

"I caught her once," Butch continued. "She said that Marty was waiting for her up here."

"What do you mean you 'caught her *once*'?"

"She got away."

"Find her! Bring her to the mansion. And turn your radio on!"

Noah hurried away.

Butch watched him disappear into the fog. His head hurt. His nose hurt. He turned his radio on.

Where is she?

Grace was curled up under a bush less than fifty feet away, trying to stifle her sobs. She had heard the exchange, but had paid little attention after Noah shouted out that Marty and Luther were dead.

It's all my fault. If I hadn't gone with Noah Blackwood, Marty and Luther wouldn't have come looking for me. They'd be alive. We'd all be —

Noah walked right by her hiding spot. If she could have, she would have killed him right there on the path, but to try would have been reckless and useless. He would grab her, haul her back to the mansion, and she'd be flown out of the country. He didn't know yet that she had actually seen Marty and had been below, but he was going to figure it out as soon as he got to his lair. He'd see that all of the bedding was gone and know that she had used the laundry chute. If he checked the desk, he'd see that the three key cards were missing.

If he checks the computer . . .

She didn't even want to think about that. It was too late for him to get back the files she had uploaded to Marty, but he could very well discover she had switched the *Wildlife First* episode.

There's nothing I can do about that. What I can do is get out of here and tell everyone that he murdered Marty and Luther with a genetically engineered chupacabra. I can tell them that the Ark is nothing more than a breeding ground for his sick collection of stuffed animals.

The only way to avenge Marty and Luther was to tell the story. She wiped her tears away. There would be time for grief later. Right now she needed all of her wits to get out of the Ark. The keepers arrived at seven thirty. They were bused in from an offsite facility near the park. Once the keepers were inside the Ark, the buses returned and picked up the maintenance and gardening staff. The last group to arrive were the concession people. Security was very careful about checking people into the Ark, but very lax about who exited. She might be able to sneak out while they were checking people in. If that didn't work, her next opportunity would be when the Ark opened at ten. There was always a huge crowd waiting to get inside, mostly school groups. Noah's security would no doubt be watching the entrance and exit closely, but it would still be difficult to pick her out from the hundreds of kids coming and going.

She looked at her watch. All she had to do was stay hidden from Butch for two hours. She guessed the bush she was hiding under was as good a place as any.

Butch can't possibly look under every bush in the . . .

"Your grandfather's waiting for you."

Grace jumped up, took one step, and fell flat on her face.

"Ouch," Butch said sarcastically. He had her by the ankle. "That must have hurt."

She kicked at him with her free foot.

"That ain't happening again," he said. He grabbed her other foot, flipped her onto her back, and sat on her, pinning her arms down with his knees. He looked at her and grinned. "Boohoo, you got a nosebleed. I know exactly how that feels."

He reached back and unclipped his radio, but he didn't get it up to his lips. It flew out of his hand, then he was plucked off of Grace as if the night had reached out and grabbed him.

"She's coming," Marty said, eyeing the Gizmo's screen. "Get into position. And don't do anything until I give the signal."

"Yeah, yeah," Luther said, finding his spot.

Marty looked at Dylan. "And you're sure the chupacabra can't get out of the cabinet?"

"Positive," Dylan said. "It's made out of heavy-gauge stainless steel. The wire's tight."

There were a dozen good places to hide in the nursery as long as Yvonne didn't start poking around, which Marty doubted she would. She looked as if she was in a hurry. She also looked ticked off. Her trademark pleasant smile had been replaced with an angry scowl. She was carrying the remote, looking down at what he assumed was the video screen. She stopped outside the nursery and swiped her key card. Marty flew the dragonspy back to the elevator to watch for Butch and Noah. The nursery door hissed open. She walked in and set the remote on the butcher block.

Marty was hiding in the walk-in cooler, watching her through the little frosted window. If she happened to open the door, all he had to do was duck behind a side of beef. The place was packed with them. He was about to give the signal, which was three clicks on the radio, when she picked up the cleaver and started hacking meat.

Probably not a good idea to make our move while she has the cleaver.

She was pretty good with it. She chopped off what she needed, tossed the hunk on the table, then expertly cut the meat away from the bone with a butcher knife. When she finished, she buried the knife into the butcher block and took her harvest into the nursery.

The hatchlings were awake, and had been for ten minutes, screaming their heads off and flipping their fisted tails around like prehistoric maces. Marty had worried about how they were going to move them without getting killed, but Luther assured him that as soon as they'd had enough to eat, they would go completely comatose until they ran out of gas.

Marty stepped out of the cooler and peeked through the door. Yvonne had her back to him and was completely focused on the feeding, which Luther had guaranteed she would be because if she didn't focus, she was liable to get her pretty hands torn off her wrists.

Marty gave the signal.

Two apparitions rose up behind straw bales on either side of her. At first, she didn't see them. She only had eyes for the dinos. But Luther got her attention by making a creepy ghost noise. She glanced to her left and let out a shriek louder than the hatchlings'. She backed away from Luther, right into the dusty arms of Dylan, causing her to shriek even louder, which seemed impossible. Luther ran over to help restrain her, but Dylan didn't really need any help because Yvonne seemed to have shrieked the fight right out of herself.

Marty walked over with the remote control as they tied her hands behind her back with her lanyard, after removing her key card. They pushed her down on a straw bale.

"I thought you were dead," she said breathlessly, staring at Marty and Luther. "I saw it. It was horrible. I felt so bad. It was all Noah Blackwood and Butch McCall. I would have called the police by now, but they've knocked out all of the phones. I was on my way out of the Ark to report these hideous crimes, but thought I should stop by here first and feed the hatchlings. Who knows how long it will take when the police get ahold of this."

"Wow," Luther said. "What a whopper! You recover quick."

Marty smiled. She *had* made a remarkable recovery from being scared to death a few seconds before. He showed her the screen on the controller. The "chupacabra" was rooting around the lab in hog heaven. "Who do you think that is?"

She turned her head away, as if the sight was too distasteful for her to look at. "I don't know," she said. "Perhaps a custodian. The poor, poor man. I'm just happy it wasn't any of you."

All three of them gave her humongous eye rolls.

"What are all these buttons for?" Marty asked.

She shook her head. "I don't know. Butch and Noah always work the controls."

"Then why do you have the controller?" Dylan asked.

She gave him an odd look, as if she were momentarily confused, but Marty didn't think it was because of the question. She didn't know who he was, or where he had come from, which meant that Butch and Noah didn't know he was here, either.

"Why do you have it?" Dylan repeated.

"I stole it from them," she said. "I didn't want them to use the . . . uh . . ."

"Chupacabra," Dylan said.

"The genetic mutation you made in your monster lab," Luther clarified.

She was obviously shocked that they knew as much as they did, which made Marty happy. He wanted Noah to think they knew more than they did, too, and she was certain to tell him.

"Okay," Marty said. "We need to wrap this up."

Dylan and Luther lifted her to her feet.

"Where are we going?"

"For a walk," Marty said.

"It would be easier if you untied my hands."

"Forget it."

"What about the hatchlings? I need to finish the feeding. At least untie me long enough to finish."

The hatchlings were throwing a dino fit.

"They'll be fine," Luther said. "I'll come back and finish up after we drop you off."

"Drop me off where?"

"There's another animal that needs your attention," Marty said. "And he's a lot hungrier than these two."

He checked the Gizmo. The coast was clear.

"You can't!" she screamed.

"Of course we can," Dylan said.

As they walked her down the corridor, she pleaded, begged, and cried. By the time they reached the lab, Marty was starting to feel sorry for her. Then he reminded himself that she helped kidnap Grace and the hatchlings, and sent the chupacabra after Luther, and probably shared a fist bump with Noah when she saw the mess on the other side of the door.

"I guess you know what's behind this door," Marty said, holding the controller. "Are you sure you don't know how to use this thing?"

Yvonne shook her head.

He shrugged and looked at Luther. "Okay, just crack the door so it doesn't get out, and shove her in."

"No!" Yvonne shouted. "I know how to use it! I know how to use it! Untie me and I'll —"

"Just tell me what to do and I'll type it in."

She told him.

"And that combination makes him go to sleep?"

"Yes. For a little while. There are electrodes embedded in Nine's brain. We can make him do whatever we want."

"Nine?"

"That's what we call him."

"What happened to One through Eight?" Dylan asked.

"They didn't work out," Yvonne said. "Now let's get away from here."

"I can't do that, but I'll tell you what I will do," Marty said. "I'll put him to sleep." He acted like he was typing in the code she had given him.

"But he won't be asleep for long," she said. "And my hands are tied."

"We're giving you a sporting chance," Luther said. "Which is more than you gave me." He swiped the key through the lock, then reached inside quickly, switched the light off, and closed the door.

"Not in the dark!"

"It's better that way," Luther said. "You really don't want to see this thing coming at you."

"I'm not sure I got that code right," Marty said, looking confused. "If I messed up, just stay away from the blinking light on the harness."

Luther reopened the door, Dylan pushed her inside, and they pulled the door closed behind her.

They gathered around the monitor. The infrared picture wasn't that good, but it looked like the potbellied pig was following her.

PANDA-MONIUM

Grace heard Butch curse, then what sounded like punches landing and a scuffle. She had no idea what was going on and she wasn't going to wait to find out. She started to sprint down the path.

"Wait, Grace! Don't go!"

She slowed. The voice was familiar, but she couldn't place it.

"Butch isn't going to be a problem anymore."

She stopped and turned. "Ted?"

"Yeah."

Ted Bronson jogged down the path to her. He was dressed in black from head to toe. When he got to her, he pulled the hood off his head. "Are you okay?"

"Yes . . . I . . . Oh, Ted. Marty's dead, and Luther and Dylan. They have a chupacabra. They used it to kill them. It's all my fault. If I hadn't . . ." She broke down in sobs.

Ted put his arms around her. "It's okay . . . it's okay. I don't think Marty's dead. He's probably in trouble, but he's not dead."

She separated herself from him. "What are you saying?"

"Someone's flying my dragonspy, and I assume it's either Marty, or Luther, or maybe even Dylan. I picked up the signal a couple of minutes ago. It blinked back out, but the dragonspy was definitely in the air."

"How did you find me?"

"Your dragonspy," he said. "It came online a few hours ago. I'll explain everything, but first tell me who's in the park."

"Butch, Noah, and Yvonne, and another man on the radio, but I don't know who or where he is."

"Where's Noah?"

"He headed toward the mansion."

"And Yvonne?"

"I think she's below."

"Good. Those are great odds."

"What about Butch?"

"He's not going anywhere for a while. I knocked him out with a couple of interesting martial art moves I learned in the Philippines a few years ago, then I tied him to the rail with flex cuffs. I'm hoping a visitor finds him before a staff member does."

"We need to get his key card. He and Noah are the only ones who can open the main gate."

"I have his gun, and his key, but we don't need either to get out of the Ark. That's what took me so long to get to you. Noah's security system is unbreakable. I got here a few hours ago, but I couldn't get inside."

"But you're here now," Grace said. "How —"

"The chopper," Ted said. "I had to go to the airport and steal it from Noah's pilots. Noah owes us a chopper anyway, since Butch pushed ours off the *Coelacanth* into the Pacific. Let's walk while we talk."

He explained that Dylan's mother had come home from the university and found a teacup poodle in her living room, a pile of orange hair and bloody tissues in the bathroom, and no son. She called Ted. When he discovered that their tags were completely off the grid, he headed directly to the Ark.

"I figured they had come here looking for you."

"Does Wolfe know?"

"Oh yeah. And he's not too happy. The military is flying him home as we speak. Tell me what's been going on here."

The story took them all the way to the keeper service area.

"Switching the real episode for the outtakes was brilliant!" he said. "I hope he doesn't figure that out." He swiped Butch's key through the lock.

Grace led him to the elevator. She got in and punched the button for Level Two.

"So you really think they're okay?" Grace asked as they dropped down.

"I hope so," Ted said.

The car stopped and the door slid open.

Marty, Luther, and Dylan were standing in front of the elevator behind two carts carrying two sleeping dinosaurs. They stepped back in shock, ready to run, until they recognized Ted and Grace.

Marty smiled. "About time you got back down here," he said to Grace, then looked at Ted. "Hey, Ted."

"Hey, Marty. Glad you're okay. Where's Yvonne?"

"Pig heaven," Luther answered.

Ted looked at Luther and Dylan. "You two look a little rough."

"That's because we've been doing all the work," Luther said. He wheeled his cart in. Dylan wheeled in the second one. "See what I mean?"

On the carts were two gorged and sleeping dinosaurs. Grace hit the button and the door closed. She thought this might just be the happiest moment of her entire life.

Ted made a face and waved his hand in front of his nose. "Wow, I'd forgotten about that part."

They were all relieved to get out of the elevator into the keeper service area where they could breathe.

"Let's get out of here," Ted said. "Keep your eyes open for Blackwood."

"We have one more thing to do," Grace said. She told them about Noah's collection and the mother panda without the baby.

"Let's grab them and go," Marty said.

Grace led them to the holding area. She used Butch's key to open the door. The panda cubs were sleeping on a bed of straw. She picked one up and handed it to Ted. She gave the second one to Marty, and picked up the third for herself.

"What's wrong with this picture?" Luther said. "Dylan and I get the gassy dinos, and you three get the cuddly pandas."

Noah Blackwood was in a complete rage. He had discovered the missing bedding and realized that was how Grace had gotten below. But how had she gotten up to the third floor? She had been at his computer. He could tell by the way the keyboard sat on the desk, and there were smudges on the snakewood that shouldn't have been there. There were also smudges on his diorama. Her greasy fingerprints were all over it.

When Butch caught her, Noah was going to make her clean the glass, then he was going to make her tell him how she had gotten up here, and what she had seen on the computer. She was obviously just like her mother after all. Narrow-minded, disobedient, and disloyal.

He got on the radio.

"Butch?"

He waited.

"Butch?"

He waited.

"Answer me, Butch! If you turned your radio off again, I swear I'll —"

He heard the helicopter rotors start. He looked at his watch. It wasn't time to leave, and his pilots wouldn't leave without him anyway. The quickest way to the main floor and the helipad was the fire escape. He turned on the lights to the cube and ran over to the thylacine panel. He put his hands on the designated spots and pushed. The glass panel swung open. He stepped inside, got on his knees, and pressed on a secret door near the wombat burrow. It clicked open. Inside was a ladder that led down to the library. He scrambled down two floors, opened the secret door into the library, and ran toward the French doors leading to the swimming pool. Sprinting as fast as he could, he arrived at the helipad just as the helicopter was taking off. Marty and Grace were looking out the window at him.

Marty smiled and gave him a thumbs-up.

CRYPTOS ISLAND

They reached the island at sunrise. Grace was glued to the window as they made their approach. She had wondered if she would ever see the little island again. They flew right over the top of the western promontory, where Wolfe's three-story house sat overlooking the Pacific. It was built out of huge moss-covered stones and looked more like a castle than a house.

Ted swooped the helicopter down toward the interior of the island, past the staff housing; the giant-sized Quonset hut, called QAQ, where Ted invented all of his wonderful things; and finally to the second Quonset hut they used as a hangar for Wolfe's military bomber, which had been converted into a transport jet. The jet was parked on the tarmac.

Ted set the helicopter down next to the transport. Several of the crew members were there to greet them, including the Bishops — Phil, Bertha, and their daughter, Phyllis — and another man Grace didn't recognize.

"Is that your dad?" she asked Dylan.

"Yep," Dylan said. "Wild Bill Hickock, but you can just call him Bill."

Marty and Luther got out first, followed by Dylan, whose dad gave him a big bear hug that Dylan happily returned.

Grace was disappointed that Wolfe wasn't there, and wondered how she would be greeted by everyone. After all, she had abandoned these people when she went away with Noah Blackwood.

She needn't have worried. As soon as she stepped onto the tarmac, the Bishops swarmed her, hugging her so long and so hard she thought she would have bruises.

Bo the chimp came hooting out of the trees.

"Crap," Luther said, and took refuge behind Marty.

"She's only after your hair," Marty said. "You don't have anything to worry about until it grows back."

Bo eyed Luther suspiciously.

Grace walked up to the chimp and gave her a scratch under the chin. "I missed you," she said, then turned to everyone. "I missed all of you! I can't tell you how wonderful it is to be back here!"

At that moment a fighter jet screamed overhead, shot out over the Pacific, then circled back toward the island. A minute later it touched down on the long runway, taxied over to them, and came to a stop.

The flight crew wheeled a set of stairs over to it. The canopy opened and a huge man climbed out of the rear seat. He was wearing a helmet and a flight suit, but Grace would have recognized him anywhere. Travis Wolfe, her father, pulled his helmet off, shook the pilot's hand, then limped down the stairway. She ran over to greet him, but stopped ten feet short, unsure of herself.

"Why are you just standing there?" Wolfe shouted. "Get over here!" He threw his giant arms out. Grace ran to him.

Wolfe held her for a long time.

"I guess we ought to talk to your partners in crime," he finally said.

"I guess so," Grace said.

They walked over to the helicopter hand in hand. Ted was standing outside the door with Marty and Luther.

"So what do we have?" Wolfe asked.

"Two dinosaurs, four kids, and three panda cubs," Ted answered.

Wolfe looked at Marty and frowned. "Pandas?"

"It wasn't my idea," Marty said. "Talk to your daughter."

Wolfe smiled at Grace.

"I have a lot to tell you," she said.

"I guess you do." Wolfe looked at Ted. "Nice chopper. Where'd we get it?"

Ted shrugged.

"So we're in huge trouble," Wolfe said. "Again." He called the Bishops over. "I guess we need to get out of town for a while. You up for another flight?"

"Sure thing," Phil said.

"We'll take the hatchlings, the pandas, and that chopper with us." Wolfe glanced at his watch. "When can you be ready?"

"Maybe by tonight," Phil said.

"Where are we going?" Marty asked.

"Right now we're going up to the Fort, where everyone can get cleaned up, take showers, change their clothes, eat some breakfast, take a nap. And then, as soon as we're all rested and ready, we're heading down to Brazil to find your parents."

MR. ZWILLING

Mr. Zwilling loved doing rounds at the Ark.

He had already spoken to Paul Ivy, assuring the poor fellow that they would have the surveillance back up within a week. He told him to come up with a completely new design for the system, and that money was no object.

He said good morning to all of the research staff, popped into security and told them they could have a few days off because the cameras were down, then headed up to the keeper area to find out how their charges were doing.

When he finished below, he went up top. It was a glorious day. The fog had burned off and there were nothing but blue skies above. He had just enough time to tour the exhibits before he had to leave the Ark grounds and head over to see the giant squid at Northwest Zoo and Aquarium. He stepped out of the keeper service area and started whistling. He couldn't help himself.

A school group recognized him.

"That's Noah Blackwood!"

"I've seen his show!"

They ran over and swarmed him, asking for his autograph. He took out his pen and signed every scrap of paper they had.

• • •

As Mr. Zwilling signed autographs for the kids, Noah Blackwood looked out the window of his private jet, thirty-five thousand feet in the air. Two rows in front of him sat Dr. Strand and Mitch Merton. Mitch had been delighted to leave the Ark and Henrico's taxidermy studio. Noah had told him that he had a new job for him . . . "One where I'll be using your mind instead of your hands."

"Perfect, Dr. Blackwood," Mitch had said. "I love using my mind."

Noah shook his head as he recalled the conversation. *People hear what they want to hear.* He hadn't said, "*you'll* be using your mind." He'd said, "*I'll* be using your mind." He had already told Dr. Strand what he wanted to do. Strand had spiked Mitch's drink with a tranquilizer and was just waiting for Mitch to go to sleep.

Butch McCall and Yvonne Zloblinavech were seated three rows behind Noah. He hadn't spoken to, or even looked at, either one of them since he had untied Butch and rescued Yvonne from the potbellied pig.

A pig, for crying out loud!

He was disgusted with both of them, but he needed them. His spies on Cryptos Island had told him where Wolfe was going. It was a place he knew well. The place where it all began.

ACKNOWLEDGMENTS

Three down, one to go. I want to thank all my fans for hanging with Marty, Grace, and me as we try to get this fantastic story into print. We've had a lot of help in our labors. . . . My fantastic editor at Scholastic, Anamika Bhatnagar, who seems to have a baby every time a cryptid book comes out. Welcome to the world, Nik. This book is for you. The amazing Scholastic editor/midwife Siobhán McGowan, who always makes me look better than I am. My wonderful agent, Barbara Kouts. The fabulous Phil Falco, who designs these books. Lori Benton, David Levithan, Ed Masessa, Robin Hoffman, Lizette Serrano, Charisse Meloto, Becky Amsel, Elizabeth Starr Baer, and everyone else in the Scholastic family. Thank you all. But the biggest thanks goes to my wife, Marie, who takes care of all the mundane details of my life so I can stand at my desk looking for cryptids.

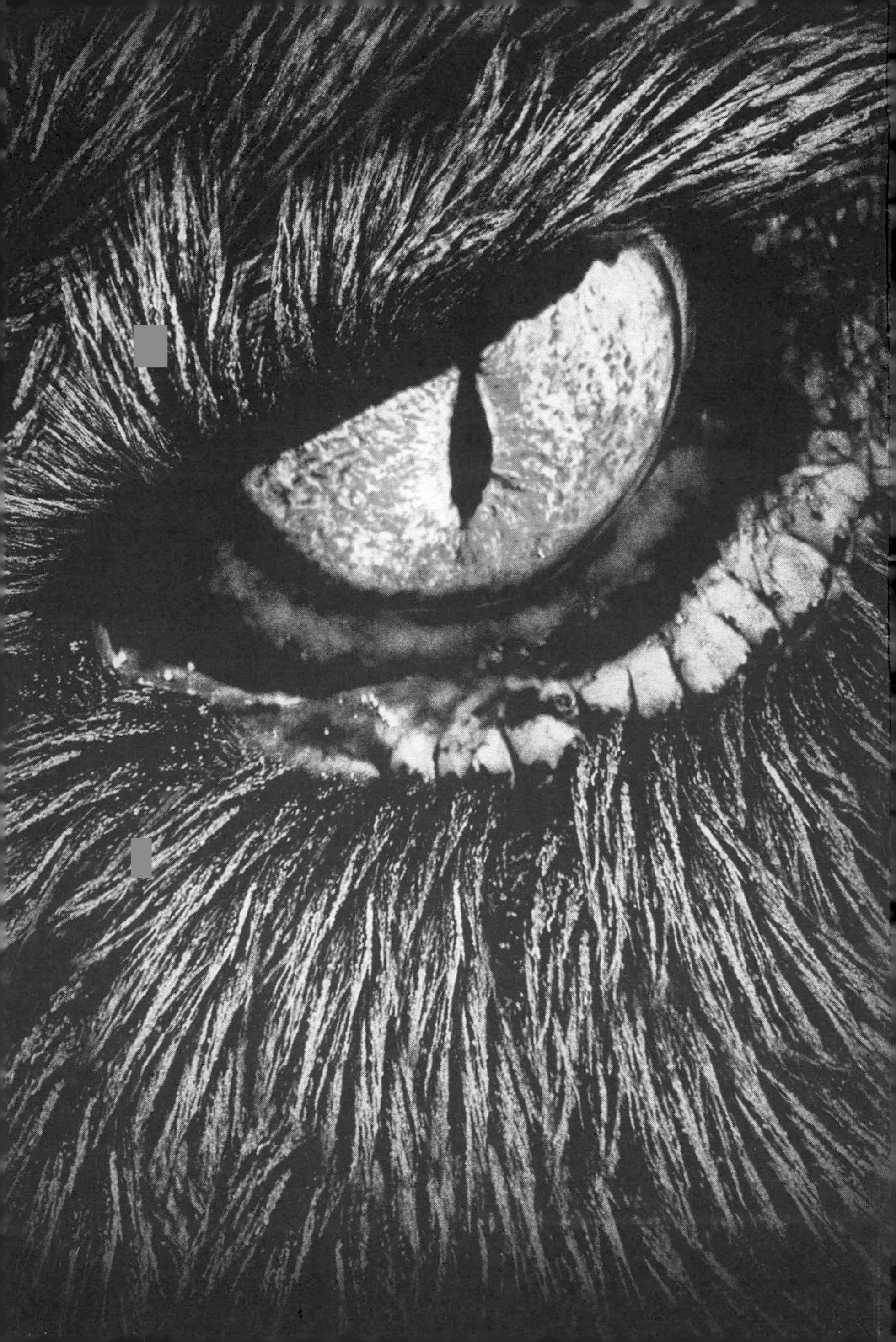